FORBIDDEN ZONES

by the same author

Pink Butterflies / Bize Dair
Turkish Speaking Communities & Education - no delight
Turkish Cypriot Identity in Literature (editor and translator)

FORBIDDEN ZONES

Short Stories & others

AYDIN MEHMET ALI

FATALpublications – LICITUS

A complete catalogue record of this book is available from
the British Library / *Forbidden Zones* / First published in 2013
by FATAL Publications in London and Licitus in Cyprus

FATAL Publications
4 Inchmery Road, London, SE6 2NE

Licitus Cyprus
2 Raktivan Street, Nicosia, 1020
E-mail: fatalpublications@gmail.com

Copyright © Aydın Mehmet Ali

Versions of some of these stories first appeared in the following publications, to whose editors grateful acknowledgment is made: *Forbidden Zone*, Kunapipi (2011) and *Going West, The Beginning* (extract, 2012), *Caught Out*, Diaspora City (2004), *Bedtime Story*, Cadences (2008), *The Midwife*, Exiled Ink (extract, 2010), *Emine's Fight*, Uncut Diamonds (2003), *The Daughter-in-Law*, Crossing the Borders (2002), *Roll-Call*, Exiled Ink (2005), *Women of Nicosia*, Klandestini, http://klandestini.britishcouncil.org/ (2004) and Cadences (2009), *London is my City*, Cultures of Memory/Memories of Culture (2007) also Evening Standard (2005), 91st Meridian, Excerpta Cypriana (2009) Idaho, USA and Cadences (2006). *The Dedication*, first published in Crossing the Border (Five Leaves 2002) and Pink Butterflies / Bize Dair (FATAL 2005). The short stories, *I could never be without you, The Nurse Mother* and *Grandma Jamaica's Delroy* are from an unpublished collection, Grandma Jamaica.

ISBN 978-0-9515656-3-6

Photos: Miriam Butler (p.268), Aydın Mehmet Ali (p.12, 330), Kathy Kattashis (p.326), MA+DIN (p.330), Türkan Tuncel (backcover), unknown artist (cover)
Concept/Design: Achim Wieland www.lookinglately.com
Design Support/Production Assistance: Navid Gholipour, Gregorio v. Hildebrand.
Printed and bound in Cyprus by Lithostar Ltd, Cyprus

–to those who wander in forbidden zones
and return to tell the stories

A FEW WORDS

This is a rescue operation for some of the short stories and other creative pieces written over the last thirty-five years. Some have been languishing in filing cabinets in suspended animation for a lifetime, others have been published in anthologies, journals and magazines scattered around the world… Some are still travelling with me across time-zones, barriers and locations.

It is time for this collection to make its own way in the world. I am confident the stories will sustain their fearlessness, the spirit in which they were written. After all, they are fictionalised realities…

AYDIN MEHMET ALI
September 2013
Nicosia

CONTENTS

Forbidden Zone	9
Caught Out	37
Bedtime Story	57
Emine's Fight	81
The Daughter-in-Law	97
Roll-Call	125
I could never be without you	131
The Nurse Mother	151
Grandma Jamaica's Delroy	171
Finding Maro	187
The Midwife	213
Conciliation is on the horizon	231
Desperately Seeking	257
Tongues of a city	269
Women of Nicosia	327
London is my city	331
Acknowledgements	345
Biographical note	347
Comments	349
Other publications by FATAL	357

**FORBIDDEN
ZONE**

A cracked skull appeared beyond the hotel… Snuggled in the shape of a foetus. A larger head compared to the body. Only the shoulders and upper torso visible. A large chunk missing. Jagged edged. The sky peering through from the other side. The sharp lines of the late nineteen-sixties early seventies hotel clashing with the smooth rounded contours of the skull. An almost square building twelve storeys high. Broad and full of bravado while facing the sea, narrow and vulnerable from the side, almost flimsy. The neat lined-up balconies as though at a military parade, reminders of the boom seventies package holidays. Maximum sun. Maximum sea. Tiny boxes. Wall-to-wall windows. Wall-to-wall balconies. Angled for privacy precariously balanced against the aim of the holiday, to be seen, to be exposed, to be noticed, to be a star for fifteen days in a year…

Drinks, sun, sea and the local tanned olive-skinned boys with erotic eyes and shy smiles. Always moving around in groups. More in love with their own bodies and each other than the tourists, peripheral to their lives but still a temptation. Doing somersaults on the beach, games, excuses for touching, embracing each other, holding tightly. Older women aware of their own attractiveness glancing, careful lest their lingering looks attract exaggerated attention needing justification to husbands. Older men wistful. 'Accidentally' the ball is kicked towards the blonde, red-skinned tourists sizzling in the July heat. Blue-eyed, loud-laughtered, bikinied girls. A few smiles, furtive looks. Seductive games while drinking bottles of coke or beer unable to quench the thirst. Laughter, movement, running. A cacophony of noise, a perfect camouflage for the hastily spoken words while picking up the ball from the blonde tourist talking to her friend. The dark long fingers gently brush off the wet sand grains from the ball, enough time to arrange to meet at the disco, at the back of the hotel. What time…? 8.00 tonight…? OK.

The cacophony has died. An eerie silence patrols the hotels, the balconies, streets, gardens, the disco. The blood-red hibiscus continue to blossom on the veranda, between two hotels half submerged in the sand. And date palms, natives and lovers of the sand dunes. The pigeons have taken over the hotels. The new tourists with permanent residences and no visas. No one can order them about.

FORBIDDEN ZONE

Red boards. Black letters with black soldiers gun in hand tangled in barbed wire guard the empty hotels. Against whom?

ZONE INTERDITE

The pigeons in defiance of orders fly in and out, settle anywhere they wish, shit indiscriminately, even worse dance in courtship and fuck all over the balconies, in full view of the guards impotent in preventing or punishing such audacious violations of morality, decency and military dictates. The quick succession of generations ensuring erasure from memory passed on by those witnesses to carnage.

VERBOTENE ZONE

Empty holes. The dark hollow body of the hotel cannot prevent the echoes escaping from all its orifices. Cooing sounds echo around the hotel corridors, bedrooms, dining room, barely audible but the woman with the dark hair and olive skin can hear them as her bare feet touch the sand, and toes sink in gently gathering sand grains and tiny ground white pink and yellow shells on her skin. She turns her face to the hotel and silently calls for the sounds to come to her... A child's voice. Laughter. Excitement. A little girl. With Daddy. A game is being played. In and out of the water. *Daddy-Daddy-look-look! Catch me! Catch me!* She is three. Dark hair. Bouncing in two bunches on top of her head. Rubber duck ring around her bottom. *But Daddy look, look at me! Look! I'm nearly swimming.* Little bare feet run in and out of the water leaving tiny footprints kissed then erased by the sea foam. Daddy is looking at the lone figure in the distance

11

on the other end of the beach. She walks without haste. Daddy holds the little girl in his arms. His eyes watch the lone woman in a white flimsy dress with fluttering tiny cornflower-blue flowers. *Daddy-Daddy-look...* Yes I'm looking. The woman is watching the little girl. Daddy is bald. He can't believe the lone woman is looking at him so boldly. Daddy smiles at the lone woman in expectation...

* * *

Planes flew over in July. Fighter jets screeched and tore the sky apart. A confused moment. *Happy birthday to you happy birthday dear Aris happy birthday to youuuu...* From the basement of Aspendia Hotel. *Wish wish blow the candles and wish... Don't tell anyone or it won't come true. Close your eyes close your eyes. Now, wish... silence everyone...* A roar whistles past. The walls shake. The crystal chandelier. A deafening blast as though the earth exploded. Clouds of dust descend. Invisibility fear seep through. A child's whimper. Adults shout orders, *get down get down...* hands reach out for each other crawling on the floor until they reach other hands, other body parts. *Hold on. Hold on. Quickly quickly let's get out of here.* Dust-covered bodies try out slow ghostly movements. *My beautiful dress Mummy... my pink fairy dress... it's dirty.* A whimper. *I won't be able to be an angel again Mummy...* loud wails. *I want to be an angel Mummy. You said you won't get me another if I get it dirty. It isn't my fault Mummy! Mummy?* An imperceptible silence. A hushed trembling voice. *Shusssh Alexia... don't cry baby. It isn't your fault. We'll get you another one baby... shuuush...* A loud explosion shakes the walls further. Windowpanes explode a rush of hot wind blows in, furniture flies off, debris falls, the stunned silence no longer contained, screams, screams fill the air, hysterical, uncontrollable screams. In between offerings and prayers to God and Jesus and to the Holy Mother Panayia, Mary. The fear of death of the adults soaked up by the young unable to comprehend the complexities of life and death but well aware of fear. With tear-filled eyes and faces the young watch the adults, wait for them to make everything all right, to stop the loud roaring, to stop the dust and debris, to get back to the party. The adults paralysed by fear become children... holding babies tightly against themselves, nearly suffocating them, searching for safety. *Get into the cars quickly get into the cars...* a man's voice penetrates through the dust and fallen debris from what was the direction of the door. But he is invisible. *Mummy my cake... I haven't made a wish yet. And the candles have all blown out, by themselves. Wait Mummy wait...*

The swings are buried under the sand whipped up by the winds from the sea sometimes bringing red sand clouds from the Sahara. They don't move. The top bar rusty with peeling blue paint stands half a metre above the sand dune; the immovable rusty brown chains hold the seats trapped under the sand. No children's laughter, high-pitched excitement, giggles. *Push Daddy push... higher higher... up to the sky...* the high pitch of excitement skirting the edges of fear. *Hold on now... don't let go!* Both *hands! Both hands! Don't wave to me...*

White sand lilies blossom at the end of Summer, their scent descends on decay, destruction, decomposed bodies, broken windows, doors, abandoned buildings, flowers, trees, prisoners of barbed wire protected by red signboards black gun-toting shadow soldiers. Visible. Impenetrable. A shrill whistle tears the silence of the day. The fight of the shrill whistle against the thousands of cameras clicked by the day-tourists from the South on their quick tour of the North to the abandoned well-guarded empty hotels silent witnesses to war and atrocities. Unmovable, unhidden, magnificent monuments to shame stand stoically while around their skirts insignificant nobodies flutter desperate to impose unimplementable rules with the help of the gun-toting-black-shadow-soldiers strapped on barbed wire. The whistle losing the battle of *no photographs* to the music of the click clicking of cameras and languages of the world whispered along the narrow beach in homage to the dead and disappeared.

His whole upper torso is tattooed. He struts, a peacock on an almost deserted beach. A few late season English tourists afraid of the sizzling July heat arrive in November with their umbrella and cool-box always at the same spot with the stones they have appropriated. A few *tut-tuts* followed by the assertive claiming of the umbrella bearing stones which may have been scattered or used for other purposes by the university students for a cheap night-out on the beach the previous night. The stones oblivious as to their constantly changing ownership by day and by night. Sunflower seed husk patterns and empty beer bottles evidence of the nightly crimes. *They must be animals these people how could they do this? Why don't they put their rubbish into the bins?* The anger and frustration from the slightly disabled young street cleaner pouring curses on the privileged spoilt brats at university while he clears up rubbish. He is luminous in his orange jacket moving around picking up *their* rubbish. A Cypriot by accident brought over from Turkey aged three by parents offered land and houses abandoned by the Cypriotgreeks after the invasion in 1974, cursing the students from Turkey who come to escape military service and in the process live envious student lives due to generous parental contributions.

The tattooed peacock struts over to the English couple settled under the umbrella ensuring high visibility from the barely five people making up his beach audience. The woman with the dark hair walks by steadily looking at his tattoos, sagging body, greasy dyed streaks of hair which travel from one side of his head over the top to the other side in a futile attempt to cover the bald patch on the move. Streaks, forever at the mercy of gusts of wind. But he doesn't see. In the mirror he only sees the body beautiful and dazzling white smile of his youth now maintained by porcelain dentures.

* * *

Yorgos runs into the room. He tries to disperse the thick dust clouds burning his eyes with futile hand movements. Gasping for air as he swallows the earth tastes stuck on his tongue and

15

roof of the mouth. His heart pounding, ricocheting echoes in his ears. He barely recognises his voice shouting into the void, "This way ... this way!" drowned by the screams and cacophony of sounds. He desperately wills himself to believe his wife and child are alive. Trying to identify scraps of nuances amongst the screams, shouts, crying children and women, shaking chandeliers and falling debris. Tears stream down leaving luminous snail trails on his dust-covered face.

"Ariii... Mariaaa..." bellows out of his lungs as he hurtles himself from one shadow to the next losing his balance, crushing into objects and bodies, falling over, scrambling up and dashing forward into the dust fog.

"Daddy... tomorrow is my birthday! You know... did you buy me a present? Mummy says it's a surprise." The previous night his son had crawled onto his lap as he was reading him a story and conspiratorially whispered, "You can tell me... I won't tell Mummy." After a brief silence he added wisely, "It will be our secret." Yorgos had chuckled at his son soon to be six playing games he had picked up from him. He marvelled and worried at the capacity of the young to pick up so much which was not consciously taught them.

"Ariiii... where are you?" his voice bellows into the hall of chaos as fear begins to wrap him up. He wipes his eyes smearing his face with salty mud aware that no one can hear him.

He jumps out of his skin as a hand grabs his arm and grips it painfully tightly. He catches Maria's scent as he wraps her in his arms breathlessly asking, "Aris? Aris?" before he becomes aware of two little hands pulling onto his trouser legs. Yorgos picks up his son as they rush towards the sea through the back entrance hoping it will save them from the wrath of the fighter jets screeching by and burning up what was spared by the heat of July. They crawl on the sizzling sand amongst people scattering in all directions and circle the hotel. They rush past the crimson-red flowering hibiscus bushes on the corner, turn left, past the date palms growing in the sand, emerging in front of the hotel. Their car is covered in debris and broken glass. All the hotel windows next door had exploded from the bombing. People run in all directions, confused as to which direction leads to safety. Where did the attacks come from? They jump in the car. Total strangers bundle in after them, with ghostly fear in their eyes. Silent. Stunned. Yorgos struggles to turn on the ignition. His fingers shaking uncontrollably like the poplar leaves in a summer breeze. Maria watches carefully without panic as he tries to spit the grit sticking to the inside of his cheeks, no saliva comes. "I can drive," she says gently touching his trembling fingers.

The roads are filled with streams of people walking, running, crying, calling out, looking for loved ones, someone they might recognise, searching, constantly searching with dazed eyes, in disbelief, trying to guess the way out, the safe passage. Cowering with every loud bang, searching the skies for the next fighter jet attack.

"What's he doing hanging down from the hole? It's dangerous..." Aris' trembling voice breaks the silence of held breaths, looking up at the tenth floor of the first hotel on the beach. Neither Maria nor Yorgos explain. No one speaks. Sweat pours down the roots of their hair, behind their ears, trickling between their breasts and down their spines, creeping between their buttocks creating pools on the leather seats of the car, drenching their clothes. A young man hangs precariously over the wall framed by the massive hole torn open by the bombing, a direct hit by the fighter jets. He was so still. Dead. Aris knew. The side of the hotel has collapsed, all the way from the top beyond the tenth floor, creating craters on the ground and mounds of crashed concrete, metal and red bricks.

The car crawls towards the new yellow painted modern church while they avoid talking lest it betrays fear. They are reduced to eye signals and quick secret hand and finger movements they hope Aris can't see or interpret. Avoiding people on foot, bicycles and motorbikes running in and out of cars is becoming even harder. They head towards the West. The safest bet, Maria and Yorgos signal to each other. The jets had come from the north so would the soldiers. The invasion had begun. For days they didn't want to believe it, for days they wished it away, they wanted to believe that diplomacy would prevail, that the big guarantor powers and the West would not allow it. Surely common sense would prevail. War was not in the interests of Cypriots. There were deliberate provocations but surely the majority of people could see through them and would restrain from reacting. It couldn't happen… They wanted to continue the normality of their lives just like yesterday. But it had happened. And it was changing everything beyond their imagination.

They approach the traffic lights by the famous Venus nightclub on the corner on the left, where the sailors of the world docked at Famagusta harbour for a short respite seeking the comfort of the arms, tongues and groins of prostitutes and delights of young olive-skinned boys willing to fuck them senseless to prove their masculinity. They were the fuckers and not the fucked. You are not a *puşt*, a Turkish word finding itself transformed into the Greek language as *pushtis*, a poofter, if you did the fucking, they said. They saw the dark clouds billowing out of the upper windows and doors of the District Court House. Tongues of fire devouring the timber structured roof with an avarice and speed uncurtailed by the absence of firefighters. Yorgos gazes at the building only for a brief moment imagining the transformation of bundles of white sheets of paper into the black flakes flying around in the skies. Records of his cases, victories, defeats for justice, fairness and equality before the law for all people; some he had defended without pay out of principle, now mere specks fluttering in the bluest of skies. He barely hears the gasps of Maria and Aris as he wonders the whereabouts of Mustafa, his friend since the English School in Nicosia and fellow barrister since their time together at Lincoln's Inn in London. He closes his eyes willing with all his powers that he be unharmed. He can hear the screams of the panic-stricken animals and their crashes against their cages, imprisoned in the small zoo opposite as he puts his foot down.

* * *

"Pull up… to the side of the road…" came the order from nowhere. In Cypriotgreek spoken by the softness of a Cypriotturkish man. All Yorgos could see was a rifle pointing at him, straight into his eyes, level with the car window. It caught flashes of light from the headlights of the car behind. The gun shook with impatience, held by a relaxed hand, pointing towards the left. There was nowhere to go. The road was blocked by hundreds of cars, small pick-up trucks, lorries all going the same direction: West. Gridlocked. Others just walked alongside cars or stood waiting. "Get out," came the order immediately after. Yorgos opened his door slowly and scrambled out of the car, loaded with some of their belongings, avoiding any sudden movement and squeezing his wife's hand gently with trembling hands.

They had managed to get back to their house in the new developing suburb of Varosha with modern houses, beautiful large gardens full of bougainvilleas, frangipani, jasmine, roses and pavements lined with trees transported from other parts of the Empire. Australian bottle-brush, South African jacaranda, flame trees from Malaysia, ficus variations from Africa, broadleafed almond from the Caribbean and purple, sometimes white flowering, legume trees, their scent descending over the streets especially during warm spring nights. They had decided to pack some things and travel by night as they thought that to be safer.

What do you take with you at such moments? Will you be away for long? Is this temporary? When will you return? Not returning, not an option to contemplate. Just a situation you need to get yourself through. And you have no answers to the same questions asked by others seeking reassurance. Maria did not ask. They packed some summer clothes, books, toys for Aris, important documents, money, passports, jewellery, ID cards and a first aid box. Yorgos wanted to take some law books and case files he was working on. He dropped them when Maria said, "But the Court House was burning." Some water and food on the way was better use of space she suggested. When Maria took her wedding dress he just looked at her but said nothing. Some photos, she insisted on taking some albums and photos off the walls. She looked around the house in desperation for what else to take. She, much more astute and quick as to what she could leave behind; he, feeling useless and detached. It didn't matter anyway; they would be back in a few weeks...

He was so young, the hand holding the shotgun. On the inside of his forearm a tattoo of the crescent and star in lurid red. They came eye to eye. He was barely fifteen–sixteen. One fully aware of his powerlessness, the other unused to wielding such seemingly limitless power. One used to operating in circles of power curtailed and limited by the laws of the land, the other operating without boundaries on that insignificant remote road leading to the village of Derhinia usually deserted, running through potato fields witness only to occasional tractor jams caused by three or four travelling together during harvest or sowing time.

He guided Yorgos unhurriedly to the side of the road before coming back and leaning down to look into the car. He noted Maria's frightened eyes darting back and forth to her hus-

21

band while she held her son's hands, squeezing, letting go, caressing and squeezing again. She heard women screaming from other cars in front and behind her. She noticed another body, the crotch level with her window, on her side of the car. She didn't look up. She kept her eyes on her husband.

"Can you drive?" the young man asked. She was surprised by his steady, unhurried voice. She nodded after a while trying to prevent the possible scenarios crowding her head, threatening to overwhelm her. She kept repeating to herself to be focused. "My husband..." she managed to say, swallowing hard to overcome the fear in her mouth but he had already moved away, towards Yorgos. She waited in the car for what seemed to be an eternity trying not to take her eyes off her husband, her ears picking up the screams, crying, curses, half-hearted scuffles betraying defeat, the guilt of self-preservation, abandonment of the self and others to fate... The futility of resistance, struggle, the surrender to what is perceived as more powerful, reluctance to become martyrs in a land eulogising 'martyrs' adorning most streets in all towns and villages with their names, where special parades and anniversaries are organised with much pomp and ceremony, where the families of the martyred are honoured and rewarded for giving birth to and instilling the sacred duty of martyrdom for the Cause. Maria noticed other Cypriotgreek men by the side of the road. Her heart beat faster but she was alert. Why were they separating the men from the women? She was startled by a scream close by. She looked towards the back of the car. A woman wearing a black headscarf and clothes, a sign of mourning, was being dragged along the road. She held on tightly to a young man wearing a white T-shirt being dragged away in turn by two men each carrying a shotgun in the other hand. Her scarf came off in the scuffle, her legs covered in blood as they grazed along the side of the asphalt. They hit her arms, repeatedly with the butts of their rifles but couldn't make her let go. "He's my only son…" she was wailing. "The other two you killed in our village!" She spat out the words in anger rather than fear. "You killed my husband! God's curses be upon you! Satans! Murderers! May you burn in Hell! I curse your wives, your children! May they be killed and raped… like you are doing to us!" The slim young son imprisoned in the powerful hands of the two men, gripped under the arms, was being pulled away, his feet scraping the ground, his face crumpled, tears flowing.

Maria kept her eyes on her husband holding onto her son sitting on her lap…

* * *

"That night the army officers from Turkey in charge of the operation made so much money. Imagine… these people were trapped! On the road, they could go nowhere. They handed everything over in exchange for their lives. The officers claimed it was for the Cause, to buy guns and ammunition so we could defend ourselves against the Greeks." He leans sideways from where he is sitting, stretches his arms, his face breaking into a smile, the folds of his face curtains on either side. Dazzling perfection achieved with porcelain dentures.

"Come... come to Grandpa *bullim*, come... come," he makes a childish gurgling sound as the thick rough fingers make waves in the air cajoling the toothless wonder on all fours crawling away speedily scattering little excited cries and giggles to his audience of one. He pretends to get up to follow the baby who becomes more excited by the chasing game scuttling off even more speedily giving out little victory cries of delight. He sits back in his seat, his eyes moist as he continues to watch the baby for a while. "Those who tried to crawl into the darkness, it was a moonless night... to disappear into the potato fields, were shot or beaten mercilessly and dragged back onto the road. A deterrent. That night was Godless... He abandoned us all. They raped women," after a brief silence, "...and girls, some as young as thirteen– fourteen." He seems reluctant to go there. He resists. But it's like a flood. Once the barrier breaks, he is swept in the torrent. That memory has been buried for so long... thirty-four years. Why dredge it out? What good would it do? The dead are dead. What's done is done.

"I will never forget this man... he just stood there, calmly, once he realised he was going to be killed. He was a barrister, I think, famous one. I knew him. He had defended many Cypriotturkish people, even when he knew some couldn't pay him. But I couldn't say anything. I kept quiet," he lowers his voice and throws a glance towards the house. A quick confirmation that no one was close enough to be listening... to what? Shame? Guilt? Remorse for his silence on the night but even worse his silence for over thirty-four years? He colluded. He was complicit in the creation of this history, he knew. But even more so the creation of the schizophrenic society of cowards his children and grandchildren now inhabited. This was his legacy and that of those still walking around free. Wherever they dug the ruins of the past… skeletons emerged with the recent excavations of mass graves. Bones, hidden at the bottom of waterless wells, under bridges, caves, ravines, remote and not so remote fields, emerged to tell half the story, the other half still a secret, safe with the perpetrators. "I didn't want trouble with the officers from Turkey or the TMT* killers they brought to Famagusta, to do the killing. They would bring in outsiders because they knew the locals would find it difficult to kill someone they knew or grew up with. It wasn't worth putting my life and that of my children in danger and be accused of being a traitor. Do you know what that means? Especially during a time of war? I'll tell you… death! They used to kill 'traitors', and you could be a traitor sitting in the café with a Cypriotgreek you'd known all your life. You immediately became a spy! It didn't take much to be one.

"I killed some myself…" he shuffles in his chair and glances over at the baby. "When you get the orders and the gun delivered in the middle of the night, from 'high above', you don't ask questions. You go out and do what you are told. It was all for the Cause. We killed many good people, some totally innocent… for the Cause. I left and went to London. Now, I know most of it was for the personal Cause… of the Leader!"

* * *

25

The body next to the passenger side of the car leans over calmly and opens the door. Maria holds tightly onto Aris. She is feeling exposed, more vulnerable; the shield created by the car door has been removed. She tries to keep focused, her heart beating like a trapped bird. She looks at her husband watching her, agitated. He tries to take a step forward, a muzzle slowly cuts across his chest, dark against his white linen shirt. The hand leans down and grabs Maria's arm. She is still holding onto Aris, straddling her lap. He pulls her out, forces her onto her feet. Maria can hear Yorgos' desperate shout, "Mariaaa…" as she is dragged from the car. A few steps along, the young fourteen–fifteen year old appears by their side. He is calm, "*En entaxi,*" he says in Cypriot-greek, "It's OK. Don't be frightened." She looks at the face with the innocence of youth. His Cypriotness a momentary comfort evaporating as soon as he leans over to take Aris from her arms. Her elegance, gentle manner, reasonableness vanish. She snatches him away her eyes scattering fire, "No! No!" she hisses. From the corner of her eye she sees the muzzle against Yorgos' heaving chest. She is on her own. She takes a few steps back and stares at the young boy. He has not changed his expression. Such calmness, control, so unnatural for one so young. The man's face a mocking leer. He grabs her hands and prises them apart at breaking point. She struggles twisting and kicking, tears rolling down her face drenched in sweat. She tries to escape by dropping her body on the ground suddenly, but the two hands hold on, bruising her forearms and burning the skin. Aris is sitting on her lap, his arms tightly around her neck, almost suffocating her. The young boy prises Aris' hands from around her neck and pulls him up into the air, like in a game of swirling around… Suspended in mid-air by his arms, he looks over his shoulder at his mother being dragged away by the stocky man with bullets strapped across his chest, wearing camouflage hunting trousers and boots.

* * *

"He dragged her into the night. A light elegant little thing she was. Like a bird. Young, barely in her mid-twenties. I heard him shout like a wounded animal, "Mariaaa… Mariaaa…" as they dragged her from the car. She was wearing a light blue sleeveless dress. You know, it was a hot summer… '74. And she was beautifully tanned, with dark hair down to her shoulders…" He pinches his lower lip and bites the tip of his thumbnail. He looks up, "You should've seen what he did to her… Sex is one thing… but this was something else! Her face was cut up, eye swollen, lips cut up, bleeding, dress torn into shreds," he demonstrates by moving his hands from the top of his chest to his knees, repeating the action a few times, his face crumples, "…soaked in blood. You could see her legs and arms sliced open…" he shudders. "She was covered in the red soil of the potato fields… she held her forearm, it dangled unnaturally… it was broken. She walked barefoot into the headlights of the cars on the road. For everyone to see… as though she wanted everyone to see! She didn't cry or shout. Nothing! She limped, dragging her foot, looking ahead, searching for their car.

"She was the symbol of our shame... of the shame of our Cause. And of those who carried out such atrocities in its name. I wasn't proud to be a Turkish man that night! The blood running in my veins was not *noble* that night... it was a stinking sewage!" After a deep sigh, "And he was Cypriotturkish, the one who did it, he wasn't from Turkey..."

He realises he is going bright red in the face and throat and sits back in the chair reminding himself not to forget to take his high blood pressure pills, as he sometimes does. The toothless wonder is preoccupied with a bright orange marigold flower he has decapitated with one flying swoop from the flowerpot next to his chair busily deflowering it, scattering clumps of petals all around him.

* * *

"What's your name then?" the fourteen–fifteen year old asks Aris. He does not look up. He keeps furtively looking in the direction he last saw his mother. "Mine is Hasan." Aris wipes off his tears with his palms. His mother has been gone a long time.

"Where do you live? Are you from Famagusta?" Aris looks at the ground, covering his eyes with his hands, his elbows on his bare knees. "I'm from Sandallar, Sandalaris... do you know it?" Aris gets up and looks in the direction he has last seen his mother. He is agitated. "Don't worry she'll be back."

"When?" Aris asks as quick as a flash. "Soon. Soon she will be back. Just sit down..." Aris does, looking at the gun the young boy is carrying.

"This is my father's gun. Do you have one?" Aris is shocked; he is not even allowed to have a toy gun. He checks that he can still see his father. He lifts his chin up, the Cypriot gesture of *No*. "I'm thirteen. I learnt to shoot when I was nine. My father taught me." A brief silence as the thirteen-year-old caresses the shotgun.

"Have you seen anyone dead?" asks Hasan. Aris jumps up, agitated, "Yes, at the hotel," he blurts out. "A man. He was hanging from the hole in the wall. After the jet fighters..." Hasan nods slowly. "Have you?" asks Aris with fear, for the first time looking at Hasan. "Yes," he says with a deep sigh. Aris continues to watch Hasan's face with fear. They are sitting on the ground by the car on the road, leaning against it facing the darkness into the fields, beyond the initial light amber headlights casting long shadows. All the doors are open, looted, their belongings now belongings of others. "My Dad," came from Hasan. Panic in Aris' eyes, he looks for his father who is still standing by the side of the road, further down, with many other men of all ages. Aris looks up to see Hasan wipe his nose, "My Mum. My two sisters. My little brother... he was your age," Hasan nods towards Aris. "My eighteen-month-old baby brother... and my *nene* and *dede*. They were old." He looks at Aris, "Why did they kill them? They are all dead..." as though murmuring to himself, "I have no one left..." Aris stands up like a shot. He starts to tremble, his eyes full of tears he does not hide, looking directly into Hasan's face which is now oblivious to his presence, crumpled, eyes shut, covered in tears and snot, sobbing uncontrollably. Aris sways from leg to leg, agitated… He must pee...

* * *

"She swept her son into her arms with that single arm, she held him. He wrapped his arms around her neck, his legs around her waist tightly and pissed all over her breasts and down her front. She took one look at her husband, put her son into the car, got in, put it in gear, put her foot down and took off with one foot and one arm into the fields overtaking the cars blocking the road, like a woman possessed. No one dared to shoot or drive after her. We watched her as the lights of the car disappeared on that lonely road going west, far into the distance into the night…"

He murmurs almost to himself, "No one said a word… but you couldn't help but admire a woman like that. I looked at her husband. A strange tiny smile on the corner of his lips… that's all." A deep sigh.

"After a while we were told to tell the women, children and the old to go. We pushed them into the cars, lorries, pick-up trucks, threatened them with guns. Some just left, others wanted their husbands and sons. They tried to walk over to the men; we turned our guns on them. They stopped. It was heart-breaking really, we didn't allow them to say goodbye.

"We were under orders. We didn't know what the officers from Turkey wanted to do with the men. Later they said they were going to be used in prisoner exchanges. It made sense…

"Then out of the blue, a young one, barely fourteen-fifteen… he went berserk! He started shouting and screaming about his father, his mother and sisters. He was crying about his brother who was six… We knew him. He was the only survivor, his family was massacred alongside thirty others, we were told, in one of the Messaoria villages. He waved his gun at the men, at the women and children who were scrambling into the cars and lorries, frightened out of their wits. He kept shouting, ' I'm going to kill you… why did you murder my family? What did we ever do to you…?' tears and snot running down his face. It was heart breaking. He had found them brutally murdered in the house and around the yard when he came back from tending his herd." He shakes his head, the confusion of the moment still lingering in his eyes.

"Then a hothead from another village shouted he wanted revenge, an eye for an eye. He was one of the sharp shooters but young, barely eighteen-nineteen. He was one of those who had heard there was a blockade and that Greeks had been taken prisoners. So he turned up for a bit of excitement with a couple of others. He wanted to kill everyone. He kept pointing his gun at the women and children getting into the cars, then at the men lined up at the side of the road. He was raging, running up and down. No-one in his family was killed… Then a couple of others also got worked up into a frenzy and started to do the same…

"The army officers didn't intervene. They let it play out. Some of us instinctively walked towards the women and children and stood facing the hotheads. We took a risk. The hotheads turned to the men. They started pushing and hitting them

31

with the butts of their guns, kicking, swearing… They were pushed against the wall of the open reservoir used to water the orange orchards. A low wall of about two feet. Some instinctively climbed on the wall. We stood back. Suddenly a machine gun rattles out. From where we don't know! Shotguns join in. It was Hell! The men didn't have a chance. They were mowed down. They fell back into the water. Again and again… they killed them all… hundreds… it only took a few minutes." He shakes his head as the image resurrects itself. "We had to let them do it… to take revenge… an eye for an eye," he says slowly.

"Some of us just dropped on the ground." A brief silence, "When we went to look, the reservoir was full of dead bodies, all piled up. Riddled with bullets. Some still with their eyes open. The water had turned to blood. I will never ever forget it…" he rubs his fingers and hands repeatedly.

"As the day began to break, they opened the sluice gates and the blood water gushed out like a river. It rushed to the orange trees a little further down," he looks down at his knitted fingers going white at the knuckles, then away into the distance. A vacant look.

"We bury them in two mass graves. Huge. We dug all night… All of us… just digging and digging. We managed to bury them as the sun was rising," he sighs and rubs his palms on his legs a few times, absentmindedly, looking down. "Some took whatever was left on the bodies… the worst was the gold wedding-rings. They cut off the fingers… The officers said it was to prevent identification but it was robbing the dead… and we all knew it."

He straightens his back, takes a deep breath, exhales loudly and looks straight ahead, "They are 'missing' according to records. No one found them, so they are 'missing'. They are DEAD! Many of us are witnesses... but no one will say. The area is under the control of the Turkish military. The 'Forbidden Zone'. No one can enter except military personnel. Their graves and our secret are safe. What a secret...! I've lived with this all these years..." an imperceptible tremble in the voice immediately buried.

"And you know... it's not very far from here. Only just down the road... Some nights it's so hard to sleep. Well you know that; I come here to talk to you. But even that doesn't help," he hangs his head staring at his lap for a while.

"Two summers ago I got really worried!" he looks up, "It was the time when they started to dig up the graves. People rang the UN Missing Persons Unit anonymously giving details of murders and burial places. Then one night, I heard what I thought were tanks in the 'Forbidden Zone'. When I listened carefully I realised they were bulldozers... they were at it... all night! Then the next night! It went on for three-four nights! I was worried... I was so scared! What if they were found?" After a brief silence as though to himself, "And maybe part of me wants them to be found." He looks around him with vacant eyes, "The following day I asked one of the TMT members, a hardcore, I told him I'd heard bulldozers... At first he didn't want to say, but we carry a common guilt... we were all there.

"Anyway, you know what they were doing?" He waits for a respectable pause, "They were digging up the mass graves after thirty-two years!" He calms down, "They scooped up the bones, shoes, rotting clothing, everything with those huge mechanical diggers and dumped them into the back of military lorries. I suppose they were afraid someone amongst us might talk... We wouldn't, would we?" he asks without seeking reassurance, then continues in the same breath, "They sent them to a stone quarry halfway up the Pentadachtylos Mountains and crushed everything into small pebble-size pieces. They loaded them up again, brought them back and laid them down as hardcore then tarmac on top... on the road they are re-surfacing in the 'Forbidden Zone' leading to the hotels the Army has commandeered for a luxury holiday resort for its officers. All under the control of the Turkish Military. Ingenious... with orders from the highest command outside the jurisdiction of the UN. All that remains is a beautiful, smooth asphalt road.

No one will ever find them..."

He sighs again and looks at the face sitting in front of him listening to his confessions. It's not the first time. He has come here before, to this safe place where he can dig, excavate in his memory where he has chosen to bury, to forget so much. He sits in the same chair and talks, sometimes losing all sense of time... he looks out for signs of disapproval, accusation, hatred even sympathy and understanding, signs of forgiveness, of guilt, of shame... in the face.

He picks up his grandson who has come up and put both hands on his knees, now standing, pleased with his creation of torn up newspapers, thrown and scattered cushions, plastic cups, boxes empty of their contents, shoes and sandals, socks, decapitated marigolds, busy-lizzies, daisies, stock flowers...

"Come here... you *maskara*, little clown! Look... look! Say goodbye! We have to go or they will be after us. It's food time." He lifts him up and holds him close to his face, breathing in his sweet curdled smells, cheek crushing into cheek, showing him their images in the mirror.

* * *

The woman with the dark hair walking barefoot on the beach notices the tattoo of the lurid red crescent and star on the inside forearm of the man playing with his daughter running in and out of the water's edge amongst the descending shadows of the deserted ghost hotels in the Forbidden Zone guarded by the black shadow soldiers on red boards tangled amongst barbed wire as the sun goes down in the West.

Famagusta-London-Nicosia. 2007-2008

---

* TMT: Türk Mukavement Teşkilatı (Turkish Resistance Organisation)

CAUGHT OUT

"They caught him with his lover. His mother and his wife's brother set a trap for him and caught him. He had this extra flat. His wife and he bought it with the money from their wedding. You know what it's like... that's what happens at weddings. They collect all that money pinned onto their clothes all the way down to the floor... and they bought a flat with it. His wife had a flat already, her grandmother used to live in it and she died or something, I don't quite know, so they had two flats. They bought both of them from the Council.

"I couldn't cope with him. He was so unpredictable, so immature. He was becoming deranged. He rang me a few times and I just gave up after a while I couldn't cope with him. It's not · worth it. You have to face what's happening to you and tell your mother at least. Fathers... never mind, leave them out of it." And he swipes his hand away as though shooing a fly. The importance of fathers could not be more powerfully dismissed than with that gesture! Shoo... out of my life! "But your mother who gave birth to you, who loved you... you have to tell her. You can't pretend."

"What about you?" she asks watching him and laughing at his humorous way of dealing with his life. He is a market stallholder. He sells women's clothes in Ridley Market, Hackney. Women come and look at his clothes while he talks to her. As the wind blows he instinctively grabs his giant umbrella handle set up to protect his wares from the rain.

"How much is this?" insists a Black woman. "Twenty-five pounds, darling," without turning his face in the middle of his story.

"What size is it?" comes another insistent question.

"Twelve," is the non-committed answer. She is too obviously above that size but does not accept defeat and defies classification by others.

"Haven't you got a size fourteen?"

"I've got a size sixteen!"

She shrinks, "Sixteen!" she says, touching her breast tenderly with her fingertips, insulted, and smiles shyly at the woman he is talking to who had turned her eyes to look at her in the middle of the story.

"If one buys one thing, they all want the same thing; if one stops to look, they all stop to look!"

"How did they catch them?" she asks.

"I suppose someone must have twigged that something was going on and they set a trap for them. They caught them in bed together, there was no denying it. Then the whole thing started... screams, shouts, the whole family became involved, a big scandal! They, the family, reported it to the police, the lover was deported. You should have seen it! It was so messy, a real

Arabesque story... the Turkish films had nothing on this!" He laughs then his face creases up again as though he bit into something bitter.

"And he was terrible. He just didn't know how to handle it. He freaked out. He did things he shouldn't have done." He straightens out a black suit with embroidery on the collar. He looks at passers-by, would-be customers, with a quick glance.

"He wanted to give his lover the impression that he was really well-off. He borrowed money from everywhere and everyone! He cheated lots of people, he did really horrible things, he swindled his friends. He was so much in debt. Then he went to Cyprus and checked into one of these expensive hotels. If he had put together four or five thousand pounds he blew it all at this hotel. Golden Sands. Trying to impress his lover. He just blew it all!" He makes an expansive open fan gesture with his hand and stops.

"Do you know it?" he asks.

She says no with the slight upward movement of her head and the raising of her eyebrows.

"Anyway, it's this really expensive place in Girne. So they stayed there; he spent all his money on his lover. They ate, drank, went to discos. As you know, Cyprus is expensive. It didn't last long. He spent it all. They were then kicked out of the hotel. He had nowhere to go. No one would have him. So he came back to London. His wife wouldn't have him back, of course. His mother didn't want to know. He'd disgraced the family! Others are after him because he swindled everyone. So he can't ask for help from

39

anyone. There he is... you see him here and there, destitute. To tell you the truth, I don't think it was worth it. Not the way he did it anyway."

"What happened to the lover?" she asks.

"Oh, nothing! What can the lover do? In Cyprus; waiting for him to sort things out from this end. The lover obviously wants to come here... but not much chance with these immigration laws as they are. And if you haven't got anyone, no one will look after you. This bloke can't even look after himself let alone his lover."

***

"Oh! *Vay vay vay!* What a surprise! *Hoşgeldiniz! Hoşgeldiniz!*"

The expansive mother contained in the latest fashion garment admired on the tall top models on the front covers of magazines opens the door and smiles. She is one of the privileged few who worked in the sweatshops making those garments for the world's elite so she wore them whether they suited her or not just like other Cypriots making other garments in other sweatshop.

She welcomes her guests. She is happy and although she had said it was a surprise it wasn't at all. She knew they were coming and she was well prepared for them. She leans over and kisses her brother who has just arrived from Cyprus. She has dressed to make a good impression on him and his family. This time he is here only with his son.

40

She doesn't like to give the impression that all they do is work long hours. She wants him to think that there are other important things in their lives, that they know how to enjoy themselves. It wasn't all about killing themselves in the shop or in the factory to show off their car, their expensively but tastelessly decorated house, the large amount of food and excessive amounts of drinks in the cabinet. Her pink painted cheeks flashed in contrast to her straw tinted hair in an attempt to hide the greys appearing amongst the dark browns. Her gold bracelets and chains and rings were ceremoniously put on to complete the picture of success if not of a comfortable life.

She embraces her brother's son, who is barely twenty, she thinks. He has a smooth skin, dark hair and dark soft eyes. His aftershave as she kisses him reminds her he is a man. She checks herself and her womanly desires. She suddenly becomes conscious that her breasts have rubbed against his body. She pulls herself away and looks at his face for signs of awareness. He smiles in the depths of his eyes at his aunt and tells her she's looking younger than the last time he saw her because he is aware of her efforts to preserve her younger self.

"What is it? Is it the water the soil the air of this London that makes women look young and beautiful?" She laughs him off, sure that he is only being polite and he has not sensed anything. She shows him in.

Behind her, her daughter kisses the cheeks of her cousin formally as appropriate between two young people in their twenties lest there is talk even from the most innocent of contacts.

People talk. People invent. People want to add excitement to life. People refuse to accept the dullness of life all around.

Wake up get the children ready send them off take them to school go to work enter that sweatshop early in the morning listen to the crap from the boss who keeps telling you to work harder or else you know there are so many people out there ready to jump in go to the shop work your guts out trying to make a living go shopping pick up the kids go home cook for the evening eat sit in front of the TV and fall into bed get up in the morning...

...and at the weekend go to a wedding and engagement reception a circumcision party sit in rows of tables sometimes not sure whether you are in a wedding engagement circumcision party unless you look in the appropriate direction the same food is served the same music played the same dance danced the same money is hung on the breast of the bride groom fiancé circumcised boy you show off your daughters ensure that their wares goods are exhibited to the world ready for the payment from the highest bidder sometimes trouble strikes these young women nowadays get off the rails fall for some penniless nobody because they are good looking what sort of choice is that what sort of life would good looks bring how long would good looks last...

...people want life to be as dramatic as in the Turkish films... ahhh! did you see how that gullible girl believed the words of the boy's wicked mother that he was already engaged to someone else he would never marry her he was in love with his fiancé the daughter of the eminent so-and-so the girl was just a plaything for him passing the time after all... didn't she know?

Cemaliye kisses her distant cousin's cheeks with the appropriate degree of propriety. Distant not because of proximity of relationship but they have not met each other often and they don't know each other at all. Cemaliye was born in London, in Islington, when it was a home for Cypriotturkish communities in the late sixties. Her father was an auxiliary policeman in Limassol. Soon after the declaration of independence in nineteen-sixty he took the hand-out package for services delivered to the Great British Empire and came to London. The package consisted of a British passport for him and his wife who was two months pregnant, two tickets and a thousand pounds pocket money to start a new life. Compared to what he would have faced it was a good package. He had to escape from the possible reprisals of all those Cypriotgreeks he had beaten the shit out of and imprisoned under instructions from the British officers. He was only doing his job, obeying instructions. He sensed that his compatriots - no matter that they are known as gentle island people more in love with life than vendettas - would not welcome him with open arms once the British Empire withdrew in nineteen-sixty leaving well-stocked well-guarded annexes of the Empire in Dhekelia, Episkopi and Akrotiri. The Middle East can still be controlled from the unsinking aircraft carrier as Cyprus is aptly named. England promised a new life where no one would know who he was and no one would care anyway.

She was born into the family as the third daughter and her childhood passed in the working men's cafe her parents ran in Islington. She forever remembers the eating and smelling of greasy chips sausages bacon and fried eggs. Greasy chips and egg came out of her pores almost. And bacon was not supposed to have been allowed in the house let alone cooked and served by Muslims. That was one of the first jobs her father had; he moved from one to another until now where he had a grocer's shop in Haringey.

Her cousin was handsome. Slim. He had beautiful eyes and long eyelashes and a very dazzling smile... and full lips. He brushed his curly black hair back. But he didn't seem to be aware of his own looks or the effect he had on women around him or maybe he was too used to it. He was so natural with women.

Behind her came her husband who shook hands heartily and welcomed the father and the son who he had not seen before and now he was related to. They had become his uncle and his cousin as well. He was also a second-generation Cypriot but came when he was one and grew up in Haringey. He grew up with African-Caribbean boys because they were more daring and would get up to more tricks than anyone else. He didn't like the English boys because they didn't like him. They called him "bubble-n-squeak, Greek", even though they knew he wasn't a Cypriotgreek, but it was all the same to them. The Black boys stuck together and didn't let anyone mess with them. There were a couple of Cypriotturkish boys in the gang and they did everything together. Not that they did anything nasty; just the fact that a group of Black boys walked together was enough to worry other people around them. He picked up Jamaican language, one of the best collections of Reggae records, swear words and they picked up Turkish ones. His mother always shouted at him for going around with those "Arabs" her word for African-Caribbean people. Why couldn't he stick with his own kind or, even better, with the white boys? But she was polite to the boys when they came to call for Ahmet and even offered them things to eat, things she had made for the family. In her heart of hearts she knew that the boys were all right and were some mother's child like her own. They were nice boys. It was just the neighbours. What would Pembe Hanım say if she saw Ahmet hanging around with these "Arab" boys. What would she say? It would be all over the community, that she, she wasn't able to control her son who was going around with the "Arabs". She would be embarrassed, her reputation would be damaged. What reputation, Ahmet would ask her when she would go on and on; what reputation indeed? It was just that the community would talk, there would be gossip, she didn't want gossip; and then it would also affect the reputation of his little sister. She was only six but as she grew up, if he continued to hang around the "Arab" boys and they were to come around when she was older... no! That wouldn't do! That was the limit! Wait till she gets a couple of years older and he would have to stop this nonsense. She wasn't going to have the kismet of her daughter cut off because of his nonsense of hanging around the "Arab" boys because he felt more comfortable or safer with them. He had to stop this nonsense.

Then he was married off to Cemaliye. It was as traditional as the marriage of their fathers and mothers except making use of all the latest gadgets, like filming the event. They met at one of those well-known weddings one Sunday afternoon in one of the big banquet halls. The Aksaray. White Palace indeed! And they had their wedding there in the end.

He gave in to pressures to marry from his mother. He tried to resist but in the end he ran out of excuses according to his mother's set of values or good reasons according to his own which he thought might be acceptable. He held out until the age of twenty-five then his father joined in.

They wanted him to stop running around with his friends, disco here night-club there wasting his money wasting his life he needed to settle down a wife would do him good and a couple of kids would settle his madness he was getting old no woman would have him soon he was wasting his life he would be too old to have children and be a proper father what did he want to be a father at forty he wouldn't even be able to kick a football around in the park with his sons if he left it any later he would be an old man his hair was going to fall out soon and women don't like bald men didn't he know his father did not feel he could support him like this any longer he had to make up his mind was he going to get involved in the business and work hard or what he didn't think Ahmet could take the responsibility like this but if he was to marry then he would feel responsible for his family and would settle down and yes they would concede to him choosing his wife as long as she was the daughter of a good family and her parents had taken good care of her he wasn't going to chose some barefooted beggar was he to leave it to them... they would see him right.

Everything was arranged; all he did was to say yes to their

suggestion when they pointed her out at a cousin's wedding. It felt like they were out shopping. She seemed OK, lively, was dancing with her friends, she looked at him teasingly across the tables when she realised his family and he were looking at her. She had guessed. The boy she secretly loved was married to a richer girl eight months earlier. She was devastated, thought about committing suicide but in the end went to Cyprus and stayed for five months. She came back knowing she had no choice but to go on. She had to find someone to be married to - maybe the feeling of being married and having children would make the heartache go away. She loved children. She wanted to have one as soon as she was married. And in time she might love her husband. That's what the elders kept saying anyway. In time she would love her husband and forget about her love.

Do you think we loved anyone, they would say, we just married them and here we are. What's so different about you lot? Just because you are younger and you have a bit more freedom to say yes or no, more than we did, nothing much has changed for women. It's the same story. In the end you will marry someone, you will serve him, you will cook for him, clean his house, have his kids, put up with his funny ways and just get on. No use moaning or groaning about your lot and think you can do something about it. He is your husband, he has to look after you. That's it! Sometimes you younger girls think you can do things differently from us. It's all the same and don't talk about love. What's love? What's that got to do with anything?

They were married six months later. That was a year ago. What was it like? She couldn't complain. He didn't have bad habits.

He went to his Mum a lot. He went out with his friends a lot, the ones who came to his wedding. Lots of people his age, some Black friends, they all seemed to have hung around since they were young. They played football together for one of the teams in the Turkish League. Most were married like him only one or two were still unmarried. Her own marriage wasn't exciting. He didn't take her out as much as she wanted. And she was getting bored on her own in the house they bought together. She was working half a day at the dry cleaners but that was almost just to get her out of the house and contribute to the bills. She wasn't enjoying it, she wasn't enjoying married life. She felt more lonely than when she was in her mother's house, at least she had her sisters when she was at home. That's why she would go to her Mum's every minute she had.

And a baby? Well, it wasn't happening. Every time she wanted it he moved away. At first he tried and she didn't know what she was supposed to do. She thought she was doing something wrong, putting him off, he gave her that impression anyway. She would hug him and caress him and he would get excited and come inside her then all of a sudden she would realise that she couldn't feel him. She would try her best and push her body against him, open her legs wider, try to hold him. He would try and they would both struggle because that's what it seemed like. After the struggle he would roll off and leave her bewildered, laying on her back in the dark, because it was always in the dark, not knowing if something had happened, if he had come, if this was all there was to it. She would lie there afraid to do anything, feeling hunger rising from her inner depths, from her cunt, unsatisfied, unfulfilled, screaming with hunger. He would say nothing, turn his back on her. Sometimes he would turn around and hug her, wrap her in his arms and kiss her hair. She felt maybe he loved her then. In time they would learn how to do it and in time they would have children and then everything would be OK. Her mother told her to be patient every time she tried to broach the subject.

She had nothing to worry about he wasn't beating her up was he he wasn't spending his money on whores and other women especially English women was he he went out with his mates every weekend and that was normal men like going out with their friends for a drink after being at home all week he was looking after her providing for her wasn't he not all of them are good at it you know they might talk about it a lot show off and put themselves about and walk around thrusting their below the belt area forward to show what a big bundle they had but when they have to do it when it counts they shrivel up don't worry about it she would laugh wiping her tears from the corner of her eyes doubling over and slapping her hands at her own explicitness secretly worrying that her daughter had not been sexually satisfied yet and was living with that frustration who knows what might happen if she continued to be sexually frustrated she can't carry on for ever can she if only she could get pregnant that would take things off her mind she would be occupied God forbid she might want to divorce him or even worse go with another man she would die of the shame of it wasn't it crazy all these years she was like a mad woman making sure that nothing happened to her daughter that nothing happened to her thin membrane her virginity symbol stretched across her vagina's entrance and here she was now that that damn membrane didn't matter she wasn't doing anything and wasn't enjoying anything wasn't life a fuck-up!

Everyone piled into the meticulously kept *misafir odası*, guest room as it is called in Turkish. No one is allowed to even walk into it during normal family life. It is the preserve of the guests.

The family can only use it when guests arrive. The best china is in the glass cupboard so are the crystal glasses of all shapes for whisky wine water perfectly lined up small ornaments of china glass tall vases figurines dancing playing the violin being hobos dogs on their hind legs an inevitable map of Cyprus made into a clock coffee cups with an ancient map of Cyprus on them colourful plastic flowers in vases dotted about the room brand new looking sparkling furniture reproductions of some heavy palace furniture... all tasteless. Finished off with the big glass chandelier maybe even crystal. And the obligatory untouchable drinks cabinet containing collections of whiskies wines miniatures all lined up leering at the guests with the knowledge that they will never be drunk, they are there to be looked at and for him to feel proud of his achievement of his collection. Everything in the room belonged to her, she had chosen it, she had arranged it, but that belonged to him. She wasn't even allowed to clean it.

"What would you like to drink? We have practically everything you might like," she says without giving them a chance to ask but also preparing the ground for him to enter and show off his collection and knowledge. Cemaliye sits next to her husband on the long sofa. The uncle and the son opposite them on comfortable chairs near each other. Mother is fussing to provide nuts and savoury nibbles while father shows off with his drinks, both giving the performance of the ever attentive generous hosts to their guests. Cemaliye's eyes keep flowing back to her uncle's son. She catches the curve at the side of his lips, the laughter in his eyes, his fingers folded around the glass. She hides her fascination with him quite well; she has had a lifetime of practice. She is careful to address him as little cousin as a term of endearment but also highlighting to everyone that at twenty-two she is three years his senior. He responds with his casual warm smile and reserved manner. He doesn't seem to need to speak in a manner that draws attention to himself or needs to impress anyone.

His father tells Cemaliye that marriage seems to have done her good, she is looking good. He then makes the usual sexual innuendo and jokes with Ahmet. He in turn confirms the correctness of the observation with his hearty laughter. Yes, indeed, once you give these women a bit of.... they blossom, thanks to us. Cemaliye shifts her shoulders and smiles as befits a modest married woman. Her eye catches her cousin's smiling eyes which move from Ahmet's laughter to her uneasy smile.

During dinner, Ahmet and her cousin sit next to each other. She watches them loosening up as the evening progresses and is pleased that they are getting on so well. She hadn't seen her husband so friendly towards her side of the family. They are drinking, she thinks, it's also the influence of the drink. By two o'clock in the morning all the men are drunk, women are tipsy and laughing a lot, humouring the men.

Men are telling stories of their youth and telling the younger ones that they don't know what life was about. Did they live through EOKA, did they live through TAKSIM and VOL-KAN? What was that... lining fourteen-year-old schoolboys in the schoolyard and telling them they had to be soldiers and protect the *Yavru Vatan*, baby country, and that *Ana Vatan*, the motherland, had ordered it.

"I shit on it! You pimps! If you thought it was easy why don't you come and do it?" demands Cemaliye's father of long-suppressed ghosts. He swings his hand across his chest pointing to the space between his feet. "Oh! Yeah! Easy innit? You send your sons to Turkey, pretend they are at college or university so that they are safe, and you tell everyone else to send their sons to fight. They are sacrificial lambs but not your sons. If your arse is tight come and fight and let your son fight too!" The uncle talks of the officer from Turkey who came to the village and threatened everyone to turn up for duty the following night. "The village shepherd didn't because no one had told him, he was such a meek person I suppose no one thought of it. They found him dead after a few days by his animals in the valley. The Turkish officer blamed the Greeks for the bloody murder but everyone in the village knew it was the officers from Turkey. What funny names they had; Wind, Storm and such like. Our people weren't such brutes to do such a cold-blooded thing to someone from their own village; he was only a poor bastard trying to earn his living."

He sniffles trying to suppress tears. "Let's drink," he shouts as he staggers across to the whisky bottle - a dash of coke takes the bitterness away. The music goes on, Turkish, Greek and a bit of English. The gathering dances, the older ones collapse on the sofa. Ahmet is trying to dance with the cousin. Their arms and legs move leisurely and exaggeratedly slowly courtesy of the drinks. They keep reaching out, balancing themselves or helping the other balance as he staggers. At one stage they look like rams horn-locked in a fight with one arm against each other's neck, the other hand holding onto a whisky glass. Once the dance finished they hug and slap each other on the back, holding each other up laughing with eyes closed, almost passing out in each other's arms. Congratulating each other for still standing. "How beautifully you dance, kid. Is this what they teach you in Cyprus?" Ahmet says holding the cousin's face in his hands close to his face in his drunken stupor.

***

"How beautifully you danced that night. I couldn't keep my hands off you. I couldn't keep my eyes off you. I trembled each time I thought of my lips touching yours. I don't know how I kept my lips off you. I don't know how I managed to control myself in front of all of them."

"You do though... don't you? You learn to do it as soon as you realise you desire someone. You must not let anyone suspect a thing..." The cousin reaches out and touches the hands holding his face.

They are on the mattress on the floor in the middle of the room. The white sheet acting as curtain at the window filters the sunshine coming into the room falling onto the bed. They are kneeling facing each other. They are naked. Ahmet holds Cem's face in his palms as he did that night they met, his heart beating wildly, his body wanting to burst out of the skin holding it in check. He breathes in Cem's smell. He touches his cheeks, eyes, nose, temples, hair, mouth, lightly, with his slightly parted lips taking in his smells. Kissing him gently afraid of the violence of his own passion. His lips move further down to kiss his neck, his shoulders, his chest. He licks his nipples. He takes them between his lips and plays with them with his tongue until he feels them harden and stand up. He moves his hands down Cem's shoulders, then to his waist, to the small of his back, exploring with his fingers the crevice between his buttocks, his other hand caressing his buttocks in circular, gentle movements. He carefully lays Cem on his back trembling, touching him gently, afraid he may break him, his fingers move to caress the smooth warm skin across his abdomen, navel, down the inside of his legs. Ahmet takes Cem between his legs and on his knees leans over and kisses this body he adores, he licks every inch down to his toes. He sinks his face into his curly sweet smelling mound of hairs and sucks Cem's offering of himself. He fills his mouth with love juices as his heart beats in his head. He turns Cem gently over on his side and nearly cries out as he enters him.

***

54

"Well they had a key didn't they. The mother had a key because it was her mother's flat. So the mother and his wife's brother found them in bed together. There was no denying it. There it was. Well, you can imagine the scene can't you! Especially from the mother... the mother informed on the boy so he was deported. Ahmet now is wandering around desperate, alone, because he cheated everyone, he owes money to so many people. And frankly, no one wants to help him, they've been stung! And he's gone crazy! He is walking around like a madman. You see him in the cafes, gambling what little money he has. He thinks he will make it big one day and he will bring his lover over. I don't know... he lives in cloud cuckoo land. As long as he stays away from me I don't mind. I tried to help him but it's no use... he is a liability, he has lost it somewhere... he should have told his mother right at the beginning. She would have shouted and screamed but she would have accepted it eventually."

"No love," his voice is impatient but gentle, "I don't have that size in twelve. It's too small for you. I have this in size sixteen, would you like to see it?"

The Black woman whispers an inaudible no, offended that anyone should take her for a size sixteen and walks away.

London. October 1993

**BEDTIME
STORY**

"Where's my son?" She looks with anxious eyes, leaning around the bodies blocking her view. Her hand reaches out pushing aside firmly, the white coats floating past her, trying not to be rude.

"Where is my son?" her trembling voice follows her eyes up to the white coat's face.

"It's all right Mrs. Ahmet. Don't worry. He is just around the corner. Here, look you'll see him," responds a gentle, clearly spoken English mouth not certain whether to smile or be serious.

She charges towards the direction they point. Her feet almost floating on the shiny floors, her head looking both ways at once. Like the chicken in her yard when it moves away from danger eyes fixed, captured but quickly scanning both sides from the sides of her head.

She sees him. He is on the left. He is lying on his back, his eyes closed. Nearest to the window. There are two more beds on that side. One empty.

She mumbles, "*Osmanım, oğlum...*" as she fights to hold

onto her tears. Her lips twist into pain. She wipes the hidden tear running down inside her nose onto her upper lip with the side of her finger. She sighs and rushes to her son.

She doesn't throw herself on him as she had imagined she would do, playing the scene time and time again in her head while she sat in her garden at sunset, watching the sea listening to the last sounds of the day, breathing in the scent of the jasmine flowers climbing above her front door. Sometimes she would pick handfuls of closed buds and put them in her lap in the cradle created by her skirt trapped under her knees on either side. The buds would open as the night came, slowly, as little funnels, then as pointed white stars releasing their scent deep into the night. By morning they were crumpled, soiled with brown stains of death on their delicate whiteness.

She walked into his space slowly. Dragging herself inch by inch. Quietly. Afraid she would scare him, startle him. He didn't know she was coming. She just came. She didn't want him to be angry with her. He was like that; unpredictable. He hadn't told her how he was or what was happening. She knew he didn't want her to worry. He wanted to control the situation and she would just behave outside his control. He would think it pointless for her to leave the house and the animals and come to London. She didn't want him to stop her.

Here he is. Oh! Son! You look so ill! So haggard. What have they done to you? My beautiful little lamb. What has happened? Why didn't you tell me you were so ill?

She fights her tears, as she gets closer. She looks at his

curly black hair. It is longer than when he left Cyprus three years ago. His eyelashes are still long. Even women used to be jealous of his long eyelashes. Full lips. Mouth closed. He used to laugh so much. Tell jokes, play tricks. Full of life. The mouth that never stopped now closed. He was the funniest of all her sons. He used to make her laugh until tears came to her eyes. He was her youngest. Her baby. She had three sons. When he left to come to London she cried all night. She walked around like a ghost for days forgetting where she was what she was doing.

"Why are you crying Mum?"

"I'm not, son," she would whisper afraid he would be angry with her.

"You are. Don't try and tell me you are not," his voice irritated.

"Well son... mothers cry when their sons are leaving. What do you want me to do? Laugh? Do a belly-dance?" she would retort defiantly.

"Mum. You know I can't stay. You know I can't. They'll drag me into the army. I'm eighteen. And they'll drag me in, shave my head, take my clothes away, put me in some stinking khaki uniform, line me up every morning and night, beat me up on the slightest of pretext, order me about, brainwash me, give me a gun and tell me to go and kill some innocent Greek young bloke like myself. Why? I don't want to kill anyone. For God's sake... I am only eighteen. I want to live, laugh, get drunk, fall in love and all that... Why should I kill someone who has done me no harm? He is just like me. He wants to live, laugh and fall in love too."

"Yes son, I know. But everyone else's son stays and nothing happens to them. Look there is no war any more. They go into the army and come out after two years and it's all over."

"Mum you know it's not all over. You know this country..." he is a little exasperated with her but he is aware of the unspoken reason she is doing it; she wants him to stay. To stay with her.

"You know we don't know what will happen tomorrow. Anything could happen. War could break out again. Look what happened to Fatma Teyze's son. On guard on the border. Sitting in his lookout on the sandbags. A bullet out of nowhere comes and finds him. And he is dead. Dead! Where he was sitting. And there was no war. And it wasn't the Greeks who shot him. It was some bastard playing with his gun, showing off. I don't want to go down that shit road. Do you want me to?" he demands looking with angry eyes at her eyes stubbornly looking down at her apron. She had just been to the chicken coop and collected four eggs. She was bringing them into the house. Her loose sandals were making rustling noises on the paved path, her blue *yemeni* with embroidered white and orange flowers dangled on its borders around her head.

He was right. But she didn't want him to go. She had a feeling he would not come back. They would never let him come back. He would be classed as an army deserter. She wondered what she would feel like being the mother of a deserter. They had instilled in her and all other mothers, to be mothers of heroes, brave soldiers. "*Asker Anası*", Mother-of-Soldier, that is what she had to aspire to. "*Şehit Anası*", Mother-of-a-Martyr, was the ultimate honour. She didn't want to be honoured if it meant her sons were going to be killed. And she told them so. They can keep their honours. They thought her unpatriotic especially when she told them to send their sons to war and let them be honoured as *Şehit Anası*. They remembered the dead once a year. And what use was it? What did it all mean? But she noticed that there were no *Şehit Anası* amongst the rich the distinguished who lined up the podiums on days of remembrance and military victories. There were lots of medals on the chests of all those generals, big shots with sunglasses, uniforms and white gloves. And their wives wearing their finery and gold all stand up majestically in the name of the dead. But then what? What happens to the *Şehit Anaları* the mothers who don't have their sons anymore; died defending the country? Defending all those standing on podiums on the days of the dead.

"But son, I don't want you to go. I have this feeling inside me I will never see you again."

"I'll come back Mum," he smiles now and moves up to her puts his arm around her shoulder and presses his cheek against hers, "of course you'll see me. I'm only going to London. I'll study there. And I can come back. And you can come and see me. I am going to stay with my *abi*. It will be a good excuse for you, you can come and see both your sons. Two birds with one stone. He always complains you have never been to London to see him."

He is relieved. He can argue with seeing or not seeing him and convince her. He can't argue with her other way of reasoning. She feels she is giving in. She doesn't want to be a *Şehit Anası* for all the glory in the land. Her older son suffered badly. He served as a *Mücahit* for eight years and in the war in 1974. He had seen young boys committing suicide or shooting off their limbs just to get out of the army. His nerves went when he saw a young boy beaten up, tortured, driven to suicide by the commanders from Turkey. He was discharged when he had a nervous breakdown and wasn't any good to them anymore. After a year or two he went to London for treatment. He never came back. She lost that son. She was afraid to lose this one as well.

He left. He laughed as he was leaving. His happiness had hurt her.

"Son..." she whispered. She reached out and touched his black curly hair. "My dearest little son," she said and saw the long black lashes tremble and open. His brown eyes looked up then moved towards her. After the momentary confusion the eyes smiled. He lifted his arm from under the sheet and wrapped it around her neck. She hugged him and breathed in his smells. "My Osman. My lamb," she cried as she hugged him tightly to herself. The metal on the side of the bed dug into her ribs.

***

He slowly opened his eyes when he heard the crying of a woman. She sounded so familiar. He had heard her before. It wasn't English. The English didn't cry like that. They were so controlled. She just cried. Her heart sobbing out. Lamenting. Almost wailing. He knew this crying. His eyes filled with tears.

62

It was his Mum crying. He let the tears drop. He could feel two little puddles of wetness on the pillow against his skin on either side of his head. They became two cold patches after the warmth evaporated. He felt too weak to wipe his eyes. The tear pools accumulated in the hollow between his nose and eye, balanced on the brink trembling for a moment then slowly and gently going over gathering momentum, rolling down at a vanishing speed. Soaked instantly by the white cotton pillowcase. Only a wet stain remained.

"Are you O.K. Tony?" he heard the voice near his ear. It was the nurse who had come to find out if he was upset by the sound of the crying. He turned his head and signalled yes to the blond male nurse. He was like the angels in his childhood storybooks. He called him Tony, anglicising his name, Antonis. Antonis Hajipavlou. Twenty-four. He didn't mind, all his friends calling him Tony. He had lived in England since the age of five. The whole family had come soon after the invasion of Cyprus by Turkey in 1974. He can't remember much. He was too young. His memories of war consisted of running away from somewhere, wailing sirens he couldn't work out where they came from and kept asking the grown ups much to their annoyance and silent dismissal. And hiding. In the darkness of night. In some sheep and goat pen for two-three days. He remembers running in all directions. A white lorry picking them up with soldiers wearing blue berets and blue flags. Different to the Greek flag. His flag. Then they came to London. That was nineteen years ago.

***

63

"Hi there Tony! Have I got a surprise for you, mate!" The angelic blond nurse is pushing a chair towards him. A young man with curious eyes and beautiful long lashes gives him a fleeting look then looks at the bed he was being wheeled towards.

"Here Tony, I've brought you one of your own, mate! You won't feel alone anymore. Great inn't! You can chat away in your language and no one will understand a thing. What'd you think, eh? You should thank me for this. I'll accept a ticket to Cyprus... that'll do. No need to overdo it no matter how grateful you are to me!" He laughed his deep chuckle pleased with his achievement as he manoeuvred the young man back and forth with great skill, put the breaks on, pulled the blanket off his lap with great flair as though he was a matador in some great bull-ring and he offered him the bed with a generous exaggerated sweep of his arm over the bed.

"Tony, this is Ozzie. He is from Cyprus too! You might even find out you are cousins. You never know." Angel was his usual cheery self, as though he had set himself the task of cheering everyone around him. He radiated joy, charm, gentleness, warmth and life as he walked through the wards. He left humming, promising he would be back and check up on Ozzie, winking at Tony and asking him to make Ozzie welcomed. Did he want anything? Could he bring him anything which he didn't have already? He pushed his chair away almost floating with it. Tony watched his movements with pleasure and turned to the newcomer.

"Hi there!"

"Hi."

"Did Angel say your name was Ozzie? Is that like Ozzie Ardilles of Tottenham Hotspurs fame?"

"No," he smiles slightly embarrassed, "not like Ozzie Ardilles."

"I thought he said you were Cypriot?"

"Yes, I am a Cypriot." He lets the other go on guessing.

"Ε, καλάν, ίντα πον' τ'όνομα σου;" Tony switches into his best Cypriotgreek and waits with a smile in his eyes.

"Not all Cypriots are Greek you know…"

Tony stops smiling. "Ah! You are Turkish," he says with slight embarrassment that he got it wrong and deflated as the guessing game had come to an end.

"Yes. Do you have a problem with that?" Ozzie challenges aggressively. "Should I ask the nurse to move me somewhere else? I don't smell you know."

"No, I don't have a problem with that," Tony can't disguise the irritation in his voice. He didn't expect the sudden attack and he was annoyed for making a mistake. He felt a fool. "You can be whatever you like. It's a free country."

His voice is cold and he has lost interest. He is in fact quite annoyed that Angel had brought this young person and put him in the next bed. He was quite happy by himself. Now he had this sour face. How the fuck were they going to get along at such proximity, side by side, in this ward. They were having enough problems in Cyprus, let alone being together in such a confined space. If he sneezed the other would hear, if he farted the same. He couldn't even masturbate and enjoy the solitude of the pleasure. And Christ save him from visiting days! It will be a disaster! When *his* family came and they found out that he was a Greek what would happen then? Anything could happen. What shit! What fucking rotten shitty luck! He turned his back to the newcomer and tried to go to sleep. It was the only way he could escape the impossibility of his situation.

***

Good job no one knows I am in here otherwise we will have great spectacles of high drama with this Greek in the next bed. Ozzie is lying back after dinner the same evening he has been admitted. He is more relaxed now that he has got used to the smells and sounds of the ward.

"So why are you here then?" he hears Tony's voice from next door. "I am Tony by the way. Antonis Hajipavlou really, but my friends call me Tony. The English have difficulties with names," he says softly afraid that the cold exchange from the morning might continue. They had not spoken the whole day. Each trying to pretend the body next door did not occupy the bed. The other bed was empty. There was one other person in the ward on the opposite side of the room. And he had been asleep for most of the day.

"I am here for a few tests," Ozzie answers with deliberate distance. He does not want to say any more. He wants to keep a distance. Tony waits for a bit more information but it doesn't come. He straightens the bedclothes slowly and waits. Ozzie is not going to offer any more. He turns his back to Ozzie again and takes one of his magazines looking through listlessly. He can't imagine the energy radiating from all these bodies when he was feeling so tired. Perpetually feeling tired. He tried to think to a time when he was so full of endless energy. Sleepless until five in the morning partying drinking smoking going home to change and then on to work, in the evening more drinking and dancing and the weekends were one long party. He didn't know how he lived through it all. They were good times.

***

"How long do you think they'll keep me in here?" Tony heard the sound coming from the next bed. It was just after breakfast. He turned around slowly and saw Ozzie looking for dirt under his fingernails. He looked up and quickly glanced at him. "How long do you think?" Ozzie repeated.

"I don't know," he said quietly and slowly.

"I hope they'll find nothing and I'll get the Hell out of here. They should tell me pretty quick."

Tony is gazing at this sudden change of heart. He wants to sustain it and not scare him away. "So how did you end up here?" he asks.

"I go to the doctor's for a few pills and end up in here. This is the last time I go to any doctor's. Half of the time they don't know what they are talking about and the other they don't even want to know you. They give you a couple of aspirins and send you off. This one got it into his head to send me for tests and put me into hospital for observations. I only have a bit of a temperature and coughing, my lungs hurt when I cough. I've had it for some time now and I'm not getting any better. He thinks it might be pneumonia." He was smiling slightly, his attempt to melt the ice between them. "And you... what are you in for?"

"The same," Tony responds quickly and quietly looking at Ozzie. He is puzzled. But pleased that he was reaching out to him in his own way.

"Good job I don't live with my brother anymore, he would make a fuss over nothing," Ozzie volunteers. "And I haven't told him. I don't want to worry him. And what about you? You have family here?"

"No. None," Tony tries to answer without showing emotion. He looks away.

"Sorry to hear that. Look, yesterday, I didn't mean to be nasty or anything but I get sick and tired of people taking me for a Greek whenever I say I am a Cypriot. As though there are no Turkish people in Cyprus. It's like we don't exist. We are invisible. I get really pissed off!"

"No problem man. I shouldn't have done it. And I have lots of Cypriotturkish friends you know. I don't know why I did it. I really don't. Look, sorry eh?"

"Yeah, what the Hell! I wish the Cyprus problem could be solved with a couple of quick sorries. I am Ozzie as in Osman. My English friends gave me this nickname and I like it. It sounds good especially with Ozzie Ardilles about..." he laughs a warm quick laugh and looks at Tony who returned his smile.

"So you are on your own here? Do you have family in Cyprus?" asks Ozzie eager to keep the thaw going.

"Yeah, everyone's in Cyprus. They were all here, they came as refugees after the Turkish invasion in 1974 but went back after a few years." He suddenly was aware of the word invasion and that some Cypriotturkish people interpreted the same event as liberation from the yoke of the Greeks and as the "Peace Operation". He glanced at Ozzie and noticed a quick blinking of the eyes and felt an effort restraining himself from comment. He continued, "I didn't want to go, so I stayed. They couldn't stay because the British government didn't recognise us as refugees. We had lost everything. We were living in a tent, so we came here. We had to stay with relatives, my parents weren't allowed to work, they didn't get any social benefits, we didn't know if they were going to deport us any minute... and where? We had come from the north we didn't know any one from the south and just because the south was now the Greek side they could deport us to the south. And we didn't want to be sent to the north because now it was under Turkish occupation.

"Anyway they are all right now. They've started a property business. I don't fancy going back. I had a good life here. I was freer. What about you?"

"I came here about three years ago. I couldn't stand it in Cyprus, in the north anymore. I had a brother here so I came to study. But I left his house after about a year. I couldn't get on with his wife and all they did was work work work. I didn't like the way they lived. On top of it all, they were trying to marry me off to some girl they had their eye on. Her father owned a factory or something..."

"Why didn't you get on with your sister-in-law?"

Ozzie didn't answer at first, he thought about it then said, "She told my brother I made a pass at her and my brother believed her. He was furious. He chose to believe her, I suppose he had to. I couldn't get him to believe me. And do you know... all the time it was her, she was trying to seduce me! Touching my hand, brushing her breasts on my arm, my hair. When he wasn't around walking around half naked, trying to provoke me. I didn't want to know. I suppose if I took her to bed everything would have been all right. I didn't fancy her. And she was my brother's wife for God's sake!" He watched Tony's face for reaction. He was listening intently with his head lowered. He looked up smiled and nodded.

"So no one is going to visit me either. And I haven't told my Mum. She lives in Cyprus. She would come like a shot if she knew I was in hospital, even if it's for tests. She would just get on a plane and fly. I don't think she has ever been on a plane.

"She didn't want me to leave Cyprus. She cried and cried when I told her I was going." Ozzie's voice fades with the memory of his mother and the image of hugging her. He suddenly misses her. He nods to Tony and lays back to rest, he is exhausted.

"My mother knows." Ozzie hears a voice in the distance. Sometimes it's quite near, sometimes it floats away. He keeps his eyes closed. He realizes that he is not aware of time. Tony is talking to him. "She knows I am here. She won't come to see me. My brother told her."

Ozzie's brain slowly deals with the information, its implication, compares it with the reaction he expects his mother to have and wonders how two mothers could be so different.

"She won't come," Tony sighs and continues in a low voice, "she has disowned me. She doesn't think I am fit to be her son. God and Jesus Christ didn't give her such a son. What were her sins that God had punished her in such a way? She went to church and pledged candles to all the saints for Jesus to bring me back to my senses and get me on the right path again." Tony stops. It is past midnight and the ward is quiet. Ozzie thinks Tony has fallen asleep. He dozes off.

"Nothing changed of course. How can she change anything with candles to the saints." Tony continues as though talking to himself.

Lit candles of varying sizes and shapes and the interior of Apostolos Andreas Monastery at the tip of the Karpaz peninsula appeared in the imagination of Ozzie's dream-sleep. Tall icons of gold. Benevolently smiling faces of men. Dark haired, curly, sometimes straight, sometimes grey. Sometimes mischievous, sometimes stern sometimes smiling eyes focused on you as you entered the Monastery. The eyes moving wherever you moved. So uncanny. Some lips were thin yet others like ripe cherries. And candles. Some as tall as a lamppost or as thick as a column. Some made into shapes of heads, feet, legs, arms. Some like hearts. Others like the fleshy mound between the legs of a woman. They were disconcerting. Organs, body parts scattered in a corner of the church, parts of mutilated bodies. The wax was dark yellow or flesh coloured creating an even more of an eerie feeling. What shape candle would Tony's mother have vowed to the saints? What colour?

"Why?" Ozzie heard himself ask, his eyes closed, his mind's image travelling around the church by the sea, one of the most revered holy places for the Cypriotgreeks on the island. They couldn't visit. It was in the north. The Cypriotturkish people visited this shrine of Orthodox Christianity and lit candles for themselves as well as for their Cypriotgreek friends in London. A few tourists also came but they didn't know about the dedications. What sense did they make of the mutilated wax limbs he wondered? The sea was beautiful, the sea rocks and wild flowers were breathtaking. It was one of the most remote corners of Cyprus at the end of the long narrow Karpaz peninsula. The unimaginative English had called it the panhandle. The panhandle indeed!

"She found out I had a Cypriotturkish lover." Ozzie's eyes flicked open into the semi-darkness of the ward when he heard Tony's words. He didn't move. Surprise, laughter, questions crowded his head all at once. Happiness, a strange sense of happiness came over him.

"So why did you speak to me in Greek if you have a Turkish lover?" he heard himself say indignantly. He chuckled, "Don't, don't answer that." He suddenly felt closer to Tony, the lover of Turks. He was all right was Tony. He smiled and found himself floating away.

"How could I love a Turk? She just would not let it rest. How could I love a barbarian, such a whore, after all the Turks did to us, to her, to me? Wasn't I ashamed of myself? Where was my honour as a man, as a Greek man? She told me she wished the milk she had fed me from her breast had turned into poison so that I had died rather than for her to live to see such days, for me to force her into such shame, such degradation, such dishonour. She cursed the day I was born and told me she would have rather given birth to a snake than to me. Wasn't it enough what they had done to her? The Turkish soldiers came and killed the village men and they took others hostage and transported them to Turkey to prison camps. They haven't been heard of since. Then they lined up the women against the wall of the house at the end of the village and raped them one by one all of them not one was spared fourteen-year-old girls in the hairy arms of the stinking Turks one after the other raping raping ten of them on one young girl of fourteen three grown up sons she was raped with a bayonet stuck in her mouth she didn't care about herself but those young ones those young ones raped in front of all the village, I, I should know I was five I should remember they raped her in front of me while I was screaming helplessly and tears rolling down my face... she said. How could I love a Turk my eternal enemy after what they had done to us? They were animals not human beings. I should kill Turks wherever I saw them not love them! I was no longer her son. She told me to get out of the house and never come back again. She didn't have a son called Antonis anymore, he was dead. She screamed the place down so I packed my one bag and left that night and that was that. I never saw her again or my brother."

Ozzie heard it all. His eyes were open. He had tears in his eyes. He wiped them quickly on his sleeve and rolled over to face Tony. He was lying on his back talking to the ceiling.

"What happened to your lover? Did you get it together?"

"Yeah. We lived together. We lived together for five years. I was so much in love. I was so young. I'd never experienced love like that before. I was nineteen and desperately in love. No one was going to tell me anything. I wouldn't listen. I was... we were so in love."

"Why are you saying 'were'... where is she now? Why doesn't she come to see you? It must have been hard for her too you know, especially as a Cypriotturkish woman!" Ozzie waited with held breath his folded arm under his head supporting it watching Tony carefully. Tony closed his eyes. Ozzie could see in the semi-darkness silver traces running down from the corner of his eye. Luminous snail trails. In the light of the early sunrise he used to look fascinated at the web of trails left behind by the snails through their night wanderings all over the garden in Cyprus. Tony didn't answer. Ozzie's arm began to go numb under his head; he changed position and lay on his back. He glanced at Tony at intervals to see if he was still awake. After a while he found he was dozing off again. At one stage he thought he heard Tony's voice. When he opened his eyes and looked over,

Tony was still in the same position with his arms folded on his chest. He looked at him closely watching to see if his chest was moving with each breath. He suddenly panicked and wanted to be assured that Tony was alive. He had that death position he saw in films. Someone laid out in a coffin or on a deathbed. He lined up his eye with Tony's chest against the light on the ceiling behind him and was relieved to see it move up and down. Slightly, but it moved. He sat up and dangled his legs from the side of the bed. He watched Tony, he took in the whole of him without feeling that his gaze may cause discomfort to the person being watched. He wasn't much older than him but looked so much older, so thin. If he ate a bit more he would look a bit better. He must tell him to eat a bit more tomorrow otherwise he will waste away in here, especially when no one from his family cared, no one wanted him or cared for him. He'll waste away if someone doesn't look after him.

"He left me," said the laid-out lips. Ozzie nearly jumped. He thought his heart hit his upper teeth. He got back into bed with automatic movements and suddenly realised what he had heard. He left me. He.

"He?"

"He left me," said Tony with a steady unemotional voice, slowly opened his eyes and turned to look at Ozzie. A steady gaze unflinching. Ozzie noticed Tony had beautiful haunting green eyes in the strip light seeping through the window blinds behind his bed. They looked at each other without talking. His eyes smiled at Tony.

"I am dying of AIDS," Tony's eyes fixed on Ozzie. Then moved his head back and closed his eyes.

***

He felt a weight on his bed. He could not work out what was happening. He was emerging from deep sleep. It was still night. He felt hands on his shoulders. An arm made its way under his shoulder and a hand emerged holding him.

"Tony...?" It was Ozzie's voice in a soft whisper. "I want to hold you." Ozzie was on his bed lying on top of the bedclothes, his face against Tony's, holding him in his arms. "Don't worry Tony, I'm here." He held him gently, stroking him, holding him against his body and rocking him gently.

"Why Tony? Why did he leave you?" Tony didn't answer.

"What are you doing here Ozzie?" he whispered slowly in mid-sleep. "Go back to your bed. The nurses will think we are having it away. Go on, go back." He smiled to himself his eyes closed. He had missed the warmth. The warmth of another body next to his. The loving touch of a hand, the embrace, the feeling of being tightly held. The warmth flowing from one body to the other.

"Go on Ozzie go back to your bed." Ozzie stayed. After a while Tony carefully removed his hands from under Ozzie's arm, turned slowly towards him and hugged him, resting his cheek on his shoulder, smelling him through the open neck of his pyjamas.

"Tony, I've lied to you. I'm not here for tests."

"I know Ozzie, I know. Shhhh! Don't cry."

***

"He left you because you had AIDS, didn't he? What a coward." Tony turned to look at Ozzie who was flicking through a magazine while he spoke. "Do you think you will die Tony?" He stopped what he was writing and closed his book, slowly. He didn't respond.

"How long ago did he leave you?"

"Six months."

"Does your Mum know?"

"No. I've told you, she has disowned me already. I'm not her son anymore."

"Maybe she would change her mind if she knew you were dying."

"I don't want her here even if she wanted to come."

"Why not? Your Mum's the closest person to you. She gave birth to you after all."

"Not mine. I don't want to see her. She lost the right to be my Mum long time ago when she chucked me out. And got that oaf of my brother to beat me up. Mothers don't do that!"

"Come on Tony. Don't be so hard."

"No! Don't even bother! I don't want to see her. If she loved me she should've come to find me when I was all right. I don't want her pity. And I don't want yours either. Don't pull the trick you pulled last night again. Do you hear me?" His eyes were scattering fire. Full of fury. Ozzie gave him a sideways glance, "Stop trying to be the hardman. It will take more than this to stop me or scare me. What's your problem? Why don't you just accept it when someone likes you?"

***

"Μάμμα... μάμμα είσ' εσύ; Μάμμα μου που είσαι;" Tony could feel the sound in his head. He wasn't sure if the sound left his mouth. Could anyone hear him? Was it his Mum? Had she come? Was this blur, her?

"Εν εντάξει γιόκκα μου. Μεν φοάσαι. Είμαι δαμαί. Κοντά σου." He heard Greek words. A Cypriot woman's voice. He felt a soft hand on his face and hair. Short gentle caresses. It was soothing. Who was she? It couldn't have been Ozzie's mother. She would be speaking Turkish. This voice spoke in Cypriotgreek.

He could hear the noise of his breath leaving him burning its way out choking him. He was gasping for air yet his lungs couldn't respond couldn't fill or empty in that effortless gentle motion anymore.

"Tony, don't worry, I'm here," he heard Ozzie's voice. Ozzie was there. "And my Mum's come from Cyprus. She is here. Don't cry Tony. It's all right. Don't cry." He didn't think he was crying. How strange that he couldn't even feel his tears anymore.

Tony died three days later. Ozzie and his mother held his hand throughout the night. No one from his family came. His mother didn't come. Ozzie's mother talked to him throughout the night. She called him son and told him not to be afraid. She told him she was there, beside him. Near him. She wiped the sweat from his face and caressed his hair. He was not much older than her Osman. She cried as she saw him slowly give up his life. She wondered what would happen to the body. Ozzie didn't know and he didn't ask the nurses.

London. June 1994

EMINE'S FIGHT

"Look at Emine... she doesn't have a worry in the world!"

Emine has let herself go to the rhythm of the music. A high-pitched female's voice lamenting the loss of her love, cursing her luck, while the instruments are moving into a frenzy of movement inviting the hips to gyrate, the breasts to shake, the arms to stretch forward, the head slightly tilted back moving in sync with the body. But the hips are out of control. They are rolling and shaking as though they have a life of their own, as though they are not attached to a body.

Emine has tied a bright red embroidered *yemeni* around her hips accentuating the belly-dance movements. She is happy. Her eyes are shining, her mouth in perpetual laughter. Every now and again the eyebrows become knitted, the look intense, the lips pursed, Emine is concentrating on the movement of the body in tune with the music. She stops on the same spot, one foot on tiptoe her hips making huge provocative sensuous swings, sharp swings and back again towards that direction. Another woman comes up to her and reciprocates the movement. She swings her hip and brushes against Emine's hip. Emine laughs, laughs to her heart's content and moves off.

She feels eighteen or is it sixteen? Light-headed. Light-bodied. Not a care in the world... Emine dreams of being young, of being loved, of being the shining moon... no one can touch her. She is the most beautiful in the village. The most desired. The subject of sweet dreams, painful dreams, wet dreams, night-mares! Emine... who doesn't give them the time of day. Emine the wild fawn. Emine the untouchable! The wild one. With beautiful eyes. And a heart-shattering heart. Who will she marry? Who will she choose? Oh! Emine oh! My wild Emine! My beauty! My dove!

Emine dances... at her sister's wedding. The whole village is at the wedding. Young men watch. Young men watch with de-sire trying to hide their desire from each other - it is improper... she will either be his wife or his friend's... in either case, signs of lust, of desire, are improper. She will belong to one of them. It is a curse on the one who owns her knowing everyone wants her and makes her his own in his bed, and a curse on those who will never touch her, who will not feel the warmth of her skin, her tender breasts on their lips, her hips against the fire of their loins. Oh Emine! Emine! She will choose someone.

They line up in the small yard in the village of Aksaray, in the province of Konya, mid-Anatolia. The sun is setting the earth is copper, it is bathed in the blood rays of the sun. The last flames linger on the *kerpiç* walls. The rays catch the straw gold strands enmeshed in the brown soil bricks used to build the houses. Fires have been lit. Food is being cooked in large pots. Everyone is invited, everyone comes, it is a moment of communal joy.

It is the women's turn to dance, the men have lined up in the yard. Emine is beautiful and barely sixteen; her father reluctant to give her away. He can't according to custom, anyway; she would bring bad luck if he married her off before her older sister. She would bring bad luck on her sister as she would not find anyone to marry her, and bad luck on the whole household. Probably a tradition set by the elders to ensure that the older, less fortunate daughter is not robbed of marriage and stays at home all her life. Now attains a semi-religious status of bringing a curse onto a household... bad luck! Now Emine, brown-eyed olive-skinned heart shattering smile Emine, can marry. She can choose the best in the village. Not only this village - any of the villages around for miles. Just anyone. Just anyone her heart desires. And her father loved her. Loved her to death. He didn't see anyone but her. Even his son was not as important to him as Emine. He had prepared her dowry. He had the plot of land and house ready for her. On her wedding he would give her the fertile lands down by the riverbed. Emine, the light of his eyes!

***

"You whore! What time do you call this? Tell me you fucking bitch! Where have you been?"

"I was at..." she says with a quiet voice. She is scared. She tries to shuffle sideways through the door.

"Come here! I told you to come here!" he roars. She doesn't

move. She stands by the door as though nailed to the floor.

"Come here, I tell you!" pointing his fingers to a space by his feet. Spit splutters from his mouth, his eyes venomous, his neck red, muscles tense, veins standing up. The children are becoming uneasy, confused. They begin to whimper. She feels if this goes on they will begin to howl and scream uncontrollably. One is in the pram. The other holding onto the pram. She looks up at her mum, then at her father. She seeks comfort where there isn't any. Emine tries to touch the little girl's shoulder, her hand moves to her hand on the pram, she feels her own hand nervous, shaking. The girl is no more than four. She senses the fear and violence in the air. She moves from one foot to the other watching her father and mother. The mother stands still trying not to show her fear, feeling the little girl watching her.

"Don't shout in front of the children," she manages to say, trying not to make it offensive.

"In front of the children!" comes the mocking roar, "I'll give you in front of the children!" He moves towards her in long strides and grabs her by the collar. "It's OK when you fuck in front of your children! When you are a whore! When I ask you a question who are you to tell me not to shout! What right do you have to ask me that question! Is that what you want? You want me to be quiet? All right... Where have you been till this time of night, you whore? Huh? Where have you been? Is this quiet enough? Is this all right then? Eh?" His face was almost touching hers as he hisses. And suddenly he lets go of her dress crumpled in his fist and hits her face. Her hair goes flying, she holds her head in place. The side of her face is burning. She feels a fist coming down on her head like a hammer.

She is aware of her daughter running away and screaming. The little boy in the pram has been jolted. The shouting has woken him up. He looks bewildered, his eyes follow the movement of legs around him. The little girl has run away to the settee. She looks at her father with large frightened eyes. She watches very carefully.

"I am listening... where were you? Yes? I can't hear you!" He mockingly pushes his ear forward with the cup of his hand and leans over her. She tries to protect her head with her arms. She uses the pram as a shield against him. She tries to squeeze herself into the corner of the room.

"I can't hear you... you daughter of a whore! Where have you been whoring?" He hits her repeatedly on the shoulders and head with his fist. He moves to the side of the pram and kicks her legs.

"No wife of mine can come home this late at night. This is not a whorehouse. This is a respectable house. Do you hear me? Do you?" He leans over to her ear and shouts with rage. He hits her again. "Do you hear me? I am not a pimp and this is not a whorehouse. Don't come back here again. You think you can walk the streets on your own? You think you can walk the streets of Stoke Newington on your own, down Green Lanes, pass all those cafes and all those people know you are my wife? Alone this time of night, you whore? I won't be able to show my face around the cafes because of you. They'll laugh and say, 'Your wife was on her own, Kemal, I saw her at midnight last night walking down Green Lanes on her own. So what was she doing on her own at that time of night in the middle of Newington Green? Where was she coming from, then?' You whore... you make my reputation shit... not worth tuppence!"

She slowly looks up as he has stopped hitting her. "You should stand up to them. You know where I was. You know I was coming from the women's centre. We had a meeting. We had a meeting with a councillor. I wasn't whoring around." Before she could finish she saw him turn around and hit her with his fist. He caught the side of her upper lip. Blood started flowing from her mouth. She could hear her daughter crying.

"I will shut that mouth of yours... I will shut it for you for good. You think you are clever don't you... you think you are clever. You think no one can shut your mouth for you. Your father didn't teach you manners... did he? You talked back, didn't you? But I will teach you to shut your mouth. What the fuck do I care about the councillor! You are my wife. Your place is in this house. Looking after me my children my house my business. You have no business going out at night and walking down Green Lanes where everyone can see you and call me a pimp! Do you get that? Do you?"

He leaned over her and grabbed her by the hair. He banged her head against the wall. She screamed as the side of her face felt the whole impact of the wall. She felt a sharp pain against her high cheekbone. She held her head, trying to pull her hair away from his grip, trying to loosen it so it didn't hurt so much as he pulled. She began to cry and spit blood over him. She wanted him to be covered with her blood. She tried to hit him at the same time trying to defend herself. Her two small hands were delivering some blows wherever they landed. She wiped the blood from her mouth and tried to smear his face his arms his white shirt with it, all the time thinking she had to wash it. She was angry. He moved away. She moved towards him in her furry, "You bastard! It's easy to hit me, isn't it. Yes, go on, go on, hit me... you are so fucking brave, aren't you? Oh, so brave! Just because your friend says you are a pimp... hit me! That's how big a man you are! Oh, yes! You are such a man... all you can do is hit me!"

The front of her dress was covered in blood, her mouth, her teeth were covered in blood. She tried to stop it, felt her teeth to see if any were loosened by the blow. They were solid. She was relieved. She spat on the floor tears rolling down her eyes, screaming and screaming at him now that she had found a voice to scream. She couldn't care that both her children were also screaming with her. She couldn't control it any more, she screamed almost hysterically. Through her tears she noticed that he had moved away from her, she noticed the blood stains on the carpet where she spat, she couldn't help thinking she had to clean it tomorrow. He had moved away now, slightly worried by the sight of blood. She screamed in anger, in frustration at her own impotence, just screaming and screaming as though she was a young girl.

During a lull she heard her children screaming and stopped. She listened to them and their sobs. She sat on the floor just listening, unable to pick them up to hug them, to comfort them. She wanted someone to hug her, to comfort her. She slowly moved and tried to get up, numbed. She went into the bathroom to clean herself up and get ready to prepare dinner as she heard him shut the front door on his way out.

***

"This woman's project is important to us. It's our lifeline!" says Emine with her son on her lap. She is holding a bottle to his mouth, one arm under his head. She is agitated. She looks at the councillor from Islington Council who has come to Newington Green to talk to them.

"You can't shut our project down! We built it. We worked for it. A whole generation of women have given their lives for this project. We had to face assaults, beatings, abuse, harassment from husbands, fathers, brothers... a whole lot of opposition, let alone the crap we had to face from racists and men in British society. What are you talking about? You don't even know the meaning of the word to face all this and still carry on..."

The interpreter interprets what Emine is saying. The councillor looks at her and makes a movement with her hand indicating she understands. "Yes, but... because of the Council Tax and government spending cuts we can't afford to fund these projects any more," she says.

The interpreter has difficulties trying to translate the intricacies of council tax and government spending arrangements with local councils. She finds a way of fudging it. The women are not interested. Emine is not interested.

"You spend thousands on useless projects, throw away thousands. We've had this project for ten years... ten years. No one did anything for us except these women around this project. You've never done anything for us... for us Turkish, Kurdish and Cypriotturkish women in this Council. Show me what you've done. We did it all. Women before us did it. We forced you to employ Turkish-speaking council officers. You sat around on your backsides telling us there were no qualified experienced people for the jobs. If it was left to you, you would have never found anyone. We set up this project, we gave a chance to young women to train, to gain experience, a chance for abused women, deserted women, single parents, some subjected to violence by husbands, so that we could keep this project open. We gave women a chance, we gave each other a chance. You took some of the women we trained and even some of those have forgotten on whose backs they got jobs. Some don't even come near our projects now... they walk around with their nose in the air saying they are professionals or they don't want to be mixed up in all this. Well yes... they have to protect their jobs and we have learnt to deal with those who have sold out. But this project is all we have and you can't shut down this lifeline we have. You have no right!" Emine was getting agitated, moving to the edge of her sit as she was talking, gesticulating in her excitement, her hand holding the *yemeni* she had swiped off her head with a quick movement. Her son was bouncing, still asleep, from one leg to the other in her lap, while she was folding first one leg then the other under her.

"Emine is right! You didn't set this project up. Other Turkish-speaking women before us did. They worked for nothing. You think it's easy to set up a project? And especially for Turkish-speaking women? Do you know what we suffer? Do you? And do you care?" Aysel jumped in, she couldn't control herself any longer. She was a mother of four and a machinist at home.

"Yes, but the Council Tax... this government has attacked..."

"We don't want to hear about the Council Tax!" Fatma said.

"Not the Council Tax again!" said Hatice.

"We don't want to hear about the tax, Mrs councillor! All we care about is our project. And anyway we pay our tax!"

This grabbed the imagination of the women crammed into a tiny room in an office in Newington Green.

"We pay our tax! And we are Islington residents. What have you done for us? And we paid our rates before then for years and what have you done for us? You come here to patronise us?"

"They are right!" A well-spoken woman with long black hair sitting amongst the women looked at the councillor and with self-assurance continued, "You continuously try to patronise us. You play games to mystify situations to make it confusing for us... as though we don't understand what goes on. You try to camouflage your racism and your tokenism. You think that women are a soft option. You think that women who are not able to articulate their needs and aspirations, especially Black and Bilingual women, are a pushovers.

"You are not even aware of the struggle women have to put up just to attend this centre. Do you know of the violence, the opposition they have to put up with just to even come here? Do you know of the isolation they suffer? The racism they face in the streets, in the hospitals when they have to go for check-ups, when they take their children to the school gates, the name-calling and racism they face in the streets around here? Do you know of the aggravation and at times violence they have to put up with in their homes from their husbands just so they can come out for a few hours each week to breathe, to talk, to share, to learn?

"You don't! How could you? As a white middle-class woman living in Islington, you don't have to bring your washing in and wash it again because it has been smeared with shit. I could use the word excrement for sensitive ears but why should I spare you the brutality of it? You don't have to live in fear waiting for a brick to come through your window or a petrol bomb through your letter box, you don't have to live in fear of your husband being picked up by the police who have swooped on a cafe in Hackney or Islington or on one of the sweatshops, you don't have to cry after someone in your family who has been deported. No, you don't have to suffer any of this, do you? There's no family around here who does not face humiliation, harassment or deportation on a daily basis... or even attacks in the streets.

"As women, as Turkish-speaking women, we act like sponges, we absorb all the anger of our husbands, our children, our sons and daughters... we become the target of frustration and humiliation that our families suffer at work, in the streets, at school, in the factories, in official places. Women suffer all this... and we set up a project for ourselves to try and lessen this burden, to try and prevent ourselves from going mad, to try and share our pain and suffering and find some strength in ourselves, you try and shut our project down and throw us out of these miserable premises, out on the streets.

"You are not doing us any favours! We have a right to services which you don't make accessible to us and a right to set up this self-help group. What you need to do is to listen to what we are saying. Stop this tokenistic and openly racist position against us. We have every right to be here and have our project funded. We have already paid for that project in our taxes and our families have paid for it in colonial history, you are not giving us anything for nothing. It is ours by right!"

She was angry, her large brown eyes betrayed her anger but she spoke with eloquence without missing a beat in the rhythm of her speech. The women clapped noisily when she finished, laughed and shouted. *"Yaşa abla!"* shouted Emine, waving her *yemeni*. They all knew she would do a good job of it. Some knew her from the old days, others had heard of her. She was the founder of the project many years ago. Although she had moved to another part of London and was setting up other projects, she still came when they needed her.

Mrs. Councillor looked a little embarrassed. She had nothing to say. All her arguments were tackled by the woman with the long hair. It would have been pointless trying to raise other objections or prolong the debate, the woman knew the system inside-out and presented her arguments with admirable force. Eloquently and passionately. She had heard her before, she was known not only amongst the Turkish-speaking communities but also in other anti-racist and Black struggles. She commanded respect from all quarters. Sometimes fear, but respect all the same. She wished she had a few like her on her side. She thanked them and said she would do her best.

***

Emine pushes the pram through the door. Her face is lowered and her *yemeni* hangs over her forehead.

"*Hoşgeldin Emine!* Great to see you! Where have you been? We haven't seen you for a few days. We thought you had forgotten us... that you weren't going to come!"

Emine pushes the pram in, concentrating and manoeuvring the wheels. They hear her say, "No one can stop me from coming to this centre... no one!" She leans over and looks at her son in the pram. Aysel and Hatice go up to help her. They are happily joking and laughing outrageously. One picks up the son and starts making baby talk and hugging and kissing him squashing his soft face against her dark skin. The other picks up the little girl and begins to take her coat off. It's early summer but it is cold. Tea is boiling, the double pot gives a slight sound which adds to a sense of security. Some women are sitting around the table talking, others are smoking. One of the advisers is sticking new notices up pulling old ones down. "Don't forget about it will you! We have a conference on Sunday. We are going to talk about lots of things," she says.

"What are we going to talk about Gonce?"

"Health, breast and cervical cancer..."

"What about virginity?"

"If you want to... and work. Different careers open to women. How you could progress, do something different in life. About racism and how it affects us. How we can increase our confidence in challenging it. That sort of thing."

"What about violence? Violence against women by their husbands?" says Emine.

"We all have that dear, dear Emine..." says Aysel laughing, "you know what they say in our community, *dayak Cennetten çıktı*, beatings are from Heaven." She turns to face Emine who had stood up and nearly drops the baby when she sees Emine's blood covered broken swollen lip, black eye and the distorted side of her face, bruised blood clots and the skin grazed off.

London. March 1992

94

THE DAUGTER-IN-LAW

- to Esen Yılmaz*

She sat in the narrow little entrance waiting room of the hospital. She was frightened. She had retracted her arms, legs and neck. Just like a turtle. Her eyes looked around with suspicion, watching anything moving. Anything that made a shadow. She held a new-born baby, wrapped in a white, soft blanket, close to her breast. And a white, plastic carrier bag dangled from her wrist.

It was early afternoon. A light day... traces of sun were left behind. Short-lived sunrays poured through the window behind her. There was no one else in the waiting area. Only her. Nearer the door, the porters minded their business, occasionally looking at her from under their eyebrows. Not knowing what to do with her, hoping that they would not have to deal with her.

She was Turkish. They knew or rather they had guessed. She wore a *yemeni* on her head hiding everything but the central part of her face. A white *yemeni*, embroidered with love. Little black eyes darted quick glances like a trapped animal. A young mouth with lines of pain and a body under a heavy coat, ready to spring into action, just like an arrow in a bow.

They had tried to understand her. She wouldn't look at

them. She looked down to the floor and mumbled something in her language. They had worked out from the name she repeated that it must have been Turkish.

"*What do you want dear?*"

"*Fatma'yı istiyorum!*"

"What dear?"

"*Fatma, Fatma... Fatma burada çalışıyor!*" She was making stabbing movements towards the floor with her pointing finger.

"What did she say?" He turns to his friend for help. Did he understand? No. Back to her, "What did you say?"

"Who? Name? Name?" the other one chips in.

"*Fatma... Fatma... Türk... Türk abla.*"

She was getting agitated, her face twisting up, her eyes watering. She was swaying from side to side, beating her breast lightly. She was so small. She was so desperate.

"Oh, you want the Turkish lady, the translator! She is not here dear. Not here!" He tried to make definite hand and face movements to indicate to her what he was saying. She didn't move. She didn't hear him.

"Not here dear! Not... h-e-r-e!" Speaking louder and lengthening the letters as though she had difficulties with her hearing. As though she could decipher lip reading any more than deciphering the words she could hear. She stood her ground. He looked at his watch. Nearly two o'clock. The worker should be arriving soon. But how to get it across to her? He pointed at the chairs in the corner and indicated for her to sit down. And she understood and moved. Walked backwards to the chairs. The baby was asleep across her arm and the plastic bag dangled.

***

"Hello! I want to speak to Fatma Beyaz."

"Yes, Fatma Beyaz speaking. How can I help you?"

It was a hectic day again. She was trying to complete a form while squeezing the phone between her shoulder and ear. The paper slipped under her fingers from haste. She pulled it back, her green eyes a little agitated, her face flushed. One of the other workers touched her on the shoulder and signalled that she had to go to the ward to deal with an emergency. Fatma signalled that she had understood. She still had a queue of women to see. Women from all walks of life. Some born in villages in Turkey, some from Cyprus, some were Kurdish women who went to Cyprus, then came to London and asked for political asylum. There was controversy about that. She knew that most Cypriots resented the easy way in which the Kurds were given land, housing, animals and farm machinery in Cyprus after 1974, and having sold off all that they were given, arrived in London, asked for political asylum and were granted it, as well as being given flats and social benefits. Whereas most Cypriots, who had lost everything in 1974 and had been driven from their homes and land, arrived in London destitute but were not recognised as refugees, fleeing from war. Some were deported back and suffered great hardship. That was the politics of government; Fatma provided a much-needed advocacy service for women who came to the hospital to give birth.

She helped Kurdish as well as Cypriot and Turkish women even when she knew, amongst them, were the wives of known fascists and chauvinists.

She didn't want to answer the phone but she was caught. She had a woman on Turner Ward who hadn't been near a doctor until she was six months pregnant. She was in her mid-thirties. Fatma didn't know what difficulties she might face. She still had to get her through all the tests including thalassemia; the woman hadn't even heard of the condition let alone the possibility that she might give birth to a child with thalassamia or even Down's Syndrome.

Another one was having her second baby and Fatma was anxious for her. Her first child was born blind. The woman was terrified. She was terrified that she might give birth to another blind baby. After the birth of her first baby she had cried for days, heart-rending inconsolable sobs, talking to Fatma through her strangled voice. Fatma was so shocked and felt so sad for the woman that she had spent hours listening to the undecipherable sounds of this deaf and mute woman.

How are we going to communicate? she had asked through her tear-stained face, her mouth making awkward noises, her hands wringing and beating her chest blaming her God for such punishment. Demanding answers from Fatma. *How are we going to communicate, he blind and I deaf and mute? He won't even be able to see my lips, so I can't teach him to lip read. I can't hear his voice, so I can't respond to teach him anything.* Fatma had felt so helpless she had cried with the woman and yet she knew the woman expected her to hold herself together and help her. Somehow against all odds, she wanted Fatma to help her.

Fatma was now praying, the unbeliever was praying, that the woman's second child would be a seeing child so that she could stop blaming herself for giving birth to deformed children. *A punishment from God for her sins!* That was what people around her had said. Every time Fatma thought of the deaf and mute woman she felt a kick in her belly.

And now the never-ending phone. She had made the mistake of picking it up. It could be an emergency...

"Yes, Fatma Beyaz speaking..."

"Listen you whore! You better watch out! If you don't stop taking our women away and putting them in houses you will be sorry! We will make you sorry you were ever born! Who do you think you are... you whore!" A man's voice. Speaking in Turkish.

"Who is this?" she was taken aback a little. She stopped writing.

"None of your fucking business who it is! You know what I am talking about! You better send our women back to their homes, back to their husbands or else... I don't have to tell you again! You know what's coming! You will pay for this!"

"Who do you think you are? Do you think this is Turkey? Do you think this is a remote mountain-top in Turkey? Do you think you can threaten me... cave man!" She had pulled herself together almost instinctively and was moving into the attack. Sheer survival instinct!

"We can get you any time we want! Whore! We are watching you! We know you are on your own! We know you don't have a husband. You better watch it, you feminist whore! We'll beat the shit out of you! You better tell that other feminist whore to stop giving speeches to our women or we will shut her up for good!"

"Go to Hell! Fuck off! You can't threaten me!" She was screaming into the phone. She had forgotten where she was. Her whole body shaking, her free hand made into a fist with a pointing finger being thrust at the invisible man on the phone. He had obviously hung up. She was shaking with anger. Her green eyes scattering furious glances everywhere, her flushed face slightly perspiring.

She took a deep breath and wiped her forehead. She squeezed her eyes. She hit the table with her fists and stood up, her head hanging low. She thought for a moment. She needed to act quickly. She stood up holding the table. She was shaking. She needed to deal with the threats. This was not the first one this week. She thought of her daughter, if anything should happen to her. She needed to talk to her friend, to warn her of the seriousness of the situation, to agree on some action with her. She would be in danger too. They were expecting the threats but every time it happened it still shook them.

***

God please help me! Please have mercy on your servant... I am so much in pain! I am trying to cook. I am in agony. I am trying not to cry. The lower part of my belly is on fire. Full of pain. Knives are cutting me up... I am so scared. Any moment the bottom half of my body will open up and I will look down and there... on the floor... a pool of blood with all my innards... on the kitchen floor. I can't sit down properly. I sit as though on a sharp piece of glass. I have a daughter now. I've called her Umut. Hope. I gave birth to her ten days ago. My nipples are so sore from her suckling... I want to scream. And my breasts are so full, hard as stones. She is so strong. She is my little pink rose.

Oh mother! Mother... mother... oh my beautiful mother! My selfless mother... Where are you? Where are you, oh mother of mine? Why did you send me to these strange lands to these strange people? Oh my beautiful mother... Didn't you feel any pity for me... pity for what was going to happen to this poor daughter of yours... So many thousands of miles away?

She wipes her tears as they fall, with the corner of her embroidered white *yemeni*. She continues to stir the pot with one hand as she holds her daughter across her other arm. Her breast is bare, full, gently moving in rhythm to the baby's lips buried into it, sucking.

I miss you so much my beautiful mother. So much... where are you? There is no one here. I can't talk to anyone. I see no one. No one comes to see me. And my mother-in-law... forgive me, I can't call her mother as I should, as you taught me to. She is not a mother to me. She is not. She is cruel, oh so cruel to me. She doesn't care. Look at me... ten days loğusa** *and I am up cooking for the family. I don't even need to cook. They have the restaurant; they can bring home all the food in the world. But they just do it to torment me. Oh*

103

my beautiful mother, merciful mother! I've worked my guts out for them. You know I am not lazy. You know your daughter. You know how hard I work. And I worked even harder, my fingers to the bone. Just so they wouldn't say I am lazy... that I don't pull my weight... that I am a burden. You know how proud I am. I would never allow anyone to say I was lazy or... oh I worked so hard, so hard... in the house, in the restaurant. Day and night seven days, seven nights a week... non-stop. Non-stop, my beautiful mother! You would have been proud of me. I did everything you told me and even more...

And I don't know what to do beautiful mother of mine... I don't know how to feed a baby. My nipples hurt and I don't know what to do. They bleed. And there is no one I can ask. When I ask my mother-in-law she gets angry and shouts, 'You are not the first woman to have a child... why do you make such a fuss... look at me... I've had five! Allah bless them and they are all like lions! And all sons! You had a miserably skinny girl and you act as though you've achieved some great feat! Just a girl, that's all you have produced! A daughter! More trouble... girls are trouble! You couldn't even produce a son for your firstborn.'

Oh mother... beautiful mother of mine... and they beat me for nothing. I don't know what to do. I can't do anything right. He tells my husband to beat me for nothing and my husband obeys and beats me and my father-in-law stands there and watches and tells him to hit me harder, like a man. Sometimes he doesn't and my father-in-law gets angry and threatens to beat him and hits him in front of me... oh mother, mother what should I do? What can I do? I wish you never sent me to these strange lands... to this London. I don't know it. I don't know its people. I don't know its language. I can't go anywhere not like our village where I went everywhere... anywhere I wanted... into the hills, down to the fields, to my friends, to the weddings, to fetch water, even to the nearest town to buy material and sweets... oh mother I miss you all so much!

No one teaches me what to do with my child, how to look after myself. I am trying to remember the customs of the village. The forty-day custom after the birth of the child. I remember all the village women bringing food to the new mother, washing her clothes, massaging, oiling the baby, wrapping it up tight to make sure its bones grew strong and straight. And what do I do with these stone-hard breasts full of milk, dripping... and I am so sore under there. Good job there is this abla *at the hospital who helps me when I need to ask something. But she is so busy she looks after so many women. And I can't go when I need her. They even complain when I ring her sometimes...*

He is at home today. I don't know why he is here... he should be at the restaurant. He is angry again. I haven't done anything wrong. I am even scared to breathe. He shouted at me when my little Umut cried. I've picked her up and I'm trying to keep her quiet. Hush... hush my little one... hush... come, have some milk. Here... there is so much of it... here my rose. Open your mouth... come.

"Yes father... I am trying to shut her up. I am trying to feed her. Don't worry she will be quiet now... any minute now!" *Come my rose... don't make me cry. Don't... look your mummy is crying... don't cry my rose... take this nipple... come, open your mouth.* "Yes father, don't worry, I'll make her quiet... don't be angry father... I am really trying..."

***

You good for nothing bitch! You can't even shut up your bastard. You useless shit! Shut that bastard up! You went and got yourself another bitch; one wasn't enough! Weren't you enough! Didn't you bring enough misery to this house! You had to go and get pregnant... not a year in this country and you go and get pregnant! You couldn't wait, could you? You bitch on heat! You had to have it, you had to fuck and get pregnant! You couldn't keep away from his prick, could you? Now another mouth to feed. Another one to clothe. You, then another one... another bastard to look after! Tomorrow or the day after you'll shit another one into the middle and who is going to look after it? Who? Who? That husband of yours? That good for nothing, that weakling? He can't even wipe the snot off his own nose! And then he wants a wife... he wants a wife to fuck, to fuck all night. To get her pregnant, and there... there it is, another bastard for me to feed. Do you think this is a bottomless pit? You think you can do anything you want, anything you feel like? Do you? I'll show you what you will get in this house... I told you to get my dinner, where is it?

"I'm coming father. I'm trying to get the baby to be quiet father. It's cooking. Just another five minutes and it will be ready."

He walked into the small kitchen on the landing in his trousers, bare feet and white vest. His short hair slightly greying at the temples, wild in contrast to his dark ordered moustache. His slim but muscular body tight and tense. He was ready to spring into action, to explode; very little held him back. She could see his arm muscles flexing, his neck going red in patches as she turned in fear to look at him. He was holding a belt as he came towards her.

***

"He beat her mercilessly. I couldn't bear to look at her. A mother of ten days and he beat the shit out of her. And she is only eighteen... so young!" Fatma's voice becomes gentle. "So young... all on her own in this country. No one but no one she can turn to... not one friend!" Fatma sips her drink, her eyes full of tears. "What about her husband?" asks Alev. They are in a coffee bar in Hackney drinking red wine aware of all the rules they are breaking, consciously. "What did he do while his father was beating up his wife? Watch? Applaud?"

"Nothing!" says Fatma. "He is scared of him too. You can't call him a man. He is only a child himself. Even worse... he is shit scared of his father. The father beats him too. If he tells him to beat up his wife and he doesn't, the father beats the son for disobedience. Would you believe it! But you know the power of patriarchy in some of these feudal families. The man is the ruler... next to God! He can even kill you... he has every right!"

"And religion is on their side, I suppose!" adds Alev, getting angrier, moving her body restlessly, squeezing the stem of the glass in quick movements. "And I suppose the husband is nineteen, dependant on the father for a roof over his head, for his food and for his pocket money. Working for it but... in the restaurant owned

by the father and the promise that one day this will all be his..."
She makes a full circle with her outstretched arms from above her
head to her sides, "... if he doesn't go bankrupt in the meantime!
Totally trapped. Even if he wanted to, at the age of nineteen with a
wife and child, what the Hell...? Shit! The fucker! Where were his
brains when he went to marry this poor village girl? Between his
legs I suppose... the bastard!" She continues unconsciously to turn
the wine glass by twisting its thin stem.

"Marry her in some village in Turkey, bring her here, make
her pregnant immediately, have a child, make her work like a slave
and have no responsibility for her... none... and when your father
tells you to beat the shit out of her, do it! AND if she dares, if she
dares to complain, she becomes the ungrateful, lazy slut, good for
nothing!" She looks at the couple at the next table who lean over
and kiss each other on the mouth without a second thought to
where they are and what anyone may think. She can't help but
smile thinking of the oceans that separate the behaviour of these
eighteen-year-olds and the eighteen-year-old young woman they
were talking about. "...and if she says, Allah forbid, let's go and
set up our own home, she is Satan herself, she is trying to destroy
the family and lead him astray; and if she dares to run away to escape the beatings and possible death, she is a whore! Straight and
simple... a whore!"

Alev is squeezing the stem of her wine glass pushing it
backwards and forwards so unconsciously that Fatma gently puts
her fingers at the base and stops her. She lifts the glass to her lips
and looks at Fatma with her black eyes on fire. "You are a whore

whatever you do in this community anyway. Just being a woman makes you a whore. So what hope..."

"You've got it in one Alev!" Fatma says subdued. She is sad and drained, drained from absorbing the pain of so many women. And it all seemed so endless. She watches her angry friend admiring her energy, fearlessness and quick thinking. Sometimes she looks at this five-foot-nothing slim body and wonders where she gets such power. On a platform arguing her case she is unstoppable, she mows down any opposition in sight. She has such power with words; it is inspiring to be around her and watch her move people into action with her eloquence. She remembers a Rastaman calling her a lioness. "Man, you are powerful! Nothing can stand up to you! Respect, sister!" He had saluted her with two clenched fists having witnessed her uncompromising challenge to some German academics, on racism.

"But we have a bigger problem..." says Fatma. "I received another phone call today. A man, of course... threatening me. And I need to take the threats seriously. And, you too. You are vulnerable. People know who you are and what you do. I know you don't move around in the normal Turkish community circles but... they know you. And they know where I am, where I work... they could hurt us if they wanted to. They are apes! They operate outside the rules."

She is thoughtful and watches Fatma's face to gauge the seriousness of the threats. "Yes, I suppose we have known it for a long time," she says. She knows Fatma will not panic and she will tell her the bare minimum not wanting her to worry about Fatma's safety, unnecessarily. Fatma will absorb the initial threats creating space for both of them to think and discuss with a handful of other women. "We have always known that we are operating at the edges of violence. It's a matter of time before they get to us, I suppose..." she looks up at Fatma with a glint of challenge in her eyes, "But let them dare... the fuckers!"

"I sometimes wonder why we take this risk and if it's worth it, you know..." Fatma says. "I mean what the Hell do we do it for? Why? Why us? Why me? What is it to me? Why don't all those other women do it?"

After a short silence Alev says gently, "We take this risk because there is no one else to take it. And we feel we need to do something, we can't just sit back, condone it and do nothing. Everyone else is doing that... no one wants to touch it! It's too dangerous, too controversial! At the end of the day you are show-ing women that they don't have to stay and be abused sexually, physically or emotionally, that they can do something about it, but more importantly, that there are one or two women who will risk their own safety to help them. That's all we are... And in our time there was no one to help us. You know we can't just sit around phi-losophising or theorising about it all, like some women who call themselves feminists, even... who can't get their finger-nails dirty... you know we can't do that! You know we can't collude..."

She looks at Fatma with deep affection and smiles. "Espe-cially you... you are on the frontline... when you face those women, you have to help them make decisions. You can't send them back to a possible death and sleep peacefully at night... can you?" she

110

asserts; it's not a question.

Fatma looks at her with tearful eyes... *no!* she signals with an upward flick of her chin.

***

"I have nothing to give you. I am a poor woman. A peasant. I live in Turkey... in Anatolia, in a small village. I have never been out of my village... maybe down to the nearest town... rarely. And now I have flown over seas and mountains, in a plane, to come here. To this London. I am her mother. I have come to see my daughter. I want to thank you... you, the good women who organised this meeting. Who invited me here... who invited my daughter to speak."

She touches her hair with the palms of her hands, pushes back invisible hairs out of place. She puts her broad open palms on her knees. She is nervous. Her left foot does a little dance and jerks. She swallows hard; spit has dried in her mouth. She looks down to the floor for one second and then closes her eyes. Her lips move trying to speak...

"I want to sing you this lament. I've put it together myself. I have nothing else to give you. Nothing. I can't give you any money. I can't give you presents. Nothing I can give you... please accept my humble gift..."

Alev is chairing a meeting. Hackney, East London. There are over one hundred and fifty Turkish-speaking women from Cyprus and Turkey, some born in London. They have come from all over London. Machinists, shop workers, housewives, students, teachers, activists, professionals... some fluent in English, others not... young, old... refugees, immigrants, Londoners. They fill the school hall on a Sunday afternoon, talking about being women, religion, achievements, work, racism, violence, sexism... six other women are on the platform with her.

The mother sits to the left, halfway down the hall. She opens her mouth and a strong beautiful voice fills the room. Women are silenced. She brings the purity and majesty of the mountains of her village of her other life into this constrained room. She weaves her daughter's story of leaving home, coming to London with her husband, being left with no one to help her, she curses the father and mother-in-law who torture her daughter, a mother of a ten-day-old baby, she praises the strength of her daughter but praises the courage of the women, the strangers, who helped her, even more. Wishes them life for a hundred years and more. Asks God to protect them for their goodness and generosity. Women cry as she sings.

***

"He beat her viciously. There isn't a single woman in this room who has not been beaten! None!"

Alev angrily cuts an invisible line across the air with her pointing finger. Her long heavy black hair falls down to her waist as though a protective shield. Every now and again she takes the two ends on either side which slowly have fallen down over her breasts, flicks them back and secures them in a knot at the base of her neck. She is concentrating and her large black eyes are scanning the women in the room.

"We have all been beaten in life. All of us. If it's not our father, it's our grandfather or our husband or our brother even our younger brother has a right to beat us and if there isn't a man in the immediate family then our uncle or brother-in-law or father-in-law or some other man obtains the privilege to beat us when necessary... and it will be necessary at some stage or another..." Women smile at her mocking tone.

"They think they have the right to protect our honour and if necessary beat the shit out of us. Who are they to claim honour? Who are they to teach us morality?" Her voice raised, challenging, angry. Women become agitated. They shift in their seats. They are stretching their necks to see her.

"It is not us, who run after any woman they see... not us, trying to seduce all woman around them... not us, who have affairs with English women and have children with them even when they are already married to Turkish women... the same men object to Turkish women marrying outside the community even if the young people love each other... it is them, who bring diseases like AIDS into the families... it is them, who do everything immoral and yet appoint themselves as the guardians of our morals! What hypocrisy! How dare they! Who gave them that right? Enough! Enough of this! Let them act morally before they can tell us what to do!"

The women were on their feet. They called out to her to tell the truth... to tell it as it is... to tell the truth for them, the silenced women. *"Söyle abla! Söyle!"* they shouted at her, applauding, turning around and talking to the women around them. She waits for them to calm down.

"They try and create the illusion that we can't survive without them." Her tone is now more subdued. "Lies! All lies! We can survive without them... and they know it! We are stronger than them, always have been... and that's what they are afraid of." She knows this is the fear of many women. She knows it is a taboo. And yet she knows that many women are on their own, but can't openly admit it. The men have long gone but the women still maintained a façade to protect themselves from the sexual advances of men who harassed women on their own.

"There is this saying where I come from, 'The main-stay of the home is the man, *Evin direği erkektir.*' As though, if the man disappears, the home will be in ruins." She smiles at them with irony and watches as they agree; yes, they nod, they also know that saying.

"I don't know about you but I've seen many homes without men and they are still standing. I've seen women on their own bringing up their children, going out to work or working as home-workers, looking after their homes and surviving! They have many problems but they are surviving.

"But I look and look and I can't find homes where the woman has gone. I don't see any homes where the man does the washing and cooking and looking after the children and going out to work and bring in the money! No! I haven't seen such homes! Not one!"

Women are laughing and jeering.

"When the woman leaves, the home collapses! There is no home! The only time a home survives after a woman leaves is when another woman is brought into the home to make it work! Don't tell me that the man is the mainstay of the home... he is not even the twig!"

The women are on their feet again applauding loudly, laughing and shouting their wishes of long life for her and power to her mouth and tongue to tell it all. She speaks their language, not posh. She looks at her papers in front of her and lifts her head up slowly. Her voice has become gentler. The room descends into silence.

"I want to tell you about the story of one of our women. She is an ordinary young woman. She came to this country just as many of us did to find a better life. She was married off to someone who lived here. She believed she was coming to a better life from the village with its harsh life and no prospects. She was only seventeen. Her husband barely a year older, eighteen. She came trusting her husband although she didn't know him. The elders had seen it a suitable match, other villagers had recommended the family of the young man... you know the story... how many of you were given to a 'good' man? I don't have to tell you what we discovered after the wedding..."

Murmurs of agreement and sad shaking of heads from some of the women... *if only I knew*, says a woman from the back.

"She came with lots of hopes and dreams. The dreams of a seventeen year-old, young, innocent, blind to the evils of life, soft, so soft... Within days she was slaving away in the restaurant and in the house. She wasn't a daughter-in-law, she was a servant. A servant to the whole family. She was the wife of the older son... they needed her to look after the younger kids as well as cook in the restaurant. She slaved day in day out... from the house to the restaurant and back again... no social life... not even a wedding once in a while.

Then she became pregnant. She wasn't well and the beatings started... they said she was being lazy. They said she wasn't working hard enough. She gave birth in the hospital and went home. Ten days later she was barely walking. The father-in-law was at home. He started shouting at her because the baby was crying. He started shouting at her bastard at her loose morals for fucking with her husband..."

Some women were a little taken aback by her raw use of words; especially her, an educated woman. They were used to hearing them from others and even used these words freely amongst themselves, but her... She was aware of the reaction she was causing but used them deliberately. She didn't feel there was a place for refined words in such violence.

"... and giving birth to a bastard. Who was going to feed another mouth? they said. And on top of it all, it was a girl, not a boy, she should take her bastard and get out if she wasn't going to work hard and earn her keep this wasn't a place for free riders she had to work how long was she going to swan around pretending to be ill how long was she the first woman on earth to have a child she was a lazy bitch lazy..." she said it all in one breath.

"He forced her to get up and cook for him. And when she was trying to cook with one hand and feeding her ten-day-old child on the breast, he came in and started to hit her on the head. She pleaded for him to stop and tried to protect her baby. He carried on hitting her face and head. She knocked the pot of food on the floor trying to escape him and protect her child. He became angrier shouting and pulling her by the hair calling her a whore, not a daughter, she was evil, she had brought the Devil into his house... He pulled her into the sitting room by the hair, her breast hanging out, her clothes pulled apart, the baby screaming, she was pleading for him to stop. He began to hit her with his belt."

Alev took a deep breath, she was angry so angry, she was living through the beating herself. She tried to calm her voice and her shaking body. Some women had started to cry, silently.

"He beat the shit out of her. That's what he did this 'father' of hers. He made her black and blue. All over her body. But most of all he beat her between her thighs... yes... yes... dear women!" Alev hit the table in front of her with her fist. "This man who was supposed to be her 'father', her protector, who had promised her mother to look after her when he asked for her for his son, who took her from her family, her mother, from her village and brought her to strange lands... he beat her black and blue between her thighs... Between her thighs leading to her vagina... and all over her belly... with a belt... a young mother of ten days! That's what her 'father' did to her!"

Alev stopped. "We found her waiting at the entrance of the hospital with her baby and one plastic bag. And the clothes she was wearing. That's all she had. She had run away. She knew no one... not a soul in this huge big London she could go to. NO ONE! Except the woman who worked in the hospital where she went to have her baby. Fatma Beyaz. My friend. She ran to her. And yes, we helped her. Yes, we helped her escape! If anyone wants to come and tell me we did wrong by helping her... let them... let them come!" She threw the challenge out to them because she knew some women might have not supported that position and argued that no matter what, women should stick by their husbands. No one said anything. Some looked up at her shocked at what she was saying, others wiping the corners of their eyes, their noses. Most probably remembering a similar beating rather than living through the young women's pain.

"We argued and fought with the authorities and we found her a house for battered women. With the help of my friend, Fatma Beyaz, she made it. She had a tough time but she made it. And she came here to share her story with us to make other women stronger." She turned around to the young woman and said, "I would now like to give her the platform..."

Their faces covered with tears, their noses running women applauded the young woman who was almost like a little girl in her pink top sitting at the end of the platform wiping her eyes. Some stood up and applauded her courage knowing that maybe at some stage of their lives they also wanted to escape but did not manage to do it. And she told them her story. She cried and they cried with her. And she thanked the women who helped her. And she told them she made it.

After she finished Alev continued, "She won and with her, many of us won! What she achieved was important and it is not easy. But I want you to be aware of the fact that women like me and Fatma received threatening phone-calls. We were told to watch out, we were called whores. Feminist whores, because we dared to help a helpless eighteen-year-old escape the beatings and torture.

We heard that religious Hodjas talked about us in the mosque, calling us sinful women, saying we do sinful things, that we are against God's will and calling God's wrath upon us." She knew this from one of the women she was teaching to read and write. She was forty-four and was being beaten by her husband. She had come into the class one day with the side of her face swollen and a black eye, when Alev asked, she had told her that her husband had beaten her up because she had refused to have sex with him at seven in the morning. She was afraid that her seven year-old daughter, who was sharing the same bed with them because they didn't have anywhere else for her to sleep, might wake up and discover them in that position. So he beat her up, sent the little girl out and then climbed on top of her. The Hodja had told her that he was her husband and that she had to obey him; the Koran made allowances for men to ensure that women did not disobey and that may involve resorting to a little physical action. The woman had told Alev that the Hodja had talked about these sinful women who were helping women escape but had not given any indication if she knew who the Hodja was referring to. She hadn't said but Alev felt that she knew, that's why she was warning her.

"Tell me... is it God's will that women should be beaten up?

That we should not help them? Is it?" She demanded from the women with anger, they responded meekly, surprised that she was asking them, then in anger, "No! NO!"

"That's what they call any woman who challenges them. We are not afraid. We will not give up helping women no matter how much they threaten us, and what they say about us! We will not give up because they are wrong! We will continue to help women." She stopped and looked around the hall. Her voice was encouraging, strong, "So, my beautiful women... don't shut your ears... don't pretend you haven't heard. Find out! Challenge what they say! Educate yourselves, become strong, become determined, learn, become independent. Live your lives the way you want to live them, not how others want you to. But always be aware that if you do, you are a threat to how things are... but don't be afraid!"

She softened her voice as she looked around the room again. She knew she had to take it to the obvious logical conclusion. Some women would have preferred that she had left it where it was. She felt it would be unfinished. And she knew that she could lose them now but somehow she felt she needed to push that last bit. She felt confident she wouldn't lose them. She had challenged the sanctity of the family, the domination of men, of religion, now the power relations in society. And she was confident that the women would not discard all she had said just because they may not agree with her last comments.

"But do you know something? They are afraid of us... those who beat us up and torture us are afraid of us... of women! They look so strong and yet they are so afraid. You know why? Because

120

potentially we are the ones who can change this society... because we have nothing to lose... because we have the worst deal possible... what else can we lose? That's why they are afraid of some of us who speak out... they want to shut us up, to marginalise us, turn us into monsters. They call us whores, call us feminists, enemies of men, enemies of family life, lesbians... anything, to try and marginalise us and prevent other women from hearing what we say. But we know, we know that women are listening... everywhere women are listening and waiting... waiting for a time which is right for them, then slowly they move... but once they move nothing on earth can stop them.

"So beautiful mothers, wives, sisters, daughters, daughter-in-laws, aunties, big sisters, little sisters all of you but most of all beautiful women and young girls don't be afraid! Life is out there! Go out there and take what is yours!"

When she finished many women came and hugged her some with tear-stained eyes. She couldn't even get down from the platform. She was exhausted. Fatma knew she was. She came silently out of nowhere and put her arm around her waist, firmly holding her up. She could feel the trembling of Alev's body through her arm holding her and she smiled at her friend. "Are you OK?" She nodded, yes. "You've done it again. You've really moved those women, you made us cry." She laughed in a low voice, "Look at them. They are walking inches taller. I pity any husband who would dare stand in front of them." She brought her face next to Alev's cheek, "But you chose not to tell them all of it... didn't you? I wondered if you were going to..." she whispered.

Alev turned slightly and looked into her friend's searching eyes and lowered her face, "No, I couldn't tell them all of it. I couldn't tell them he raped her!"

London. October 1992

---

* whose battered body was found on 10 March 1993, eight years after she spoke at the first women's conference in Hackney.

**loğusa - a woman recovering from child-birth.

ROLL-CALL

"She committed suicide!"

"What! I've got to sit down... you shocked me!"

Her hands, carrying the twists of years, reach out. A slight quiver, a slight shake. The fingertips reach the chair. The blue veins stretch out under the transparent skin. The years have taken their layers with them. The fingertips search for, almost caress, the top of the chair. The body does not move. The legs shift slightly. She does not sit down.

"She had this lovely flat. She had everything going for her. The silly cow!" A pause, her mouth is dry. "She was in Bournemouth... wasn't she?" she looks into her friend's face, questioning. The other nods in agreement without turning her head. She turns away with a slightly puzzled look on her face.

"She moved there. Really comfortable but she came to me and complained. She couldn't move about, she couldn't go out. Couldn't go shopping. Nothing!"

There is pity, empathy in her voice. She can understand that. Of course. She is worried about the same thing. The other day, only the other day, she suffered the same humiliation.

She pauses for a second. Silence hangs between them.

"She had all those diamonds!" floats away from her. "Oh, why?"

"She was a nice girl," responds her friend as though feeling the necessity to state a fact. Not much emotion in the voice.

"Yes... and whenever she had troubles she came to me! But she should have lived her life out." She had no right to do that. No right. She had no right to take her life. The Lord, God had given and He should take. Only He! How will she face her Maker? And talk about irresponsibility towards the rest of them... Those left behind living with the reality of her death.

Silver, thinned-out hair, beautifully kept. The tender care of the hairdresser watching it change week after week, over the years. She had a bag on her lap, holding, re-arranging it with every new sentence. She must have had long hair, trying to keep the spirit alive. The hair unable to oblige. Struggling to reach the neck, with a silver rinse. The other, trying to keep the curls of her youth. Little purple rinsed curls dotted all around the skull. Grimacing like false teeth in a glass of water. Pale freckled skin stares out between the gaps of the curls.

Jewish women of Hackney. Living out their days in foreign lands. Transported by wars, out of lands they did not want to leave, into languages they did not speak. Dying in Hackney, dying in Bournemouth having escaped Nazis, fascist attacks, ghettos, concentration camps, gas ovens...

"And where is Lucy? Have you seen her?" the one standing up, with the purple rinse, asks.

"She is all right. She's got a flat in Stamford Hill."

"And Amy, that crazy old girl?" She does not wait for an answer; she speaks excitedly, searching the face of the other woman, watching even the movement of a hair on her face. The other keeps looking ahead, not much emotion, a nod every now and again indicating agreement. She continues, "What was her name? ... Ester! She was nice. Where is she now?" A slight quiver, tension, fear of hearing the unwanted. A momentary silence.

"Oh Ester! She is all right, she is still at the flats!"

The Samuel Lewis and Evelyn Court flats where thousands of Jewish refugees found shelter from the wars and the fascists. Where, in the summer on sunny days, a line of silver-haired, well-tanned faces compete with each other for the darkest skin. Where camera holding, broad American voiced mouths smile and pose for the folks, in front of the Art Nouveau iron railings of Lewis Trust buildings on Dalston Lane. All recording moments of death.

A roll-call begins of the dead, of the living, of the dispersed, of the lonely. The doctors' buzzers go on all around them, patients wait for their turn. They continue the roll-call oblivious to the world. Checking, counting, re-arranging the list of their friends waiting for death.

"But she should have lived her life out!" a weak, thin voice persists on her lips. As though taking her own life was shortening every one else's. She had no right to bring them closer to death. The dead woman's length of life would have kept a certain distance between them and death. That is the secret pact between people in the queue for death.

An inaudible whisper mingles with confusion, resentment, sadness and a floating back to the past.

"Silly cow..." drops from her lips, almost in a whimper, finally grieving for her old friend.

London. June 1986

**I COULD NEVER BE
WITHOUT YOU**

He looks at her carefully. Twists his head, focuses with one eye then the other and looks intently. He is dashing in his immaculate blue-grey rich suit. She is lying on the table. She has been lying there for the past three days. Still.

His head moves in quick little darts. Making sure his vision takes in the scene. He holds tightly onto the flimsy young shoot of the elderberry-tree. The ripe wine-coloured elderberries have gone. They used to come together to feast on them. The end of the season. One or two single berries left. Yes. She is there... He rushes off after a while through the gap between the houses.

She has been lying on the table for the past three days put there by the woman with the long dark hair. She had picked her up from the ground and laid her gently on the table in the back garden. She looked so peaceful. Asleep. Her delicate neck not even stiff but her body without warmth. A young female. Grey suit with white trimmings. She lay uncomfortably on the table with her long-nailed toes stretched out showing from the edges of the light grey suit.

Today, he couldn't recognise her. But he knew it was her from the space she occupied. Her suit was in tatters. She was torn apart. He could see her bare bones, the flesh torn off. The dark wine-coloured flesh, in parts, going putrid grey. Individual feathers plucked and scattered all around. The flies had danced on her eyes yesterday. The woman with the dark long hair had seen them. She was so young. Her beak still flesh-coloured.

And today all her inner organs were gone. Pulled out... Had they been eaten? Her neck twice twisted, her pale throat looked up at the grey sky. Her ribcage protruded. She was flattened. Her tail feathers still beautifully symmetrical stretched out like a small delicate fan. The exposed white inner soft feathers were drenched. It had rained so heavily last night. Torrential, pitiless rain. She looked so undignified sprawled on her back, on the table. The beautiful suit in tatters and drenched. Maggots busily eating away her flesh...

He looked at her from the flimsy branch, focused with one eye and then the other. Yes, it was her. His partner his mate for life. There she was... a carcass mutilated lying on a table. Yesterday she was still beautiful. Lifeless but beautiful. Still intact. She lay with her sweet face and beak on the table. An unnatural position but still graceful creating the illusion that she might get up. Shake her grey suit be alive again. Fly with him. Go elderberry eating again. He would look behind him and she would be there following him. He would look up from his elderberries and she would be there eating daintily, gracefully. An illusion. Today it was no longer her. He had known it wasn't her yesterday, but she still looked like her. Today she was decomposing. She was half eaten, devoured. Only pieces of her lay on the table. He studied her carefully. He was alone. Then the woman with the dark long hair saw him fly away between the houses.

***

"You don't want to stay do you?" The woman with the dark hair watches his back. A white vest constricts his skin. She reaches out and barely touches his shoulder with her fingertips. She senses he is in a state of flight. She has missed his softness, warmth, smells of his body. He sits at the edge of her bed. She has been there since she came home from the hospital. She acknowledges but resents her weakness, her vulnerability. Yet, she seeks tenderness, being taken care of, rarely admitted emotions.

"I did," he finally says, exhaling, "I did want to see you. But truth be told now I don't know." He talks through his back. He does not turn around to look at her. His voice wanders into the middle of the room and echoes back to her from the walls. She catches glimpses of the side of his cheek, lips, corner of his eye. She can sense he is agitated but does not want to be understanding. His voice carries the irritation of indecisiveness. His head darts this way then that. He is almost trapped. Should he go? He has just driven across London in heavy rain to be with her. Should he stay? He had to arrange so many different things... pack his belongings, sort out the house, ring his wife, feed the cat... the traffic was solid, immovable... He was tired. So tired.

All he wanted was sleep. He could do without all this. He had to get up at four in the morning to drive across London again.

"I looked forward to this weekend so much! To be with you. Now... I don't know," he says almost in defeat.

He wanted so much to be with her, love her. And now he was with her he didn't want to be there. When in that mood, she always found something to make him feel uneasy about. After all the running around, he had made the time and had come. Why didn't she just enjoy his presence? Why did she feel she always had to be so critical? He wanted space.

"Stay if you like. It's pointless for you to drive all the way back across London in the rain again," he hears her say over his shoulder. He already knows. "As you don't want to sleep in my bed maybe you would like to sleep in my study." He can't bear it any longer. Now she is saying don't sleep in my bed. "It's midnight already and it's raining," he hears her voice becoming gentler. She has sensed his desperation; she doesn't want him to go. But she knows he won't sleep in her bed now he is wounded. She touches his back through the white vest wanting to disperse the tightness and knots. He doesn't feel the warmth of her skin. Emotions of suppressed anger mingle with uncontrollable tenderness towards him. He feels trapped.

***

I am becoming conscious and I am suffocating. I struggle to breathe. I am choking. I cough violently. My throat is on fire.

I cough again. I c-a-a-a-n't breathe! I am gulping helplessly. Air! I need air! There's not enough air! My hand goes to my mouth.

I pull off the mask I didn't know was there. A hard rim touches my fingertips. I yank it. I want to spit the sticky substance stuck in my throat having travelled from my lungs. I am trying to dislodge it to get to some air.

"Don't do that," he calls my name. "…you're just coming around, dear."

"Give me a tissue please," I hear myself say into the void. There is a cacophony of sounds and lights. I can't open my eyes, they feel stuck. Something lands in my hand. A rough tissue. I spit. My lungs trying to come out through a chamber of fire. My throat feels as though it's been cut open, petrol poured in and set on fire. I can't breathe. I can't! I speak in my head. I am choking. I am trapped under a heavy weight. My lungs are rebelling. They are trying to help me breathe. They are blocked by mucus. My windpipe is blocked by an invisible heavy curtain. I am suffocating I am trying not to panic I am trying to control my lungs calm them down I am trying to think soothing things for my throat trying to calm it down I am trying to breathe slowly rhythmically calmly I am trying to calm my whole body which is in chaos...

I cough repeatedly violently. The choking sensation is back. I can't breathe. I feel pain in my belly somewhere near my navel. I feel wires coming from my body. I can't see them. My hand is entangled in wires from my body as I bring it up to my mouth. I want to breathe. I can't. I cough and dislodge the invisible curtain pulled across my windpipe choking me. I try to pull the mask off to spit. He firmly catches my hand and stops me. I relax for a second, he lets go, I yank the mask, it comes off. I've learned this trick from self-defence classes. *I want to spit,* I say. *Open your mouth,* he says. A suction pipe is put in my mouth. I feel it vacuuming the inside of my mouth, the inside of my cheeks, over my teeth. The mask is put back on roughly conveying annoyance. I know it's him. I try to open my eyes. I want to see him. I want to look at him. I am not an idiot. I am an intelligent woman. Don't treat me like an imbecile. I don't want to make life hard for you or for me. I speak to him in my head. My efforts to open my eyes only yield a yellowish light from the strips on the ceiling and a blue blob moving somewhere near me. The blue blob has a white mask. My eyelids close and take me back to darkness.

My throat is on fire again. The temporary respite is gone. My eyes in darkness. I can't bear the pain. My lungs are ready to explode. They are holding, holding, holding... but can't any longer. They heave, they are going to erupt and all my mental powers are useless I can't control them. I can feel the acute pain coughing brings me before it comes. I fear my stitches will burst if I cough, I feel the stretching on my belly every time I cough and yet I can't hold it back. I cough. My lungs erupt. I go through a violent coughing fit. My mouth is full of sticky lung liquid. I want to spit. I quickly pull off the mask. *Stop it! You don't have anything to spit.* I hear the annoyed voice. *I have,* I talk to him in my head and in a split second without further hesitation spit it out onto the pillow. *Indisputable fact you shit,* I continue to speak to him in my head. *Who knows about my body, you or me?* I hear the suction machine hoovering over the pillow by my ear and hear the order, *open your mouth.* I open. He hoovers inside my mouth again in quick movements. Roughly he pushes the tube deeper into my throat and sucks stuff from my windpipe. He is careless, he is rough. I wretch and want to vomit. My whole body convulses in a spasm as though it has received an electric shock. I think of my stitches in this involuntary movement. *Give her a tissue,* I hear another blue blob say behind me with slight irritation in his voice with the actions of the first blue blob.

I am laid on my side my face on the pillow. The ECG machine bleeps out a continuous sound every time I convulse in a fit of coughing. Death signal. But I know I am not dead. I am momentarily choking trying to dislodge the sticky mucus curtain smothering me... I imagine I am either in a milking barn or a cheese factory. There are clanging and electrical machine sounds all around me, the atmosphere is hygienic and smells disinfected... the wires from my body to a machine are probably the cause of my hallucinations of my life juices draining away from my body. Echoes of squelching rubber boots following the blue blobs walking around find echoes in my head.

The blue blob is at the bottom of my bed at my feet. I feel him touch my feet. I am trying to look in that direction. I can see a hazy figure in the blue blob. I become aware of wetness under my buttocks. I know it's blood. I feel its viscidity as distinct from all other liquids on my skin. The hospital gown I am wearing and the bottom sheet stick to my skin. And there is a cold wetness...

sticky wetness. *Here put these on,* he says. I don't know what they are. *I'll start you off,* he says as there is no reaction from me. I can't see him let alone what he is referring to. I feel my feet go through some flimsy material a sensation of elastic on my legs. *Disposable pants,* I hear the blue blob's voice, *not much good but they will do. Now pull them up,* I hear an embarrassed blue blob voice. He has gone up as far as my knees, just above, under the covers. I obey and lean over trying to twist on my back to pull them up. I feel the wetness of blood between my legs down inside my legs. Sticky wetness. I leave them when I feel they've got further than where they were. The indignity of it, I think, as I lose myself...

***

My pager is going. I know that sound. It's mine. It doesn't belong to any of the doctors or nurses on the ward chattering talking confirming calling out numbers of people in the ward. *Has B6 gone yet? Where is B7? Oh yes, no one escapes,* says the porter as he wheels the trolley bed for the operating theatre around the ward. My pager is in my bag. I look at the distance of one-and-a-half feet with disbelief. The unreachability of such close proximity. My arm stretches to the tan leather bag on the bedside cupboard and touches it. I look at my stretched arm for a few seconds and close my eyes accepting defeat.

I glance up and the Jamaican nurse smiles at me gently from above my covers. I smile and flop back. She covers me. I tell her I am cold. Could she bring me another blanket. Especially my feet. *We don't have another blanket but here's a cover*, and she tucks it around my feet. I ask her the time and she says it's ten. I went in at eight-thirty in the morning. I think I am speaking but in fact I am hissing as my throat is on fire again. I am trying to stop my coughing and convulsions. I know it's you. I know you have paged me. I need your message. I need you. *Could you bring me a glass of warm water for my throat*, I hiss at the Jamaican nurse.

The Sister holds my arm and puts her hand protectively on my waist as I shuffle across to the toilet a thousand miles across from my bed. I struggle to see things which insist on being invisible or in a haze. She takes me inside the toilet and helps me sit down. I pull up my hospital gown and look at my legs. I open them and look at the blood smears stuck on the inside of my legs. Caked blood with some brown substance. I look up at her and lift my hands in distress. *Would you like to clean up? Just hold on. Don't move until I come back*. I nod assent. *Don't lock the door*, she says as she goes out. I wipe off the smears of blood and brown substance she tells me is antiseptic. Momentarily, I like the sensation of freshness I give myself.

On my return from my hazy wanderings I hungrily grab my bag and find my pager. "Best of luck for today. I will see you at the weekend... lots of love," it said. You said. I don't want lots of love, just one. I don't want good luck, I want you. I don't want to see you at the weekend, I want to hold your hand when I am coming out of the anaesthetic...

***

He is perched on her bed. His head on a pillow. He is un-
comfortable lying on his back. She watches him next to her, her
back against the wall. Her body seeking the least painful position. His arm covers his eyes. She touches his lip on impulse,
a tiny bubble on his lower lip. It bursts. She smiles at her own
pleasure. He momentarily slowly glances up at her surprised
at the tenderness of her touch. He hasn't touched her since he
came into her room having driven across London in the rain.
He is afraid to touch, his emotions confused. He might hurt her.
He doesn't know where he can touch her where he can't. This
creates fear of rejection of anxiety in him. He can't touch her
with his hands he can't touch her with his eyes... she longs to be
hugged. He can't bear pain. She wants to be touched. He is tired.
She wants to be loved. He escapes into the comfort of tiredness.
She screams silently.

"Why did you say good luck? What does that mean?" she
hears herself ask out loud amongst the endless questions she had
asked herself. And it wasn't even the most important. Her tone is
not submissive. Not hurt. Not gentle. He shifts his arm slightly,
exposes his eyes and looks up at her trying to gauge her feelings.
The light falls on half her face, the other side is in darkness. He
moves his arm back into position across his eyes.

"It means I am thinking of you. I hope everything goes
O.K. It means all those things," his voice is impatient.

"But it doesn't mean anything to me. It is so bland. So standard. Good Luck! What's it got to do with luck? Good luck for what? It lacks feeling..."

"Well, I couldn't put all that into a short message could I?" he shifts his body visibly annoyed. "I was trying to make it short."

"But, I am thinking of you, is short and it means something to me; more than good luck. It has feeling."

She begins to feel his annoyance through the small gap between their bodies.

"There I am thinking of you... thinking of you really with all that feeling and want to send you a message and you criticise me for saying what I say! I can't say anything right can I? I can't do anything right!" After a short exasperated silence he glances at her with malice. He already knows the effect of what he will say to her, "It must be a problem with language then..." her brain is already stinging with the blow, her first language is not English. "... maybe you should have stayed with your lover the poet..."

She moves her feet and pulls the bed clothes violently over them forcing her hands to do something rather than lash out at him for his cruelty. She tries to collect her brain scattered by the impact of the precisely aimed and pitiless blow, hold her hands in check, control her body which wants to fly out and jump on him wanting to smash him to pieces.

"You are such a cruel fucker!" flies with anger from her mouth. She has not sworn at him in the two years they have been lovers. She resents him for the humiliation he is putting her through. For being forced into a position of swearing of degrading what she loves. She is angry at his cruelty, the depth of his venom. She rebels against the injustice of it. The pain and anger in her explode, "You have to be cruel to me don't you? Whenever I am vulnerable, whenever you become aware that I may need you, that I may need looking after, you become cruel. You can't bear it, being needed. The lower I am, the harder you kick! Without pity, without compassion! As though you want to take what remaining life is left in my body. What makes you so cruel?" Her unrecognisable wheezing voice came out in coughs and convulsions. "You can never accept my vulnerability, weakness and most of all that I may need you. I need you..." squeezes past her vocal cords, a brief silence adjusting to her own admission and its implication for her. "You can't allow yourself to accept that can you? You will need to change your whole life if you allowed that reality to sink in. That's the problem. So every time I am sick you run... you run... trying to find a way of getting out." She stops, calming herself, allowing more of the anger to come through rather than the pain. "I must always be superwoman! Independent... strong... invincible... always! In my existence there must never be a moment of weakness, never a desire to be cared for." She stops for the briefest of moments and aims fearlessly, "Like all men you are such a coward!"

He sat up quickly taking deep breaths. Angry. She felt his anger matching hers. He dangled his legs from the bed. Indecisive. He didn't want to answer back. He wanted to escape. He didn't want confrontation he did not want anger he did not want violence... images of his father's anger, violence, brutality, of being beaten up by him flashed through his mind. He must escape... he felt the violence closing in all around him. He must run.

She felt the stitches, the soreness of her throat and her belly and a total surrender to pain. A tear dropped and she wiped it quickly with her finger. No crying. She didn't want any more humiliation. She was totally exposed. She wanted him to stay but to stay because he wanted to be with her, to understand what had happened to her in the last two days, to understand her pain her desperation, to hug her gently; the unquenchable desire to be hugged.

It was all so simple. After a while she became aware of his desperation and couldn't bear his sense of being trapped. She didn't want to fight. She stretched her hand and touched his bare skin not covered by the white vest. She caressed his arm. He didn't turn around, he didn't respond. She spoke to him in her head. She called out to her lover. She told him she was hurt. She was in pain. He knew she was. She asked him to turn his head. She wanted to look into his face. To look into his eyes. To see his tenderness. Could he hear her? Where was this great love of his? Her hand fell onto the bed. He stayed frozen with his back to her.

***

She wheels me into the theatre, the Jamaican nurse with false hair. Her neck is stiff, she can barely move it, she says. I want to tell her about you. "Where did you go in Jamaica?" she asks because I've told her I've been to her homeland. I reel off Mo

Bay, Negril, Savannah-la-Mar, Blue Fields, Portland, Port Antonio, St. Ann's as I re-live them in my head while she is wheeling me in. I think of you. My lover. I think of the red ebony shine of your skin in the sun and its silky sensuousness. The sensation against my cheek against my body. Your laughing eyes honey-green or maybe moss-honey. And your lips, I can kiss for ever.

"You belong here... you fit into this place," you tell me as we walk up the hill to the hotel left over from the plantation days. "You seem to belong here," you say softly almost to yourself and you are puzzled by it. Below us the harbour lights, white pearls against indigo blue. Colonial banana boats still come and go where the slave ships did come. The sky clear, deceptively velvet. And the Jamaican earth-smells, grass, flowers of the night and the balmy night itself. Dogs barked at us unwillingly fulfilling their obligation as guardians of houses and property. Scared, ran, as soon as you leaned down to pick up a stone... And you were beautiful calm serene at peace with yourself holding me against your body.

"My wife doesn't fit in. She tries, she tries hard. She will come and live here. She will do it for me... and that's the greatest sacrifice you can ask of anyone," you say, "It is the ultimate sacrifice to uproot someone and take them half-way around the world. You and I have both done it." I know. We both came half way around the world and we met and fought for life in London sometimes together sometimes separately. I agree it is a sacrifice and smile at the matter of factness of our comments. We deal with the surface and not what churns deep down. "That's what she is doing... for me!" and I sense a hidden pleasure in your voice. Someone is sacrificing themselves, their world, for you! And I half imagine that you are sending me secret messages of, *... and you are not... look at what this other woman is doing for me.* And I think of the transience of life and smile at you, knowing your secret. You touch my face, "But you... you belong here. You can just come and live here and people and the land will just love you." I laugh and I am touched by your efforts to make me part of your imaginary life in your homeland.

And yet Jamaica surprises me... she surprises me with her acceptance of me. I don't feel a stranger. I don't feel a visitor. I am not afraid of her. I am not afraid of her violence. I've been here before. I stand and she moves around me, absorbs me, makes me part of herself. As though I've always been here or that I'm returning to an old familiar place, but I've never been. The sounds smiles smells the touching the slow gentle attraction delude me into thinking I've been here before. I don't understand her, I feel her... I tell you I don't understand this feeling. Another island woman. From half way around the world. In the warmth of the Mediterranean Sea. With a spirit from Africa where she lies near. Another language another history. Is it an ancestral song through history which welcomes me in this land of yours? I am talking to you in my head as the Jamaican nurse wheels me into the theatre. I see you in my arms under the stars on a hillside in Jamaica. I breathe you in with the warm night and I sense that you will come back to your land, and face my forbidden desire to come with you.

***

I know I am not dealing with it really. I have not accepted yet that it has happened. They faxed me from Jamaica two days ago to let me know but... you know what it's like... you make yourself busy. You don't allow it to sink in. I just can't quite accept it. I suppose when they send me the contract or letter of confirmation I'll believe it. Finally, I will believe that they are offering me the job. The job I've been working towards for the past few years. It will then be more real.

But I can't be happy about it... I look at you sitting across the table from me... touching your cup to your lips... see your brown eyes look at me with that secret smile... your long dark hair over your shoulders and I don't want to accept it. The rain falls on the roof like a monsoon. A grey autumn London day. They listen briefly. *I thought I would be over the moon when I imagined it happening. It's not what I thought it was going to be like. I wanted it so much, so much! And now it's here I can't be totally happy about it.* The rain raucous, pitiless.

Do you remember I left you in the park in Kingston on your own that day and I went to talk to the head of department and his wife? I knew you were angry with me for coming back late, for making you wait in the park. I knew you were in pain and you were unhappy. I really couldn't leave them any earlier. They invited me for a meal and I couldn't say no. I suppose I could have said I am travelling with a friend and she is sitting in the University Park

waiting for me on her own. I suppose you would have done that...
that's the difference between us. If I had done that I would've had
a lot of explaining to do. They know my wife and we have common
friends both here and in Jamaica. I couldn't risk it. I know you
don't accept such conventions. You think all this family life and
marriage is rubbish, false, unreal... but you don't know the power
of the institution of marriage, security... I suppose we build our
golden cages. She is watching him intently, unable to prevent her
spirit flying away leaving her body sitting across the table under
the cacophony of the rain song.

Now that I have been offered the job I suppose I am not
dealing with having to leave you behind. I am avoiding it. I
couldn't ever imagine not having you around me, in my life. You
know when we tried to separate before I couldn't bear to think that
you wouldn't ever want to talk to me again. I couldn't bear it if you
cut me out. I can't imagine a stage in my life when you wouldn't be
there. I see you when I think of getting old. You are always there...
I could never be without you.

***

He slowly got off the bed and went to his clothes on the
other side of the room. She felt his movements more than seeing
them.

"Are you leaving?" she asked. He didn't answer. He began
to put his clothes on.

"Please don't do this to me! Please..." she pleaded. "Please don't go... please don't do this!" She was getting weaker and weaker. She held her long dark hair away from her face in exasperation. She wanted to scream at him but she was pleading... feeling his every move designed to humiliate her without pity. She felt nailed to the bed her body unwilling to react to any commands. Her head was full of action. Angry passionate loving action. She was up walking towards him holding his arms back looking into his eyes challenging his insensitivity looking for his tenderness and loving of her... firmly stopping him. Her body didn't move as a response to the images in the head. She felt her stitches stretching and hurting. She couldn't move. She looked at her motionless body, helplessly. Resenting it. Her vulnerability her rejected need of him. She sat in the corner of the bed, where he had left her, unaccustomed to her acceptance of her vulnerability. She tried to use the power of her voice to stop him. The operation had broken that too.

He put his clothes on methodically, meticulously, piece by piece, in silence, without hurrying. She watched him in silence feeling every action a piece of torture on her body. He leaned down took his bag and walked out of her room. He left the door ajar. Without a word.

***

A few days later he came back. The woman with the long dark hair noticed the immaculate grey-suited woodpigeon with the orange beak perched on the roof looking at the table below where his mate lay. She smiled at him through her window high up. He focused with one eye then the other. He looked intently. The table was clean. There was no trace she was ever there.

London. October 1992

THE NURSE MOTHER

"Iris! Iris! Come here! I-r-i-i-i-s!"

No I don't want to be here.

"Iris!"

The screaming echoes through the house. Her vocal cords are at their limits.

No. Go away old woman.

"God damn you! Where in the Hell did you get to!"

As far away from you as I can you Devil of a woman.

"I-r-r-i-i-is! Iris!"

Yes I hear you. I wish I didn't. God give me patience! Or one day...

The old woman fumbles with the wheels of her chair. Slightly perspiring. Her upper lip and underarms are beginning to feel moist. She can smell her own odour. How she hates it! Under her breath, "Iris! Damn her! She thinks she can mess me about like this!"

Then a scream disturbs her face, "Iris! Here! I want you here! At once! Here!" as though commanding a dog.

"Yes Ma'am... you've called?"

She appears in her white uniform. Breezes through the sitting room door. Her white figure in contrast to the rich reds, browns, rusts of the sitting room. Rust paisley, velvet, seat covers, curtains, deep wine-coloured carpet, mahogany and dark brown stained furniture. Her white uniform and white shoes out of place. She is a stranger. She is artificial. An ill-fitting addition. An after-thought. Not part of that world.

"Damn it! Where have you been?" She barks. "You know I can't move myself. You know my hands are useless. Damn you! What do I pay you for?" Iris looks at the squinting eyes and twisted mouth. The most movable and expressive parts left behind by the years. Scattering bitterness, venom, fire in an American drawl Iris resents.

"Yes Ma'am! What can I do for you?" Measured. Restrained. Resigned. A machine voice. No interference from human emotions.

She comes nearer and stands next to the old woman in the wheelchair. She does not attempt to touch her or the chair. She stands close. Her brown-green eyes watching. Detached. She is far, far away. Alive eyes shaded with long lashes. She watches the little angry moves of the wheelchair-bound woman. Her lips set somewhere between annoyance and pity.

Yes, here I am. Here I am old woman. What is it? What do you want? You have called and I have come. Tell me! What is it you want done? I don't want to be here. What? Your cushion is straight! Your legs are not tangled. Your body is upright. You have not wet yourself. Have you? There is no place for you to go. Here you are in your big house. In the middle of this United States... Palatial! From end to end. All yours. There is the garden. You don't enjoy. There is the tennis court. You can't play. There is the swimming pool. You can't swim. There is the kitchen. You have never cooked. Not a grain of dirt crept under your nails. The nanny looked after your kids. And they don't come. Unless they want something from you. If you could have done it, you would have let her give birth to your children for you. Ah yes, but what about the element of sex? What would you have done about that? How did you get along with sex? And what about... love?

"Yes Ma'am! Can I help you?"

"Don't stand there stupidly!"

I don't want to be here.

"Straighten my cushion! I don't pay you to stand around!"

She leans over to straighten the straight cushion. Screams of protest crowd her lips. She is aware she screams, as she doesn't utter a word. Gently her black slim fingers straighten the pink velvet cushion. Smell. Oh, no! She hasn't! Again. She has already changed her this morning. It's only lunch-time.

"Ma'am... I think we need to..."

"Yes I know! You don't need to talk about it. God damn you! I've called you already! I don't call you for the sake of it or... or your brown eyes... there, you see! There! Just get on with it... and don't take your time!"

Me don' want fe be here! Oh Lord! Me don'! Where me children? Where me people? What me doin' here? Lord give me patience wit 'er! One of these days me goin' fe smack 'er one right in

153

she twisted mout'! Lord have mercy on me!

"Yes Ma'am! Don't worry... I will change you in a tick! Just patience now."

***

"She rang me the other day; in fact it was yesterday. That was really strange," he says.

"Why?"

"Because she never rings me! In fact she has never rung me! She rings and talks to my wife but never to me. It was a real surprise. She just started talking to me as though the last time she spoke to me was last week."

"When was the last time?"

"Years! I haven't spoken to her in years! She came for the summer last year. I picked her up from the airport. And that was it. I was too busy. I didn't see her. I didn't feel as though she was my mother. I didn't feel anything about her. She was... well, she was my mother but I didn't feel it."

She looks at his face for signs of further explanation. His jaw is tight, his eyebrows slightly puzzled. He keeps his eye on the wheel, driving carefully in the busy roads of London. It's sunny. The soft roof is rolled back. Rays of sun reach the top of their heads and faces. She leans her head back on the headrest but keeps her eyes on him.

"Why? What happened between you?" she asks gently.

"I suppose I haven't spoken to her for years. I've decided I could leave her out."

"Hmm... I can understand that. But how do you feel about it? Are you comfortable with that decision You seem to be hurt by it."

"I suppose I am. I suppose I don't think she ever thought about me. She always wanted to do what she wanted to do. I never mattered. What I thought or felt... I just didn't count. I didn't exist in her calculations."

She watches him drive. Listening to Pavarotti wrenching his heart out. He leans over and ejects the cassette.

"That's my opera hour for the morning. Not now! It's funny watching the faces drop when cars pull up at the traffic lights and they see a Black man and hear Pavarotti. Now I am in a rebellious, flying mood." He looks at her as though she is the cause and smiles. He puts on a Bob Marley cassette.

Stand up stand up
Stand up for your rights

...wail the Wailers. She is not sure whether he wants to continue. It's his way of playing for time. He dives into something not too near the bone. She looks away and watches the street life. Notices the curious eyes watching them. They draw attention in their togetherness.

"Do you want to talk about her?" she asks.

He takes his time in answering.

"I've told you about her anyway! You know what I feel!"

"So tell me... what did she want to talk about?"

"She is talking about her house in Jamaica. She bought this house in Montego Bay. When you get there you'll see the soft drinks factory on the left as you go into Mo Bay. About eight years ago she bought this house. She's rented it out. Now she's talking about getting the tenants out and going back.

"She phoned up to tell me that she's missing Jamaica. That she's had enough of America and wants to go back. Even last year she was saying how she wouldn't go back. She was running everything Jamaican down. Nothing was good enough for her. She is such a snob! And now, all of a sudden, she wants me to talk to Nemie, my cousin, and start getting those people out so that she can go back.

"She couldn't get out of Jamaica fast enough. She didn't care about anyone, not about me or my sister. No one! She was prepared to leave us behind and go to England. Jamaica wasn't good enough for her. People were just no good!"

Anger swells in him. The memories of a five-year-old choke and constrict the voice of the thirty-eight-year-old man driving his car in the streets of London. The sense of abandonment crowds his emotions. The sense of being deserted, left behind, overwhelms him as he concentrates on using the steering wheel with flair and skill.

She watches his fingers grip the wheel as his lips tighten and he frowns with concentration. His cheek muscle dances as he bites his teeth. She reaches out and lightly touches his fingers on the wheel then the side of his face. Caresses his cheek. He touches her hand, kisses it and holds it for moments against his cheek.

"God, I resented her so much! And she went... she upped and went to the States... well, that was it for me! If I had anything

156

left for her that was the end of it. I just cut her out. I didn't want to feel anything for her. And I'm O.K. I don't really feel much for her. I've come to terms with it all. I don't let it get to me. But it was a surprise to talk to her, out of the blue... as though nothing had happened as though we had a normal relationship as though we were a normal mother and son!"

She smiles at his last comment at the impossibility of 'normality' in relationships. At the improbability of their own relationship. The abnormality of being lovers. And yet the naturalness of being lovers. Of being together, laughing, the fun of talking. Loving.

***

Iris! Man... Iris was something! She was beautiful! She was so beautiful! She used to walk down the road and eyes used to go with her! Straight down the road... as far as the eye could reach. If she was around, you couldn't take your eyes off her... no man! You couldn't! She used to live up by the school. And she used to walk down past the shop to go to her aunty's. Aunty Mavis. And that's when him used to see she. And him an old man now! Him thirty-three and she seventeen! And him have two young ones from that other woman already. Two sons. Oh, she was beautiful! She walk like a queen... down that road. Just like a queen! She was the Queen of Sav-la-Mar, man!

***

She screams. The neighbours can hear her. There is a light in the window above the garage. The shutters are closed. It's eleven at night. A balmy night. Full of the sweet scents of the night flowers busily visited by long-tongued moths.

Another scream. She falls on the floor. He is at it again. He is beating her up. She tries to struggle to her feet. She has fallen on the floor by the bed. She leans on the bed trying to pull herself up. Confused. Unsure of herself. Unsure of what to do. Should she stay on the floor? Would that signify less resistance? Acceptance of her guilt? Submission? Would that spare her from further blows? Will he stop hitting her? Would struggling to get up symbolise resistance? Challenge? Standing up to him? What should she do? Get up? Stay down on the floor? Her belly is paining her. It's too swollen to lie on the bare floor. She can't get comfortable. She touches it as she tries to get up. She is out of breath. She holds the curve of her belly almost lifting it up as a separate object. Settles it on her lap still holding it from below. The side of her face where he struck her is stinging. Tears are running down. She sniffs as her nose runs. She wipes her eyes with the back of her hands and squeezes her nose. She wipes her fingers on the hip of her floral skirt.

She looks up to see where he is. He is standing by the door looking at her sideways. His dark face cloudy. Green eyes invisible. He looks down at his feet. His hands are clenched into fists hanging loosely on either side. He is wearing long dark trousers and a white vest. He hesitates. He doesn't move. He leans his hands on the dresser where her perfume bottles, lipstick, nail-varnish, hair-comb lie. Little crocheted circles are placed along the glass, with the perfume bottles placed carefully centrally on them. He can see the reflection of the bric-a-brac in the round mirror. He can see her.

He breathes heavily. He is sweating. Sweat droplets have stuck to the back of his vest. Droplets are sliding down his temples and forehead. She is whimpering, crying as she wipes her eyes with her hands.

"So help me Lord! I love her so! Lord, Lord help me! Show me the way! I can't stand it! I can't stand it no more! She is making a fool of me. She is playing with me. She's nineteen and making me foolish. And I, I, a grown man! A little more and I be her father let alone father children for her. I, a grown man of thirty-five. And look at me! Look at me Lord! Reduced to this. Reduced to a wreck! Reduced to hitting her. Reduced to beating her about. And she with child. And she with child. Oh Lord, forgive me for my sins. How? How could I be this? Hitting a woman? Hitting a woman with child? Hitting my woman carrying my child? Oh Lord, forgive me! My child! I don't know any more Lord! I don't know. My child? I don't know... if it is my child. Help me bear it Lord! Help me bear it! And I love her so! I love her so, Lord! Help me, oh...help me Lord!"

He suddenly moves towards her. She cowers. Almost crawls under the bed. Puts her hands up to protect herself from the invisible blows.

"Whose is it? Who...? You tell me! You-tell-me... you little whore!" He grabs her thick hair with one hand and her raised hand with the other.

"Tell me whose is it? It's not mine! Not mine!" He lets go of her hand and hits her across the face. She screams as she tries to lie face down to protect her face and pregnant body. He pushes her face into the floor. He is afraid, his hands tremble but pushes her face down. She groans and reaches out searching trying to grab his hand. She finds it and frees herself from the grip. She wriggles away. She brings her legs between him and her body. She is ready to kick.

She screams at him between her tears and fear yet defiant, "Yours! It is yours Norris!" She watches him carefully and then whimpers, "I swear! I swear Norris. There is no one else. Your child!"

He kneels and suddenly crumples on the floor. He sits back on his legs. He hits the floor repeatedly with his fist. Then stops with both his fists on the floor. He suddenly begins to cry. He pushes his fists into his eye-sockets. And cries. Dry, short sobs. His belly quivering heaving with the sobs through his white vest.

***

"He beat her throughout the pregnancy. When she was carrying me, he beat her nearly every day. And when I was born, when I was a few weeks old... I don't know, maybe a few months... she took me to my Granny's. And that was that. My Granny brought me up. He just didn't want me around him," he says as he drives around the corner.

"Why? Do you know?"

"No! I never found out. But he never loved me. To the end. He always denied me."

"There must have been a reason..." she blinks in the sun.

"Yes, I was his." He is smiling. He has anticipated her question. "There is no question about it. I was. I am. Everyone remarks on the similarity of our looks. There is no question about that."

"Was he jealous because your mother loved you or paid you too much attention in his eyes?"

"No, he beat her up while she was carrying me. She thought it might change after my birth, but it didn't. So after a while she took me to my Granny's."

"Maybe he was jealous that you were going to take her away from him. Demand her time. Tie her up. He wouldn't have her all to himself. Some men feel that. Maybe that's what it was."

He looks at her and can't help but smile. He appreciates her attempts at explanations which might give a logical reason to unsolvable actions and alleviate the sense of rejection he has felt all his life. Even if reasons for actions could be worked out with hindsight the lived emotions cannot be unlived.

He looks away, "And all I wanted from him was to love me. But he never did. Right to the end. He never did!"

***

I knew he was older than me. But I didn't care! I used to see him working in his garage. Stripped to his waist. Wearing shorts. And he used to have a good body. Sweating and covered in oil but he had a good body.

He had two boys with the woman up by Piper's Corner. I knew that. I'd seen him go up there. But he lived above the garage. The boys used to go and see him after school. And then go to their mother's house.

He had the garage and a shop. And he used to have a bus. He was well off... comfortable. He had more than most of us. He had nice clothes. He was a nice dresser. He had style. Other women used to talk about him.

After a while he began to look at me. I could tell. I used to walk by the garage to go to my auntie's and I used to go by slowly looking in but not looking. I didn't want him thinking I was after him. And I wasn't. I liked it. That a grown man looked at me. I could turn his head. But he didn't do it openly, he didn't say a word. He just look. And look. And I knew he was sweet on me. It make me feel good. So, I past by some more and look his way. And walk past real slow and look at him... And I was sure. I was sure I got him... hook line and sinker. He wanted me. He wanted me, bad!

And me think to myself. Iris! What you want with a young man? What good is a young man? He only love you and leave you. Best take this man. Older man. Good for you. Settled. He has his business, a garage and house and a bus. What else you want now? All there. All ready for you. You have a good life! Older man appreciate you more, look after you.

So I decide to make myself a good life!

Love him? Don't know. Don't know about that. That's not important anyhow. What me do in that small town? Who me marry? Make somethin' of meself? No family. What me family give me? Nothin'! Nothin' to give. So me tell meself, Iris, you only have your face and this body, girl. Use it now! Use it for yourself! That all you have. That what will save you. Save yourself girl. And he, the man!

So I married him. He was a good man. Good looking man too. He was a redman. Nice colour. Light. His eyes green. Like my son, he has green eyes. And his hair light. A little bit of ginger in it. He was my ticket out. I wasn't going to find better.

So one night I went to him. I just open the door and went upstairs. He trembled all night by my side. He touched my face, hair and breasts and caressed my back and thighs and he trembled all night. You'd think he never had a woman before...

We had Lorraine. She was light skinned. She was beautiful. He doted on her. Then I fell with child again. And he changed... he wasn't the same man. He beat me all through the pregnancy... all through. I don't know how I managed to give birth to the child. My son, he was beautiful. Red like his father and green eyes. I had to take him to my mother when he was about three weeks old. Didn't even manage to breast feed him properly, my poor child. I was afraid of Norris. There was no telling what he would do. I was afraid for the child. And my milk was flowing. My dress wet from the milk. And I used to sneak out of the house and go to my mother's and give him my breast. He was so hungry. He was a hungry baby for the breast. My poor child...

Then one night... he gone! Norris gone! Just gone! Just disappeared! I hear he gone. Gone and left me! His friend, Mr. Jackson, he know, he tell me! I am panicking! Mr. Jackson tell me he owed money. The garage, shop, bus all useless. What could I do with a garage... a woman? He was bankrupt. Nothing! He had nothing! Everything was gone! And him too! And me left with two kids in Sav-la-Ma'... with nothing!

So I took Lorraine and the boy to my mother and went to Kingston. I found a job. My mother looked after the children. I would come back once a month and bring money and food. Kingston was a long way in those days. I became a nurse in the hospital. It was still easy in those days to become a nurse without any qualifications. I suppose it wasn't much of a respectable job. Good family girls didn't go to work in hospitals, washing patients, emptying their spit and potties and cleaning their wounds. It was still being like a servant. And almost the only thing available to single mother's which paid a wage and was nearly respectable as a government job. The British trained us and paid us.

About six months later I heard from Norris. He was in London. He wrote and told me he was working on the buses and when he had enough money he'd send for me. So I went on working in the hospital in Kingston and watch to see what would happen.

***

"My grandmother brought us all up. There were lots of kids about. There was us two, and our cousins. And we all used to be with Granny, we used to sleep in her house. We used to lay in bed cross-ways so that we could all fit in. And she used to feed us. I don't know how she did it, where she found food, but she always found something to feed us with. My mother used to bring things from the hospital and give her money... but it wasn't much.

Then he sent for her. And she went. She got on the boat and went. We didn't even feel that she had gone to London. It was like she was going to Kingston. And we didn't miss her. By that time there was my sister and me and Michael." he says.

"Who was Michael?" she is suddenly surprised.

"He is my brother."

"I thought she only had you and your sister...!"

"Yes, from my father she had me and my sister! But afterwards, when my father was in London, she had Michael."

"Who was Michael's father?"

"We don't know! She never said. But Michael was a love child. She never told us who he was but she obviously loved the man. And yet she left him and went to London to someone she didn't love. I think she really was an opportunist. She didn't love him, she went just to save herself. He was offering her the best deal!"

"What's wrong if she was trying to save herself from a dead-end life? It couldn't have been all there was to life, to slave away in a hospital, for pittance, so that you could feed three kids and a mother! Maybe she didn't have much choice!"

He smiles with amusement at his lover's defence of his

mother and does not answer.

***

I arrived at Southampton Harbour. My God, what a God-forsaken country! January and freezing. It couldn't be worse! We set off from Kingston, sunny, warm, sunshine and sea warming us up. I had my best suit on. I had a hat but it wasn't enough. I couldn't warm up. People were coughing and sneezing. Their eyes watering, blowing into handkerchiefs. It was miserable. I regretted ever setting foot on that boat in Kingston. I wished I never set eyes on it let alone my foot on it. I somehow knew it. I just knew it was wrong...

And everything was wrong. The house was damp. Smelling of paraffin from the stove trying to heat one room for us to sit and sleep in. The shops selling no vegetable or fruit I knew. The white people being hateful and rude. As though we'd come to take their country from them. They aks us to come... Signs everywhere on flats, pubs and shops: 'No coloureds here.' 'Whites only!' And they aks us to come and work here! My God! What a God-forsaken country! What misery! What an endless misery!

And I lived with it for so long, so long, till I'd forgotten what it was like being warm. What it was to feel the sun on your face to smell the flowers and see the birds and pick the ackee and mango and sink my teeth into the flesh of a rose apple drink the juice of soursop! Oh... I'd forgotten it for so long. So long...

The children came. All of us in that damp room trying to

keep warm. My God what misery! And Norris... I didn't need Norris any more. I was working. Earning my money, what do I need the misery Norris bring me?

And his children! Mine too! But I'd given him two, a girl and a boy. He loved the girl but he still hated the boy. He couldn't do anything right. No matter what that boy did he got a beating. He couldn't do anything right. He never showed him any love. And that boy was desperate, oh my poor son, he was so desperate to show him how much he loved him. But Norris wouldn't have it! He also started drinking. He would drink and get drunk. Start on me and then on the boy. There was never a day without a bashing!

And I just had enough! I had it! What was I doing getting beaten up? What for? What do I need it for? Lorraine had gone off. She was sixteen. She enrolled at a college to train as a nurse. And my son was fourteen; he could take care of himself. He didn't need me to look after him. He could get his own dinner, iron his shirts, wash his clothes, take care of himself in the streets and even against Norris. So I decided to go. I wanted out. I'd had enough of Norris and his drunkenness and everything else. That wasn't a life! I'd had enough!

I didn't tell Norris. I just wanted to go. I told my son. I wasn't prepared for it though. I wasn't! He just cried and cried. A fourteen-year-old boy, a grown man I thought. I thought he was old enough to take care of himself but he cried like a baby. He didn't want me to go! He just wouldn't let go. He said how could I leave him and go! How could I do it when I knew the way he beat him up he could kill him. Where would he go? What would he do? He was only fourteen and nowhere to go! How could I leave him with such a man and go! Leave? Leave him with a father who hated him!

He was right! He was still only a boy! And in my eagerness to escape from a life of Hell, from this drunken, violent man, I was leaving. Trying to save myself, just run and leave my son behind to his own fate.

Yes... it was selfish! Very selfish! But I didn't have a choice. I couldn't take him with me. Where could I take him? And in fact we weren't very close. He always kept me away. I gave birth to him but with the threats of violence from his father, I hardly saw him. His Granny looked after him and then when Norris went to London I was in Kingston. I had to work. And then I was in London he was still with his Granny. He was eleven when he came to London and the same story, his father rejected him again.

How he survived all that rejection I don't know. I suppose children are just resilient, they survive. They don't think much about life they just live it. They are not like us, grown ups, who think and ponder about things and suffer from thinking about it all!

***

"She stayed that first time. She didn't go! Apparently I just cried and cried and I don't even remember that! It's strange! She told my wife I had cried! Then she went. Her son Michael, the love child, went to the States. He works there. I think he is in computers. He has a comfortable life. And he sent her an invitation and some papers and then she went. I think I was at college then. I don't even remember it."

They had stopped at the traffic lights. A Rastaman with beautiful eyes looks at them and smiles at her. She returns the smile. She is curious about the loved man.

"Did she ever tell him who his father was?"

"No, she didn't! It's interesting. Granny brought Mike up too. And no one knew who he belonged to. You usually know who the children belong to."

"So what did you tell her when she started talking about returning to Jamaica? What do you feel about it?"

"I just listened. I didn't say much. I didn't know what to say. I suppose I still have some anger against her for leaving me. And I don't care what she does."

"What is she doing in the States?"

"She is a nurse! She continued with her profession."

"What... in a hospital?"

"No. She works with a private nursing agency."

"What does she do?"

"She looks after rich American old people no one wants to look after. Their relatives, sons and daughters hire a nurse to look after them, clean after them, wipe their nose and bottom... you know the type!"

London. April 1991

GRANDMA JAMAICA'S DELROY
- to Busha

"Son, me want you go find him! Delroy the only grandson me not seen. Me want you to go find him. Me want you to see how him is. Yes..." She takes her eyes away from his and lowers them to her hands. Wrinkled hands laying flat on the bare wood of the table in the back garden.

She sucks her teeth, her cheeks sink momentarily, her eyes move up and look away, bright small black eyes covered over with a film of opaqueness, signs of old age, signs of having seen too much, experienced too much. Her laughter lines have permanently settled around her eyes inseparable from her lines of sorrow. Her thick lips long lost their fullness with the loss of her teeth. Some, overlooked by the passing time, still hang onto her gums at times paining her.

But her skin is most beautiful. Velvet smooth despite the years. Thinly draping itself around the sculptured high cheek-bones reaching to the edges of her greying African hair around her large ears down both sides of her neck still holding that old wise head.

"Busha...?" she looked up with twinkles in her eyes,

twisted the old plain silver ring worn down from years of washing clothes on her middle finger, "... you hear me? You go find him! Him the only one me not seen. Me only grandson." Her insistent voice as soft as her skin. He looks at his Grandma, the great-grand-daughter of the slave.

In her memories she must still carry the emotions of slaves. She must carry the sustaining songs, the songs of resistance, the music of heartbeat, the terror, fear of slaves. She must have heard stories from her father, from her grandmother, stories of being chased, knifed, butchered, raped. She must have heard of the footsteps in the night echoing in her nightmares coming to take her away. She must have lived the fear of her mother's mother being raped by the plantation owner or his sons or his hired hands. She must have seen in her mind the brutalisation, violation of her mother's skin, breasts, the forceful pinning down like an animal the forceful entry into her body, the casting out into the dark night once they had finished.

She must have heard the moans, the wailing, the screams, the crying in the night... all others, even her husband must have heard... that brutalisation that aloness of a woman. She must have heard of suicides of beatings whippings lynchings of manslaves. She must have heard of beatings of the womanslaves by their man for being raped for being too beautiful for attracting attention of the slave owner of the sons of the overseer... She must have heard the sobs of the manslaves listening to the screams of their wives and daughters being raped. She must have seen manslaves beat their women desperately trying to alleviate their

172

own degradation and humiliation.

So grandmother under this Jamaican sun, great-grand-daughter of a slave under this guinep tree what else did you see? What else does your memory hold onto? What else are you not going to tell? What else, what pieces of history will you bury with you?

"You do it Busha?" her penetrating slanted eyes fix on his, not asking but commanding.

"Yes man, Granny! Don't fret now. Me said me do it!" comes his gentle voice.

"Don't forget now! You tell me all them things now and you go and forget. Soon as you get on that iron bird you forget everything! You fly away and you forget everything me ever tell you. You forget all this..." her hand sweeps from earth to sky, her eyes following her hand, "... you forget your old Granny! Even forget who you are, son! I knows London... no use telling me not so! Yes, you all goin' to forget who you all is!" She looks at him in the knowledge that she is teasing him, teasing this grandson of hers who is not going to contradict her. His respect is one reason, his fear of the wisdom of her words is the other which keeps his tongue tied. He flicks his head away from her and smiles, "Not a chance of that Granny! You'd give me a good lickin'... me just wouldn't dare bring your wrath upon me you know!"

He hears her give a deep chuckle. She gathers her loose skirts and wraps them around her legs showing her smooth black skin going down to the cracked centuries-old skin on her feet. She looks at her bare feet and thick twisted nails for a second. She rubs her toes against each other to flick off a speck and rests them back on her worn sandals on the earth. She rubs her eyes and squeezes her nose driving away thoughts crowded around her head. Loosens her headscarf and re-ties it letting out the troubling thoughts, almost as though putting the finishing touches to the chasing off of these invaders.

"So why you go marry a white woman now? Why you go and do it again?"

He lets her question hang in the air for a while. He wipes the table with his hand and looks at his palm, his finger nails and soft hands. He notices the cracks in the wood, a fly running on spindly legs across the table. He feels the urge to catch it, with one hand in his palm, just to test his reactions. Was he as fast as when he was a young footballer with what seemed a fantastic future before they cut him down, dragged him into a hospital operated on his knees and told him he could no longer dream of being a star... a rare Black football star in London.

That was nineteen-seventy, twenty years ago. He still lives through those days as though they were yesterday. He almost wakes up in that hospital with the smell of disinfectant in his nostrils as he tells his lover about it. When they are together, he runs on the beach, the quick steps of a footballer on training.

"Grab him! Watch that little left-winger! Get in there! That's it... that's it... cut in front of him! You fool! You've missed him again!" He is imitating his coach.

"This football coach put one bloke to stop me after he explained how to tackle a winger... and I went forward and got

174

through. Then he puts another two on me and I still beat them... he had to put three defenders to stop me!" And the great smile of victory breaks out on his face.

He plays ducking, false little dives to the left then to the right, then charges through. Run. Run. Run. Backwards. Turn around. Charge. Jump up. Head the ball.

He tells her with a gleam in his eye that his son is such a natural and he is only three. His older son was not interested. They are both from white women. He tells his lover one was a marriage of convenience the other of two families congregating for the occasion from all over the world. A marriage for everyone.

"My family all thought that after Margot I would fall in love with a woman of my own colour. A Black woman. They were surprised when I married Sibyl." He kisses her shoulder and the drops of water on her brown skin under the shower. He holds her tightly his hands resting at the small of her back. His lips move down from her cheek towards her breast gently brushing against the nipple kissing the fullness of her breast. His hands stroke her arms and shoulders. He pulls himself away and caresses her with his eyes aware that her large dark eyes are following his every move. She smiles at his desire and uncontrollable eagerness to love her. She slowly brings her wet body against his. She sculptures it into his body-scapes.

"Well Granny, you know what them say, love is blind! Just happened you know... me fall in love and she a white woman again."

No she didn't want to know. *Why in the name of... did he go and marry another white woman now? He had enough prob-*

lems with that Margot... no respect for tradition. Didn't want to go to work and didn't want property or a house. Woman is mad. And older than him. Much much older. Him young enough to be her son and him looking after her children. All four of them. Jesus bless me! And him only a twenty-four year old with four children of another man who didn't care none. Busha what you gone and done son? How you going to cope with these young ones when you is a young one yourself? Tell me that now. But no use tellin' you... you not listenin' none!

And now married to another white woman. This one his age. Nice. Now them have baby Busha. Boy, him like his Daddy! Look at them ears and them eyes ready to gobble up the world. Look at them just turn around and around. But she done him proud. She a good woman. Married him proper and look, him bring his son back to our Church to christen him. All the way from London. She a good woman to him. Good wife good mother to his child. Old Busha done well this time. White woman but good woman to him.

Oh the lickin' he had, oh the lickin' boy! And them big ears... times me had to pull them! Poor boy... my poor boy left on his own when my Iris gone and left him. Gone to London after that no good man of hers. Gone and left him. And she didn't shed a tear to leave him. Busha had a tough time, boy! Tough!

"I remember screaming when they came to take me. 'I want my Granny-y-y-y! I want my Granny-y-y-y...' And apparently I cried and cried. They couldn't stop me. I didn't want to part from her. I didn't want to go to London. I didn't want to be torn away from Jamaica, from my Granny. I didn't want to go. I didn't want to go and live with my mother and father." He looks away for a second, far, far away.

"I don't think my father ever loved me. Somehow I was never good enough. And my mother..." he searches for the right words which never come. Silence descends. "In fact I think I've dealt with my father but I think even today, I still can't deal with my mother. I thought it was him but once he was out of the way, once he was dead, I realized it was her..."

He looks at his lover listening to him absorbed, watching him with a tiny smile on her lips and twinkling eyes of affection. They sit in the garden of a pub by the river. The sky is an exceptional blue, the river dazzles and it is summer. She rests her head in the cup of her palm leaning over the table, listening. He reaches over and touches the skin of her cheek, takes her hand and kisses it as he usually does gently savouring the sensation of her skin against his lips. She smiles and sends him an intimate signal of affection with her eyes. They talk of childhoods, he of Jamaica, she, of Cyprus. Unloving or dead fathers, grannies who have brought them up half way around the world. They talk of London where they grew up, lived their politics, lovers, lives, had their education in its schools, streets, fought their battles against racism, fascism, pains of being strangers in strange lands, where they became lovers...

"You would have liked Granny. She was something else!"

"Mmmm... but maybe she wouldn't have liked me!"

"I don't know, I think she would... I think she would have."

"Did she used to cuddle you?" she asks almost certain of the answer.

"No! You know what it was like... She was always there. She cooked, washed, cleaned and if you needed her she would be there, but..."

"... but," she picks up, "it wouldn't do to show affection openly like that... right? And there was never any time, was there? But if you happened to be near her and put your arms around her round belly, it would be alright for just that short moment."

He laughs and nods at the similarities of their experiences separated by half the world. "I used to hide under her skirts... that's the nearest I got to her, to her smells. She used to wear these petticoats and I used to hide between the skirts and petticoats. She used to smell nice... of bay rum." His eyes are lost in memory.

"I buried her two years ago. I went back. I just had this phone call and I dropped everything and went. And it was something... I never thought I had it in me but there's always that something left in you from your upbringing. She was a real church-goer. All my family are into the Church. I suppose it's a way of life. And they asked me to say a few words at the service. I suppose I was the most educated in the family and it was my place to do it. And I sat down to write it, to write what I was going to say... and I sat there and..." he looked up, his pain-filled eyes searched her face. Silence. He didn't continue he looked at the other tables in the pub, at other people.

She reached over and stroked his hand, "... and you just cried and cried..." His brown-green eyes filled with tears, well controlled. The control of years. The tears kept walled in, not a drop found itself trickling over the brim.

"Yes, and I sobbed and sobbed like I hadn't from when I was a child! Just totally out of control. I suppose just like a child..."

"Maybe you were... may be you were crying the last tears of a child for his Granny."

"But later on in Church, during the service I didn't cry. I was amazed at myself, how I got into the swing of it and just read not even looking at what I had written, I delivered this sermon. And I remember people saying, 'uhummm... uuhumm... praise the Lord,' every now and again. And I found that repetitive delivery mesmerising, very powerful, '... uuhummm... Amen!' I was surprised that I had it in me. It made me wonder if I could have been a preacher. I enjoyed it." He looks at her to see what her reaction would be to something he knows she abhors. "It was also a release, there was a finality about it. I could lay her to rest, in peace and move on."

***

"George we should. I think we should!"

"Well, I don't know Mary! I am just not sure."

"He is a lovely boy! Look at him, he is gorgeous! And not a soul to look after him. We have looked after other children, he'll fit in just right. He'll be no problem! You'll see..."

"But Mary he is a Coloured boy! We hadn't had one before. We don't know! We don't know if it will be different, they are different, you know. Even if we bring him up as our own, you know he can't be. He will be different to the others. We would have to face it sooner or later."

He looks at his wife who is beginning to look sad and downcast. He puts his arm around her shoulder and kisses her cheek. He is convinced she would see reason. It is the best thing all around.

"You think you can do it? You think you can bring him up properly?" he asks a few minutes later.

"Yes, George! Yes! I am absolutely sure! I know we can do it. He is only a human being. And it depends on how we bring him up, more than anything else. It depends on what we teach him, how we educate him, give him a sense of what is right and what is wrong. That will make him what he is; not the colour of his skin.

"We are equal in the eyes of the Creator anyway. And anyway, I just love him. I want him to come and be with us. You'll see he will be a lovely boy. No trouble, no trouble at all. He'll be our pride and joy! I feel it in my bones! So come, say yes."

"I don't know Mary, I really don't know. I just feel he might be better off with his own people. They would know how to look after him, teach him about his own way of life and all those things. They will be important to the boy as he grows up. They might not be important to him when he is a baby, when he is growing up but it will matter as he grows older."

"I know, I know George... but what's the choice? What's facing him now? Do you think anyone will take him? I don't think so. You've heard what the Welfare lady said, Coloured people are not fostering or adopting these children. No one wants them. They are left in the homes to grow up as best they can.

"Think it over love... do you think he will be better off in some children's home? Do you think he will get a better deal there than being in our family? Because that's where he'll end up. It's not fair, is it?"

"I don't know love... I just don't want us to cause him any more harm than he has already suffered. The little fellow suffered enough as it is. Not a good start in life is it? Losing your Mum as you are being born and no father to claim you. Sometimes I could wring the neck of fathers like him. They think it's just a quick bang and that's it... get up wash your hands and go home!"

"So we'll have him?"

***

"Delroy was adopted by a white family. One of those ever adopting families. Adopting and bringing up many children. They went to live somewhere near Hastings where, especially in those days, hardly any Black people lived.

"When I came back from Jamaica I went to look for him.

I wanted to find Delroy. I'd promised my Granny I would find him. After a while I tracked the family down. They were surprised about it but I arranged to see them.

"His mother had died in childbirth. She was my aunty. Aunty Naomi, my mother's sister. He was the only child. And you know, I think he was a mixed-race child. I think the man was white. I never knew who he was. It was quite something in those days, in the early nineteen-sixties, you know?"

She listens to her lover without showing much emotion. Yes... she knew, she knew what was with race in the early sixties. She tries to imagine the Black woman who has a child from a white man. She wonders if she loved him or was it just a one-night desire. Did she love him? Was it intentional? Was it an accident? Even more important; what was this white man doing fucking with a Black woman? A one-night stand? An uncontrollable desire? Is that all it was? Did he even know they had created a child together? Did he know her at all? Did he know he had a child who was adopted? Did he know she died in childbirth... his child? Transitory lives coming together, loving for moments, parting, going their way and in the process creating something not so transitory. A child left abandoned.

"My mother wanted to adopt him, but my father wouldn't have it. I remember the rows about it. But he wouldn't have it. He had six children in two rooms as it was... I think I even remember visiting him with my mother and father, getting on a train and going somewhere to see him. I suppose he knew he was adopted."

***

"Hey Blackie boy! Who's your Dad then?"

"Who is your mother more like... Who is she then, eh? eh, eh?

"Some whore who got fucked by a Black man? eh? eehh? Blackie? Where is she then? One look at you and she screamed and she just dropped you and ran. Didn't she, eh? I don't blame her!"

"Ugh-ugh-ugh-ugh- want a banana jungle bunny?"

"Here, here here's a tree for you... swing monkey swing!"

"How was school today Delroy?" his mother asks.

"Oh it was alright."

"Just alright? What did you do? Did Mrs.Chapman give you any homework? "

Mrs.Chapman... Mrs.Chapman... what do you care Mum! Mum? Who are you anyway? Where did you find me? You don't even know how to comb my hair, you scrub my skin and it dries and cracks. You know nothing! Please God, if you exist... please tell me... please let me find my Mum and Dad. They say she died but maybe she didn't... maybe that's what they want me to believe...

***

"Delroy never went near that cliff! And he never walked anywhere. He always took a taxi... we just don't understand it," she says looking at the brown-green-eyed Black man who is asking for Delroy. She folds her arms around her breasts and sinks into the settee, her watchful defensive eyes catch glimpses of his face.

"In fact we used to be so angry with him that he wouldn't walk even down to the bottom of the road. He had to take a taxi everywhere. We just don't know what happened! We just don't know. Delroy would not go anywhere near that place. It just wasn't a place he would go to. He wasn't unhappy or depressed or anything. Just his usual self. A bit reserved but a lovely and well-liked boy! Everyone knew him around here."

A twenty-year-old young man, adopted son of George and Mary Brown, living near Hastings, was found dead in the early hours of this morning. He was found at the bottom of the white cliffs near a well-known beauty spot by early walkers. It is thought that the young man was suffering from depression and recently had lost his job. He had withdrawn into himself, refusing to go out of his room or see his family and friends. It is thought that he committed suicide as a result of severe depression.

***

"I couldn't bring myself to write to Granny directly. I

wrote to Nemie, my love cousin, and told her to tell Granny. I couldn't tell her. I just couldn't..." he reaches for his lover's hand and whispers, "I just couldn't..."

"You couldn't tell her that Delroy had a shorter life than hers."

"No I couldn't. Maybe if I had got to him earlier," he shakes his head sadly, "if only I could have let him know that he was not on his own, that he belonged, that there were people who wanted to know him and cared for him... that he was not alone in the world." He looks at the dazzling river for a while in silence. "Maybe that would have made a difference," his voice tapers off. "If he only knew that he had a Granny in Jamaica who loved him and asked for him, wanted to see him... maybe that would have made all the difference. If I could have got to him sooner maybe he would have been alive today..."

London. October 1990

**FINDING
MARO**

She came to find you, says the note my lover slowly lifts up to my face. I touch the corner of the paper he holds onto. My eyes race across the first line. He is still holding on as I lift my other hand to hold it, preventing it from trembling in mid-air. He is watching me, expectantly. I feel the camera interfering with the space between his eye and my face. The white sheet of paper between us.

"Hold it! Hold it! I've got something to show you!" he had said excited, agitated when earlier I was pushing my bike through the door. "I'm so excited!" he had murmured and moved out of my way. I was too preoccupied with manoeuvring the bike through the narrow door in the semi-basement, careful not to scratch the paint on the door, forever disappearing flake by flake and watching out for the pedal ready to spring into action and wallop me on the thigh or the shin in the blink of an eye. He probably wants to show me the octopus he found in the market or even better, the giant prawns, crossed my mind, which lead him into an ecstatic dance of words describing, comparing, imagining these animals leading into a crescendo of styles of cooking and even more so the feast of the senses once morsels are in the mouth. I smiled at his childlike excitement.

He ushers me upstairs. "Wait, wait!" I look amused. He runs upstairs and comes back with the video camera on his shoulder. Now he is ready. He hands me the sheet of paper.

She came to find you after the borders opened, in April says the note. I am puzzled. I feel my eyebrows crushing into each other. Who? I look at the lines. *Even our mother got excited, and you know our mother doesn't get excited about much these days,* the printout continues. My eyebrows continue to push against each other. I realise I am reluctant to speed up, to reach the end. I look up at him and back at the paper. *Maro came to the mahalle. She came to the neighbourhood to find you. She went to the house and found my mother.* I realise I haven't quite registered what was on the page. I look at it and feel a desperation beginning to rise. I feel my breath escape. I look up at my lover's face covered with the lens of the camera. He momentarily takes his eye away and looks at me, his eyes moist. Waiting.

I reread the words. I realise I am no longer playing in my lover's game and tagging along. Suddenly it has all changed. Suddenly I am caught in a whirlwind. Thousands of images descend, smother me, flashing back from childhood to being a young woman, to being a woman. All those times in between. Attempting to fill in the missing, the gaps. The unreachable missed, unshared years and lives.

She asked about all of us. She remembered all our names, continues my sister's message on the sheet. I look up again and back. I realise I've frozen where I stood and yet I'd been to a thousand places, worlds, times and lives within those seconds. *She wants to see you. Here's her number.* I put the paper on my table, the late afternoon sun falls through the arched window, above the lime tree in the front of the house. I pick it up and read it again just to make sure and turn away and whisper in a voice I barely hear myself, "She is alive… she is alive." And then everything else fails me. All the anger, the sadness bottled up for years, just explode. All I can feel are tears bursting, escaping through my fingers pressed tightly down my eyes trying to control the escape. I cannot command, nothing is going to stop. Tears squeeze through my fingertips, through the gaps between my palms and fingers, down to my chin. My voice joins in. I can hear myself crying like a child, sobbing. And yet I don't want this to be recorded, not this side of me. No. This is too private. After a while I pick up the paper and look at it again. I can hardly read the lines through blurry eyes. Relief. Disbelief. She is alive. I have been looking for her for forty-five years.

***

I don't know how to do this. Should I ring her? How would it feel? What would my first words be? After forty-five years. We were ten and eleven. Now we were fifty-five and fifty-six. Women who are getting older, what do they say? We don't know these women each has become. We knew the little girls, inseparable friends in the neighbourhood. How would it feel to be ringing from London, a place she doesn't know? How does she imagine me, where does she imagine me? I didn't want to be the stranger, in a strange place, she would inevitably imagine me to be. I was desperate for the familiar. And yet the familiar was no longer. Intellectually, I knew that I wouldn't recognise her if I had passed her in the street. But there was a Maro who was still my best friend, no matter how many years had elapsed. It wasn't a romantic notion. It was a refusal, it was a rebellion against what we were forced to live thorough, against the dictates of those with other plans for themselves, which involved misery for us without our knowledge. They made us part of their history without our consent.

I had waited for so long. I waited. I didn't ring. The moment had to be right. The place had to be Cyprus. I couldn't ring from London. I hung the sheet of paper on my wall and looked at the words every time I went past. It was April. I would be in Cyprus in May.

***

I arrive into the early dawn of Cyprus. A breeze brings the scent of wild thyme and sage from the mountains. The early daybreak light is seeping through on the horizon. I take a deep breath. She is on my mind. I look at the mountains. For so many years reachable only with my eyes. This time I can walk there if I want to. This time I can cross the borders and the minefields and get there. I smile at the sensation of that. The sensation of my feet crunching the mountain soil, my body suspended amongst pine trees and *sistarga* of my childhood, the pastel-flowered Cistus bushes. And the smells I've missed. It feels good.

I escape to the remote part of the island in the north, to the Karpaz peninsula before I do anything else. Away from barbed wire, six flags representing… what? Nation statehoods of foreign lands? Nationhood of a state torn apart after three years? Nation statehood of invaders? State nationhood of a non-existent, non-recognised state? Nation statehoods of United Nations, powerless guardians of nation statehood? Nation statehoods of ex-colonial powers in new roles as global rulers?

I don't want the mental pollution. The reminders of divisions and loss. And yet I can't escape it. Indelibly scratched on everything I look at, everything I touch and derive pleasure from. The old yellow-stone houses, in the remote village I like, were built by Cypriotgreek villagers, some killed in wars, others are in exile yet others dead in exile. Their children and grandchildren only now beginning to see what was in the imagination of their grandparents. And it is no longer there. They try to reconstruct the ruins they stare at trying to see where grandma said the bed was, where her wooden bread-making trough was hanging, where the almond tree and the carob and olive trees were. Where the earthen wood oven was, where she baked *phlaunes* for Easter. *And where was her bedroom, where she gave birth to mother?* The lime has been washed away from between the yellow sandstones of the walls. The stones lie scattered in disarray amongst spring flowers of narcissi and pink, lilac and violet anemones. Most have gone to build distastefully enlarged village houses leering like false teeth out of new walls.

And the restaurant on the beach belonged to the Cypriot-greek man who ran to save his life and his three daughters from rape. I look through his eyes when I look out to sea, fingering my badly cooked fish. And I turn my gaze to the mountains covered in a haze. Did he say, *Ah, the rains are coming. There will be a storm by tonight.* Could he read the sky for what was coming any better than I did? It's difficult living with ghosts. Crushing into you each time you look at something in wonder. What do other Cypriots do when they see these ghosts?

I celebrate my birthday by the sea thinking of Maro. Next time we will be here together. I walk into the azure sea and enjoy the sensation of being alone on this sandy bay. Within half hour it turns windy and cool, unusual for the end of May. Usually, hot days and refreshing seas. I smile a lot thinking of meeting her. Yet I don't ring her. Intellectual gymnastics can't justify my actions. Nothing. I discover I don't even ask myself if she married, if she had children, what she does, where she works. I know nothing about her. I find I resist wanting to know about her. Am I trying to preserve the little girl of ten who was my best friend? Her, I know, this woman, I don't. I don't want to pollute the images of a past life together. I am struggling to hold onto them only too acutely aware that they will disappear once I meet her. I know I am running away. But I am carrying her with me.

I go back to Nicosia. The town where we both lived. I look at her house opposite ours and images of a neighbourhood peopled with characters no longer there come to life. We are running in and out of each other's houses, her mother is sticking heated glass goblets on her grandmother's back sliced with a razorblade to suck the illness out, my mother ministering injections to the poor who can't pay, Maro's father brings us roasted peanuts and brightly coloured wrapped sweets from the factory he works for, Laikon Kafekoption. Forever indelibly written on my mind as his factory as though he owned it. Over the years I have never managed to look at any product carrying the logo of the man with buttons running from the shoulder to the waist holding the tray of coffee cups without thinking of Maro and her father. Coffee cups in cafes and bars were the worst culprits leaving my companions' words suspended in mid-air while I touched the image. The coffee which suffered political humiliation and from a multiple-identity syndrome: was it Turkish coffee or maybe Greek or Cypriot coffee? Which was the least unlikely 'trigger' word, in the crazy world of conflict resolution industry experts?

I cross the border of the north without a trace of the old humiliations dished out by their police, to buy a telephone card in the south. Telephones and cards from the north are not allowed to transcend the border twenty meters away. I cannot ring Maro from a phone in the north. I discover people walk around with two mobile phones and two SIM cards to sabotage arbitrary bans imposed by the telephone companies from Turkey in charge of communications with the world in northern Cyprus.

I walk through the UN buffer zone in the shadow of the bullet-poked Ledra Palace Hotel, once the queen of hotels. Now

193

she houses UN soldiers only aware of her shabbiness and their precarious position as sitting ducks in a buffer-zone between two unstable sides until recently pointing guns at each other. It's sizzling hot. Human traffic moves both ways. As though they have always walked through this border, as though these policemen have never captured people and imprisoned them because they had dared to cross over 'illegally' through a border no legal entity recognised. Memory is so short and yet I am a long-memoried woman.

Metaxas Square. Lines of public telephones on either side of the square raised above the passage-way linking the children's playground created in the moat of the old Venetian walled city. My mother used to bring us here to play on the swings, merry-go-rounds and the helter-skelter. It used to be such a treat. That and the Iraklis ice cream. Now Philipino and Sri-Lankan women and men lie on the grass under the trees on their day off from being the servants, au pairs, cooks, cleaners, carers of the disabled relatives and night-club workers of the well-off Cypriotgreeks and twenty thousand or so Russians. I join them in the phone booths, ringing home and loved ones left behind. But I am home. Maro's phone rings. My mouth dries. I adjust the earpiece to ensure I hear her clearly over the cacophony of the traffic. It rings. I look through the glass at the old Cupressus trees, there since my childhood. I smile, with the thought that we know each other. I haven't planned what I will say to her. The phone rings. I turn around and face the road. I watch the blond dread-locked tall skinny man with a pale face sit astride his bicycle one foot on the pavement, to my left. Cars move along. The phone rings. I swallow to ease the dryness of my mouth. I relax my tight grip of the receiver. The phone rings. I turn towards the park again. Listening to the click which will mean she will respond. Tense. It rings. And I slowly realize there will not be a response. I let it ring for a while longer without emotion just to reassure myself that I had given her enough time and put the receiver down. Deflated. Covered in sweat. I stare at the phone for a few seconds. I had worked myself up to it and she wasn't there. As I walk along I wonder where she is in this divided town which belonged to both of us.

Next day I travel to Limnidi in the north near the western border with the south. Closed border, there are no crossings. I sit under an indigo sky in June. Star hopping, sipping sparkling wine, dream-talking with my lover, Mamu, in the silence of the night. Ringing from the depths, puzzling two people unused to interruptions by borrowed mobile phones. His eyes apologise, hands fumble to find the perpetrator of the shrill noise. "From Germany," he says. "A film-maker has been given your name by three different sources. He wants to talk to you…"

It will be in July. About a woman who has lived outside Cyprus for a long time, preferably in Britain. And is returning home. They have a Cypriotgreek man. He lives in Germany. They are looking for a Cypriotturkish woman. She should be active preferably in London. An artist perhaps? I was recommended by people living in Holland, Paris and Cyprus. What did I think? Could I help?

I look at the stars and then at my lover. "He rang before, I forgot to tell you," he mouths.

The filmmaker from Germany talks, I barely listen. Being in two places at once, Germany, Frankfurt which I know well and have memories of another life and the now, in Cyprus under the stars. *It's for Arte TV, it will be shown in Germany and France* comes the voice from the depths of the phone. I am not impressed. *The* channel for the Arts! My friends chime later back in London. *Maro* I say into the unimaginable depths of the phone while I know the movement is towards satellites amongst the stars I am looking at. Now, he has a story, before, he had a vague idea. He does not want to lose it, he is hooked. *She found me after forty-five years. I am going to meet her in the next few days...*

***

The camera crew arrived at my house in London, in July. An Englishman and a Brazilian together with the Turkish director from Germany. After a few shots in front of my laptop, facing the lime tree, I am declared a *natural* by the cameraman. I enter the repetitive minutia of the world of film and capturing images telling a story which is not the story. I pack some clothes, the book I want to give Maro. I wrote her story or rather our story which was published. I have been reading it at international festivals, events, gatherings. I choke every time I read it. I struggle to hold back tears, a lump in my throat, taking imperceptible seconds as long as centuries to find my voice, for the tear blurs in my eyes to disperse, for my hand curled up beating lightly against my breast to stop, for the swaying of my body to lull... In the stillness that follows I hear those who sniffle, wipe off tears, clear throats. She doesn't know that and neither do most who listen.

Two days later we are in Cyprus. I've landed in the north which means that I am not allowed to cross to the south with my British passport. The filming is gruelling in the heat of July. Normally I'm in my element in the heat. I am going down with flu carried over from London. I fight to keep on my feet and to film schedules. My head keeps ducking and diving into the haze of high body temperatures. I don't recognise my own voice anymore tearing past vocal cords on fire and the constant night coughs keep me awake until dawn. The director and film crew think it's an emotional reaction. An indication of their ignorance of who I am. But they are *nice* to their star.

After a few location shots in Nicosia we drive to Apostolos Andreas (St. Andrews), the monastery at the tip of the island. A lonely monastery, as they all are, in the most tranquil locations. I came to see the sunrise here in the year 2000, on top of the cliffs, to celebrate the new millennium, a new dawn for all Cypriots. While they film the Cypriotgreek man I've known for two days, I walk around the back of the monastery and find the candles. I know this place well. They are piled high under a low arch running across the building. Legs, heads, hands, arms, babies made of wax. Sexual organs in dark yellow wax. Candles of differing sizes and colours from white to almost brown. Thin as straw candles, to those a foot or more in diameter. Tiny ones of finger length, others nearly two meters high. I pick up a torso. Of a baby. The size, shape of the body, position of the legs slightly bent at the knees, resembling a chubby baby on her back. The warmth and give of the wax sends strange sensations of a living body through my fingertips. I hold her from the narrow shoulder and put her in the cradle of my arm. I imagine the woman who wanted her, to hold in her arms, who pleaded with Ayios Andreas to grant her the wish of a baby. She could have been Cypriotgreek just as well as Cypriotturkish. Ay Andreas doesn't make a distinction. Her decapitated head is amongst the other candles a foot away. I lean over and gently pick it up. I turn it around to look at her chubby face, the mouth beautifully crafted by the wax-artist and the eyes looking afar into oblivion. I place her head on the neck and look at her aware of the macabre, surrealist picture we have created. I can't help thinking this would make a surrealist art movie. But I don't tell the filmmakers interviewing the Cypriotgreek man from Germany. I put her back into her anonymity amongst the discarded dismembered wax body parts from the monastery. Later, I see the Cypriotgreek man walking around with the torso in his arms and the head in his hand. He took it back to Germany with him. It would make a good story. I couldn't take her away from where she was created, even though she was destined for the melting pot, as were all the others, to create new representations of the desires and wishes of other Cypriots asking Apostolos Andreas to intervene on their behalf and grant them their wishes.

***

I return to Nicosia after two days in the Karpaz having suffered a total collapse. Filming begins in front of our house looking towards Maro's. The neighbourhood has gathered to watch the filming. Smiles on their faces. *Yes, it's Leman Hanım's daughter. Yes, they are making a film about her, these Germans. She is well known, she did tell us. She lives in London. What does she do? I don't know but she is something big, that I am sure of.*

Today is the day. I am going to meet Maro. I can now allow myself a sense of excitement. I don't need to constrain myself. The crew ask me to ring her so they can film it. The international phone of the Germans doesn't work. As soon as the code of the south is dialled the telephone company from Turkey blocks the call. Everyone who is gathered to watch the filming is mobilised to find me a phone that gets through the barriers and borders less than a hundred feet away. The owners of international mobile telephones look at their phones in disbelief, frantically pressing buttons, refusing to accept that German technology has let them down. They think it incredulous that anyone can interfere with their right to ring anywhere in the world. Surely, 'they' cannot do that. I go through all the German mobile phones handed over to prove that 'they' do. *But it works on the other side when I ring this side and when I dial anywhere in the world*, come the disgruntled mutterings. The locals sagely nod their heads. One hands me a mobile and says this will work. It's a phone with a Cypriotgreek SIM card. I get through on the first dial. I smile at

199

the ingenuity of the car mechanic putting us university degree holders and technicians to shame.

It's nine in the morning. The day is getting hot. I talk to Maro who asks where I am. "In front of your house," I say, "looking at it." She understood I was referring to our childhood homes. "When are you coming?" she asks. "At eleven," I say. "I'll wait for you," she says and I swallow hard.

The crew want to film more locations. *Somewhere which has meaning for you and is not too crowded* they say. I suggest part of the old city, they don't want it, too tourist guide type. *The old public gardens by the general hospital where I was born,* they like. I spend two hours of repetitive actions walking behind the tall grey-bodied palm trees of my childhood and next to the pool built after my childhood with fountains programmed to shoot up into the sky from different places at different times. It takes the filmmakers half an hour to cotton on to the different permutations and combinations having got me to walk past various points, setting the angle of the camera and sound recordings only to change it and repeat as the water shoots into the sky from a different place. I keep thinking of my brother whenever I see these palm trees; he likes them. He calls them the English dates. Wanting to see Maro is becoming urgent. The time wasted trying to catch the cycle of the fountains is beginning to become really banal and exasperating. After four-five days of humouring the filmmakers, this is now real. My patience is beginning to wear thin, even thinner than my state of health. I want it over with. I want them to get on with it, get it right, stop wasting time.

The July heat is eating into the skin of their foreheads, shoulders, hands and cheeks despite the highest factor sunscreen. They are sweating, getting flustered and making more mistakes with the takes. I keep my cool, walking up and down the places I am asked to, looking in directions pointed. Good job the director is astute enough not to say anything about changing expressions.

Eleven o'clock has come and gone. My agitation is increasing. I promised her I'd be there. Could I do an interview sitting on a bench? Time passes as the camera is set, reset. Questions asked and repeated. The director senses my growing irritation, he tries to placate me with assurances that he has worked with the two women camera crew and they are the best. They will do a good job he assures me. I'm no longer concerned with quality of the job but the passing of time. My frustration begins to show in the interview. I feel tears of frustration and anger well up. I could just get up and go… no one can stop me, arguments circle around in my head. The thought calms me and I focus. Arguing with myself that this is not just a personal story, it's the story of so many Cypriots. It needs to be told. The story of two women torn apart by wars, just like so many others, finding each other against all odds. Others were not so lucky, some killed, some disappeared, some buried in exile. The story is bigger than me, bigger than my anger and frustration.

Is there another location we can film the director asks. I take a deep breath and take them to the inner city. I think they should film the old Venetian walled city, whether it is tourist-guide-like or not. We walk through narrow streets with dusty

201

deserted shops abandoned in the economic miracle. The walled city now inhabited by Philippinos, Sri-Lankans, poor Russians and other East Europeans who share the narrow streets and houses embroidered into histories. Ottoman Kiosks (small palaces) with courtyards nuzzle up to Venetian yellow stone arched houses. Both hemmed in by the houses of the poor built with bricks of mud and straw, sun dried and covered with a thin layer of plaster against the rains. Nineteen-fifties houses of the artisans with door-knockers shaped like a delicate hand with a ring or Art Deco geometric styles alongside doors covered in metal studs with the typical Ottoman rings used both as knockers and handles. The Art Deco style nineteen-fifties blocks of flats with balconies all along the blocks support washing on lines flapping in the famous Nicosia evening breeze despite the heat. An odd date palm stretches into the sky heavily laden with bunches of green-yellow dates waiting to ripen into dark orange with the first rains. Dates and white myrtle berries, the fruits of late autumn.

I ask them to film a wall of graffiti as I walk past. I want them to record that the anarchist squatters are claiming the streets, wresting it from the right-wing fascists opposed to any agreement with the Cypriotturkish and the presence of these 'foreigners'. The contested spaces battle it out on the walls, crossing out each other's slogans and logos. The familiar Ⓐ I've seen all over the world, and the blue cross in a square I am newly becoming familiar with.

They film as I walk past the famous Faneromeni School

behind the old church; names from my youth. They've erected a woman's statue in the front and hung a stone wreath of laurels around her neck. The style makes me wonder if she was an EOKA luminary. I sit at one of the outdoor tables of the little restaurant at the end of the square, these days frequented by artists and professionals and not workers. The tables are lined up in an alleyway between the restaurant shop-front and the little mosque which used to be a church which became a *hamam*. The Greek owner of the restaurant has the key if you want to visit. He is an old Egyptian, the land of Cavafis. He is in his seventies. He frantically plants in pots, pans, barrels, car tyres, white jasmine, red pink flowering cacti, carnations, daisies, roses, busy lizzies. He tends them lovingly. He has a washing line with red, pink, yellow and blue plastic bags above the flowers, hooked into the yellow stone of the mosque. A huge old TV sits on the ground with enormous enamel washing bowls on top filled with pink busy lizzies in blossom.

They order me a Turkish coffee with water as they film. I laugh and tell them I don't drink Turkish coffee. *Pretend* they say. The coffee stays on the table as my exasperation begins to match theirs. Just as I feel I am hitting the limits, I see my loved friend from London who settled in Cyprus some years back and I escape. He is sitting two tables down. I jump around his neck, a lifebuoy. I need his reality, hug and kisses. He laughs pointing at the film crew rushing over to film us and turns his back on them. His presence reminds me of who I am which this film is unable to capture.

It's three o'clock. I insist that they stop whatever they are doing as I want to see Maro. They hand over one of the German mobiles, which works in the south. "Where are you?" she says, deep hurt in her voice. I wince. I tell her I am at Faneromeni being filmed at a café. "I'll come and get you," she says impatiently sensing the frustration in my voice. "They want me to come and find you," I say exasperated. Silence. "It will be hard to describe it," she says confused. "I'll find you Maro! Just tell me how to get to you." Suddenly I feel I've taken control. I frantically scribble directions in my diary as she talks, checking and double checking instructions, names, landmarks. She tells me it normally takes twenty minutes if I knew the way. I tell her to wait for me; I'll be there in thirty. "I've been waiting for you all my life," she says. My heart sinks. She had been waiting for five hours, not knowing where I was, unable to leave the house.

They gather their equipment hastily as I head to the parked jeep at the end of the square. We pile in. I am in the front with instructions on my lap. I guide the driver through the walled city towards Metaxas Square. He keeps asking me if I know where I am. I am getting annoyed. "This is my city," I say, "I was born and grew up here." I am amused by his insecurity, slightly annoyed by his assumption that I could not possibly find my way through this complex maze of streets, *especially on the "Greek" side* is lurking just under the surface of his questioning. Have you been here before he asks. I look at him and say nothing. The camera crew and the director joke in German, laughing, teasing each other, flirting. Their voices and jolliness grate as I try to focus on the instructions. He drives too fast at one stage. I can't keep up with trying to identify landmarks and follow the instructions. I ask him to turn around. He complains and tells me to ring to get further instructions. I insist that he slows down, follows my instructions and turn around. He suddenly realises I have taken control. He slows down, we find the turning. I am distracted by the raucous jumble in the backseat and annoyed that they are not filming the journey. The director had insisted that he wanted to give the sensation of looking for Maro. After all this was the reason for all the delays. We find the street. The driver looks at me expectantly and tries a joke. I ignore him. I dismiss him for thinking he can make a joke about this moment in my life. He drives slowly looking for the house number. I see it on the right and point it out. He says he will drive on and double back and tries to prepare me that I will need to wait for the camera crew to get ready. He has obviously sensed my impatience and exasperation with them and that I could bolt at any time. We park a little way down from Maro's gate. A warm sensation wraps me up and an inner smile spreads. I am here and she doesn't know...

They attach the various bits of equipment and microphone on my clothes. I wait for them to get ready and for the instruction to walk. They want to capture my walking into the house. The sun is beginning to descend. Shadows are longer. I stay by the car, waiting for the signal, holding onto the bag with Maro's book inside. I've been carrying it around all day. Ten minutes have gone by. I still wait. I calm myself reminding myself that it is nearly over. My back is turned to the filmmakers. I don't

want to see their chaos. This is now my world not what they've
been creating over the last week. Back to my reality. I hear their
voices, flapping around, muffled anxiety, noise of equipment. I
resolutely keep my back turned. I look at the gardens. Frangipani
flowers in bloom in the opposite garden. Jasmine hangs over the
wall next to me. Last night's blossoms an intricate lace on the
floor. The houses are silent. Not a soul on the street. I look along
to see if I can guess which is Maro's gate from this angle. I can't.
German voices continue giving instructions to each other, footsteps rushing back and forth. A frustrated cry. I wait. An inner
calm has descended on me. I am determined they will not shape
this moment for me. It's mine. How many more minutes passed?
I no longer know, as though I have passed into a timeless zone.
I wait. The voices and rushing subsides. *Ready*, comes the voice.
I turn and ask, "Ready?" They nod. I turn back, look at the floor
and take a step. And with each step the calm seeps out of me, re-
placed with a strange excitement tinged with anxiety. The uncertainty of letting these strangers step into my world, filming this
moment. This very private moment, the one I wanted so much to
share only with Maro, suddenly is going to belong to everyone.
This moment, only hers and mine, reached from different directions, life pathways, travelled over the last forty-five years. Part of
me regrets allowing them the privilege of sharing that moment.
I can hear them walking behind me, another commotion. My
strides continue. "Stop!" comes the desperate cry from behind.
It is the camerawoman. My eyes blink. Nothing else responds to
the call. My footsteps don't falter. I continue. "Stop! Stop!" the

cry even more desperate. I continue without looking back. Then the voice of the director. Louder. Making sure I hear his call. I continue. I raise my hand above my head and make an *over and out* sign with two fingers, a line into the air. No force on earth can stop me. My feet continue. After a momentary confusion I hear footsteps running after me. I continue. I come up to her garden wall. I check the number of the house. A simple gate. Jasmine hanging down above it. I slowly turn the handle and push the gate. Jasmine tickles my face. I find myself smiling as I take in the garden and the veranda. I am now in her world. No one else exists. I walk up to the veranda as though I've done it countless times before. And suddenly I realize I don't know what Maro looks like. Will I recognise her when she opens the door? Will it be her? What if it's someone else? I reach the closed front door. I put my hand on the wall and lean on it for a second. I look sideways towards the gate to see if the film crew have caught up with me. In my sense of euphoria I am forgiving towards them. Intellectually, I know that this story needs an end. The whole purpose of the film is this moment. I want to give them a chance to capture it despite my misgivings of their intrusion into my private moment.

I ring the bell. A few moments later a woman opens the door. She is wearing a white sleeveless blouse. I look at her eyes and then at her lips. Such huge sadness in those eyes, such reproach. Then the light enters them, the lips smile shyly. We fall into each other's embrace. All I can feel is her softness and the tightness of her embrace. Tears start to run. I feel her belly tremble against mine, mine responds. My eyes are closed. The moment is ours. We tighten our embrace, locked, eyes still closed. For how long? I don't know. Only the silent tears and an odd sob escapes. At one stage we pull back, only far enough to look into each other's tear-stained faces. Smile at the implausibility, yet the reality of it all and lock into a tighter hug. I catch her smile. The smile of my ten-year-old friend. Yes, that's her. The eyes, that look of gentleness and the light. They are not as green and honey coloured as I remember them but still look at me with wonder and love. How long did we stay wrapped up in each other's arms, crying, sobbing, stopping and starting again? I have no idea.

We slowly unwrap each other. I open my eyes. I gently disentangle myself as though waking up from a dream. Our hands hold on. They are not letting go. I look around and notice the camera crew are in the house having manoeuvred themselves around us. I hadn't felt them. She holds my hand as I lean over to get my bag. She leads me into the house. There is a young man, looking at us in confusion, stunned almost from the depths of the room. We still hold on tightly to each other as we walk to the settee. We are holding hands not as fifty-five-year-olds but as ten-year-old little girls. We sit on the settee not letting go of each other's hand. Then we both reach out and hold each other across the other hand, across our laps. We sit there tightly squeezed against each other, holding each other tightly by both hands across our laps. There is a silent determination not to let go. We talk gently. About what? No idea. I am aware of the tightly held hands. Sweating. Rea, her older sister, walks in, sits down and looks at us sitting so close as though our bodies are stuck together. I learn later that she now lives in Greece. I am aware of Maro's son looking at us from across the room trying to fathom out what is happening, the intensity of what he had just witnessed. Addressing him with a trembling voice she says, "Here Nico. This is Aydın. You see, she does exist." He looks at us with such compassion and helplessness rarely seen on the face of a young person in his twenties.

I remember the book and I untangle myself to get to my bag. I tell her I had written a story about her and that I had read it at festivals and events and that so many people knew about her in London. She smiles. I open the page of that short story with such a long history. And although it is called Dedication, everyone calls it Maro's story. She snuggles up and we begin to read it together silently still holding hands tightly. At one stage she begins to tremble and cry. I know they are the same lines I can't read beyond without choking and trying to control tears. We wipe our tears with our shoulders so as not to let go. She looks up and whispers, "I knew you loved me just as I loved you over all these years." She wipes the tears and calls her son over to read it with us.

"... *Maro! How I had loved you! How I had missed you! One day you were my friend. You were there. Then you were not. The rules had changed. You disappeared one night. I woke up and the night had taken you away. Not even a good-bye! Not a hug! No tears! The uncried tears of losing you. The unshed pain of thirty years overwhelms me.*

The morning came without you. As though you had never existed. But you are there. In my photographs. On my eleventh birthday. May 29. By July you had gone, you had become part of history.

Where did the night take you? Where? Did you live through the wars? Did you survive? Are you forty today just like me? Where are you Maro? My other self. The child inside me escapes from the mask of the grown up and howls..."*

London. June 2004

*from *The Dedication (1987)*

THE MIDWIFE

She hands me eggs over the garden wall. They keep coming. Her large soft work-weary hands and homemade sausage thick fingers effortlessly hold and cushion the eggs as in a cradle. Mine, small and bony, have difficulties in embracing them. Seven eggs. I can barely hold them. Juggling not to drop them into the flowerpots on the wall. My arms stretched meeting hers on the other side of the wall trying not to touch the cacti in the flowerpots below. Mamu, my lover, comes to help me as they precariously nestle in the crevice I have created with my cupped hands against my belly, just below my breasts. I couldn't resist her offer when she had asked, "Do you like eggs?" I was holding two, one in each palm, when she had come up to the wall earlier and asked me. We had boiled them for breakfast and forgot to eat them. I hid them quickly behind my back before I even realised what I was doing. Suddenly, I felt caught out, like a child. How could I be eating substandard, shop-bought eggs? I had turned around and rushed into the low-ceilinged kitchen to put them in a saucer while she went to bring me her offerings. One of the eggs still had a strand of straw and a fluff of feather stuck on the light-rust shell. We are due to leave tomorrow.

***

They came to get her in the middle of the night. There was a loud knock on the door. She froze. She was so scared. She waited. After a while there was another knock, louder, she heard a voice shout, " Κυρία Γιαννούλλα είμαι εγώ."

But she didn't recognise the voice although the caller had addressed her by name. She blinked pulling the bedclothes closer to her chin desperately trying to pierce the darkness, as though it would yield the identity of the caller. In those days, people just disappeared. They would come and get people in the middle of the night and no one would find them again. It was the late nineteen-sixties. They had heard in the village that Cypriotturkish families had been found dead. Buried, some while still alive, they said. In one of the villages on the other side of the island, in the Famagusta district, to the east. Mothers, children and elderly people. Paphos was in the west of the island. But news travelled fast. They knew there would be reprisals. Cypriotgreeks would be killed for revenge. For sure. You couldn't trust even people you knew. Unseen faces would threaten them or their wives and children. They would tell them to get the victim out of his house on some pretext and on a deserted street, road or in a field outside the village a body would be found by a child or someone going to work in the early hours of the morning. There was terror everywhere and fear of terror. As her mind raced from one

214

possibility to the next she wondered how anyone could do that. How could a human being do that to another? What monsters! And all in the name of love for the motherland. "Animals!" she says almost spitting it out.

"Είμαι εγώ, ο Χασάνης." She hears the desperate voice coming from the street, telling her his name; she senses he is trying to reassure her. She notices he has added –is to Hasan to accommodate Greek grammar, a common device for bilingual people switching between languages. The night was cold. The wind blowing from the sea. Seeping through the cracks of the door with a big black metal bolt drawn across it. Blue paint flaking off in sections. A February night when all the mountains around Lysos were covered in snow. No moon. Pitch dark. The roads between the villages blocked or iced over. She realised she was trembling not because of the cold but from fear. "Ποιός Χασάνης?" she manages to ask, trying to steady her shaking voice and body.

The man begins to tell her about his wife. She is pregnant. "She is in labour Kyria Yiannoulla. She needs you. Please. I am afraid something will go wrong. Please come." He apologises and pleads as best he can, not so much in words but with the tone of his voice allowed within the rules of social relations, as a man. A man calling outside the door of a woman in the middle of the night. She recognises his voice. He lives in Melandra. The Turkish village four or five miles further into the mountains.

She jumps out of bed. Puts on the light. Electricity had just come to the village. The surrounding Cypriotturkish vil-

215

lages were still waiting, she knew. There was a deliberate policy of those in authority not to connect those villages to the national grid. They were punishing whole villages and innocent people for the actions of their self-selected political leaders. She grabs her clothes from the chair next to her bed and the thickest socks and moves towards the fireplace seeking the remains of warmth from the previous night's dying embers while she dresses quickly. She goes into the kitchen and grabs her bag, draws the bolt and she is out of the door.

She finds Hasan sheltering from the cold wind, leaning on the wall by the door, trying to warm up his fingers with his breath. He smiles anxiously, relieved to see her. But he is worried about the journey back. He helps her climb on his tractor. She finds a place to perch on the mudguard over the huge tyre as tall as her. She feels the coldness of the metal penetrate the folds of her skirts, reaching her buttocks. He jumps onto the single seat. He looks shyly to make sure she is all right but doesn't speak. She indicates with a slight blink of the eyes that she is fine. They can go. The engine roars. She ties her headscarf tighter covering her ears and pulls it up to cover her mouth. She places her bag on her lap and holds it tightly, one hand holding the mudguard. They travel in silence. He is humbled by her courage and the level of trust signified by her presence.

***

"The roads were treacherous," she says. She had begun

to tell me birthing stories. "He couldn't go fast. We could end up skidding off the road and roll down to the bottom of the ravine. It was so slow. And dark. And I was thinking of that poor young woman in labour all on her own in that house… We got there about four in the morning. It must've been three when he'd come to get me. I was with her for hours. There was no electricity in the village; we had to work in the light of a paraffin lamp. It was a difficult birth. Poor woman. She was exhausted. After I 'birthed' her, I went and showed him his daughter. His eyes were full of tears. And he thanked me and thanked me. He was really in love with his wife. He was worried sick about her. I comforted him and assured him she was all right and not to worry. After I made the new mum comfortable I went out to see the father. He was nowhere to be seen. He'd disappeared! I thought it was very strange. It is an old custom around here for the father to treat the midwife and everyone in the village and even beyond, offer them a drink or something to celebrate the birth. I joked with the wife saying, 'I see, Hasanis disappeared to avoid treating us…' She was too tired, she just smiled. Someone else took me back to Lysos later that morning."

She went regularly to tend to the *loğusa*, the new mother. She noticed the new father was still not around. When she asked the villagers no one would say. She was annoyed that he wasn't around to help the new mother who was struggling on her own although the village women had gathered around her, some washing the cloth nappies of the baby and others the blood-soaked towels between her legs. It was her first child after all.

Typical of men she kept saying. They think it's easy, have their pleasure, you get pregnant, you have all the pain of giving birth and they can't even stick around to share the work afterwards. He should have been there!

On the twelfth day of the birth, she was in the village again making sure the new mum knew how to suckle the child, look after her breasts and eat properly. She heard a commotion and the roar of a tractor. She went out of the mud-brick house and saw the father coming along the road singing at the top of his voice, a bottle in his hand, swinging around on top of his tractor. His clothes were dirty and he was unshaven. She was relieved. She waited for him to come to the door of the house,

"So here you are Hasani! At last… you have decided to grace us with your presence… my, my, my… we are privileged!" Then her voice scolds him, "You come and get me out of my bed in the middle of the night. I ride along on that God-forsaken tractor of yours, freezing to death, fearing for my life just in case we roll over into some ravine, I come and help your wife give birth to your first child, we struggle for hours… and what do you do? You disappear! Puff, into thin air! You didn't have to go to such lengths to avoid giving me a treat, you know…"

He hears the playful sarcasm in her voice but ignores it. He comes up to her and with a merry gesture takes her hand, "I kiss your hands Kyria Yiannoulla. Health to these hands that delivered my first-born. And don't worry, your wish is my command… whatever your heart desires, it's yours."

"Where have you been? Your wife needed you…" she says gently.

"In prison," he replies.

She thinks he is joking. He realises she doesn't believe him. "They put me in prison," he repeats, looking her straight in the face.

"What have you done?" she asks, worried.

"They put me in prison for calling you to help my wife give birth to my child. The pimps!" angrily, swinging the bottle, "*I pezevengi!*" he shouts in Greek towards the village crowd that had gathered, daring them to hear and report it if they so wished that he was swearing at those 'above', calling them pimps. Then he turns and sees her look of astonishment, "They put me in prison for twelve days because I refused to bring a Turkish midwife to my wife. They ordered me to do that. That I went and got you. You, a Greek midwife! That I was a traitor to the 'national cause' because I refused to obey their orders... and their campaign of 'From Turk to Turk'. I shit on their campaign!" he hisses. Then he smiles and turns to shout for everyone to hear, "And you know what? When my wife gets pregnant again and when she needs a midwife again, I will come and get you again! They want to put me in prison? Let them! *Pezevenkler!*" He spits out the last word in Turkish.

She laughs as she tells me the story. "And you know what? He was part of the TMT, the underground Turkish organisation terrorising the Cypriotturkish communities and ruled by Denktaş under the command of officers from Turkey. They'd made them all join; the teachers, policemen, mukhtars, village elders... all of them!" The TMT, a murky, invisible, yet known by everyone, organisation of my childhood. Later on in my adult life I would discover it was responsible for putting the fear of Denktaş into Cypriotturkish people, manipulating and controlling all aspects of their lives. They came to fear Denktaş more than the 'enemy', the Cypriotgreeks, from whom he was supposed to protect them. The organisation was responsible for the deaths of lawyers, trade unionists, eliminating anyone who could challenge his position as self-appointed leader, spreading fear and chaos by bombing mosques, beating up those who worked with the Cypriotgreeks or shopped from their shops. And with their 'From Turk to Turk' campaign forcing people to buy from Cypriotturkish shops and merchants who had bought the very same goods from Cypriotgreek shops and merchants, adding twenty-five or fifty percent on the retail price, giving them a hefty profit on the backs of the Cypriotturkish communities. And all of this and more, in the name of patriotism, love for the motherland and for the 'national cause'.

She is telling me stories of being a midwife, here on the mountains of Paphos, in Lysos. The stories of those she had birthed, travelling all around the mountain villages. I have only just met her. Two days ago. After the balancing act with the eggs we talk about political generalities, the monstrosity of the situation, the division of the island, the suffering of all Cypriots, the manipulation by the military and the politicians of settlers from Turkey and the new communities, in the north and south. She is Andreas' *mammou*; my friend in London for thirty years. She helped him into the world. He has lent me his house; she lives next door.

She tells me about the baby who had an additional digit on his thumb; he was Cypriotturkish. Over the years she had spent long hours with his mother reassuring her that he would be all right, that the defect was not such a shameful thing and no, it wasn't God punishing her and no, she wasn't paying for her sins. That he was a beautiful child. "He came last summer after the borders opened in April and found me," she says. "He brought his mother, and his three children to introduce them to me, to his *mammou*. His *ebe*," she uses the Turkish word, "He was crying," she says with tears in her eyes. She talked about those who had come after thirty years to see their villages, to Melandra, Istingo, Meladia, Zaharga and other surrounding villages now abandoned and derelict. Cypriotturkish people used to live all around these villages. Now only goats and sheep roam. Cypriotgreek shepherds use some of the empty houses as sheep and goat pens. "They cried," she says, "thinking of the old days, their lives, remembering lost lives, friends, villages, houses, lands… all gone… and the disappointment for what came after the invasion in 1974. Nothing but hardship instead of the promised riches and good life. They were refugees from the south to the north. Some got nothing. And many had to leave yet again. This time for foreign lands… to London, Canada, Australia." She is saddened by the images and ghosts hidden in her head of people fleeing their homes, the destruction, the dead.

She tells me she is a Maronite from the village of Kormagitis, now on the 'other' side. I have been there in previous years, in my stubborn quest to find, experience, acknowledge

221

to imprint in my memory the fact that Cyprus was always multicultural with our Maronite, Latin, Armenian communities alongside Cypriotturkish and Cypriotgreek. We were used to sharing our religions, places of worship, festivities and festivals. And used to speaking a number of languages delighting in the play on words special to multilingual communities. We were not just Turkish or just Greek. After 1974, she tells me she wanted to go across the border to visit her family in the north. She heard by word of mouth from people who had managed to come to the south through illegal routes that they were all right. But she wanted to see with her own eyes. She knew her family would say they were well so as not to worry her. Letters could not be carried otherwise you would be charged with being a spy and there were no postal or telephone connections. After a while the Turkish military gave her permission to visit her family. She had to be registered with the police in the north in order to cross. Even if they had given her permission there were no guarantees that she would have been able to cross; they could withdraw the permission without warning or reason, at any time, sometimes an hour before the actual time of crossing. As she walked nervously towards the checkpoint at Ledra Palace in Nicosia, the policeman on duty walked towards her as she emerged from the militarised deserted dead-zone. She stopped. He looked straight into her face and slowly a smile spread across his face. Before she knew it, he was hugging and kissing her. He had recognised her. She had brought his sister into the world. He was overjoyed. "He forgot he was a policeman. He was supposed to give people a hard time, check their papers, make them wait," she says. Maybe it was his individual resistance, deliberately doing what would have been regarded as an act of betrayal to the 'national cause' kissing the 'Greek' enemy. He told her that even if she wasn't registered in the computer, even if she was refused entry into the north, he himself would still take her to her village. When she joked that he would get them both killed, he told her that no one would dare touch even a hair on her head as long as he was alive. Her eyes were smiling full of love and lingering tears as she was telling me the stories.

"I used to work in Athalassa," she continued, "and when they closed it down I went to the General Hospital in Nicosia because I was a midwife." Suddenly my heart jumped, my eyebrows knitted. Had I heard right? "Athalassa?" I asked, searching her face. She said yes. I told her my mother worked in Athalassa in the nineteen-fifties. She stopped and looked at me in disbelief. Confusion in her eyes. Up to then we were two strangers. I was a woman from London. A Cypriotturkish woman. A very old friend of Andreas, a Cypriotgreek. I was his guest, staying in his village house. She was being friendly, polite to his friend. And I was leaving the following day. "My mother is Leman," I said hesitantly watching her with curiosity and a tremble in my heart. Something had happened. I didn't even finish my words. "Ωχ Θεέ μου! Are you Leman's daughter?" she cried out in disbelief. Almost like a painful moan. Suddenly she was confused. Emotions rushed her all at once. For a few seconds she was lost. Agitated. Her eyes filled with tears, her voice trembled. She looked

223

away towards the mountains and the sea, her eyes probably seeing as far away into her past life forty-three years ago just as far as the horizon. She caressed her arm, "My God! My hairs are standing on end. I've got goose-pimples," she said her voice trembling. Tears rushed to my eyes, through the blur I became her, seeing her/me as a young nurse, my mother as a young nurse, all working at the Athalassa Sanatorium, full of life, full of love for life amongst the dying TB patients. And I remembered the fuss nurses used to make of us when we used to visit the hospital. Their presents, laughter, jokes, the joie-de-vivre, the camaraderie amongst them. She tells me their names. I had asked my mother before but she had forgotten most; she only remembered Panayiota from Limassol. My mother, she has developed this habit of forgetting. Now Yiannoulla Skoullou, the midwife, in this mountain village, was filling the gaps in my memory and history. They were all single apart from my mother, a widow and Xenoulla who had children. I ask if Xenoulla had a boy and a girl. She says yes and tells me where they used to live. There is a photograph in the family album, of my mother and the woman with the two children, me and my brother. I remember the son's name: Gogo. "Then there was Colombo," she says, the older man who used to dig into everyone's secrets, "He knew all the secrets," she says with a bittersweet smile of remembrance. Andreas and Ahmet the two male nurses and Nitsa and Nikki the other nurses. She tells me Panayiota who I remember very clearly died in Limassol of cancer about thirty years ago.

Once she got over her initial shock and located me in her

past, that we had shared spaces and a life together, she wanted to come closer. Until then she was in her garden full of flowers and I, in Andreas' concreted courtyard. The wall lined with cactus pots was in between. The large leaves from the mulberry tree turning golden brown kept falling around us. She rushed around the garden walls and I rushed to open the blue courtyard gate for her. She entered and almost fell on me; she hugged me tightly and cried. She held me in her embrace, Leman's daughter, she whispered. I kissed her on both cheeks and held her, breathing in her unfamiliar but comforting scents. Yiannoulla talked about her days as a young nurse, what a happy family they were at Athalassa, her room was next to my mother's. After a while she couldn't sit still, she wanted to get back to her house. She wanted to show us photographs, other things. She wanted us to follow her. She showed us her photos on the walls and then stood still in the middle of her sitting room as though listening to some faraway voice. She began to hum shyly and her hand moved as though conducting an orchestra. "*Koklamaya doyamam... Benim güzel manolyam...* (I can't have enough of breathing in your scent... My beautiful magnolia...)" She suddenly remembered the words, after forty-three years, and began to hum the melody and then sang. We sang with her. She said my mother loved that song and sang it all the time. She had taught her the words. Listening to her suddenly brought back memories of my mother singing with a beautiful full voice. She doesn't sing anymore.

I suggested we ring my mother. I managed to get through after the third try, dialling an international code just to reach a number in the same country but on the 'other' side. Where was I, she wanted to know? Why had I disappeared without telling her? She was worried, and why was I so insensitive to her worries? The previous week I had run a photographic project with my team from London for the children of Ayia Driada village, in the Karpaz peninsula; we were harassed by the military and the secret service police. It became front-page news. The authorities wanted it shut down because Cypriotgreek and settler children, whose parents had settled from the Black Sea area of Turkey, took part in the joint project. It was declared a state security issue needing special permission from the Ministry of Foreign Affairs at such a critical time, a few months before the general elections! And in any case, the incognito, CIA self-styled 'colonel' who was unused to a challenge to his authority, especially from a woman, was determined that we were not going to run such a popular project in his backyard; an affront to his authority.

After listening to her torrent of worries, I told my mother I was in Lysos and that someone wanted to talk to her. Yiannoulla took the receiver with shaking hands and with the gentlest of voices called her name. My mother didn't remember her. It was so heart-breaking seeing Yiannoulla's face, her disappointment, when she was trying to help my mother remember her. I felt saddened because in Yiannoulla's memory it was so clear, so fresh, so alive, so moving; her eyes brimmed with tears and she laughed with tears as she spoke of those days and of my mother. Slowly she got my mother to remember something but I couldn't bear her disappointment, her sad face. I told her my mother sometimes forgets the old days. Maybe it is intentional.

Yiannoulla said she would dig out the Athalassa photographs. They must be somewhere, she said, "They might be at the village. I must find them." I caught a glimpse of her in my child's eye as I was looking at her photographs on the walls. I remembered her as pretty tall, with long, long dark hair in a single plait. A thick plait dangling against her white uniform on her back, down to her waist, snaking around with her every move. We photographed the photographs of her youth hanging on the walls. One taken at age twenty, the other at twenty-four, just around the age I knew her. I remember the twenty-four-year-old face but thinner. She tells me she used to come to our house on the council estate in Omorphita, Nicosia. She used to feel so sorry for my mother left on her own after my father's death, with three children, barely aged three, one-and-a-half and five days old. Trying to look after them with the little money she used to earn as a nurse and no one to help her. "You were two girls and one boy, weren't you?" she affirms, "And she, all on her own, trying to look after you at such a young age..."

Later, we show her my mother's photograph when Maro, my childhood friend I had lost for forty-five years because of the conflicts in the late nineteen-fifties, came to find me after the gates had opened in April 2003. She looked at the woman in front of our house, "Of course, I wouldn't have been able to recognise her," she said with a crumpled voice. I didn't want to show her the photograph until after they had spoken on the phone. I didn't want the magic that had taken her to Nicosia, Athalassa, to her youth, to the youthful nurses full of life, laughter, jokes, tight loving group, where they had shared all their pain and joys, to be spoilt. I wanted her to speak to the Leman of her memories, because she had become Yiannoulla of the late nineteen-fifties and early nineteen-sixties. After the phone call, I felt I had added yet another disappointment by showing her my mother's photograph. But I reasoned it was OK as I was also responsible for her experiencing the euphoria of finding Leman after forty-three years, who used to be her very close friend, who she talked about with tenderness and tears in her eyes. The stranger who came to stay in Andreas' house, who turned out to be Leman's daughter, led her through that journey. I told her I was very lucky because I had met a very nice Kyria Yiannoulla and now had discovered she was my Aunty Yiannoulla of lost years. She smiled.

It is such a crazy story. I come to a village I've never been to before and end up next door to a woman separated by a wall with flowerpots of cacti who offers me fresh eggs in the morning who turns out to be one of my mother's most intimate friends after my father died when she had no one to turn to. The Athalassa friends were the only people who took her into their hearts and cared for her trying to make life a little more bearable for her. And they were all Cypriotgreek. Yiannoulla told me Leman was the only Cypriotturkish woman working as a nurse. My mother was brave.

I want to look through my mother's Athalassa photographs to see if I can find Yiannoulla and send her copies. It is strange to think that I am now nearly twice the age my mother and Yiannoulla were, when they were nurses and friends at Athalassa. It saddens me that they have missed the years in between. They have missed the years of getting old alongside each other just like I have missed the years of growing up with Maro, my childhood friend. And all because we were Cypriotturkish and they were Cypriotgreek or Cypriotmaronite or Cypriotarmenian or...

Lysos-London. November-December 2003

**CONCILIATION IS
ON THE HORIZON**

"I wake up. It's morning... I am lying on a single bed. It's not mine. A man's body is lying next to mine. He is motionless. He could be lifeless. The bed is in the corner. There is a brown patterned blanket on it. I put one foot on the floor. Only my toes touch. I retch. And I vomit. I vomit!"

She stops a while her head in the vomiting position, her dark brown hair hanging on either side of her face, her hands suspended in mid-animation. "And, this thing fills my mouth and pushes its way out... and the spout and the bulbous section of a Coca-Cola bottle fall out. Not all of it, just the top bit. Amongst all this vomit.

"Then I retch again...

"The bottom bit comes out in three pieces. Three broken bits with sharp edges. I inspect them. I pick them up one by one, looking closely..." she mimes picking up the broken pieces oblivious to reality. " ...I look at the sharp edges thinking how could they be in my stomach? It's illogical. They would cut up my stomach. Blood. Lacerated pieces of flesh. The stomach contents would spill all over my abdominal cavity. All my intestines would be covered in blood and half-digested food. Then I notice that the sharp edges are blunt. The brain has re-adjusted reality to accommodate logic. It controls the dream and brings it back into the realm of what is possible. The Coca-Cola writing is almost rubbed out and the patterns are not so distinct. Ah yes, I think to myself... like the sea. The sharp edges are worn away by the sea. My stomach gastric juices have done the same..."

He is smoking silently. His head to one side he holds the smoke in his lungs. Index finger touching his lower lip. His roaring laughter has subsided, he is watching her intently.

She looks up at him, "I don't even drink Coca-Cola. How does the bottle get into my stomach without me being aware of it and why do I vomit it?"

"What's your interpretation of it? Don't you like the poem? You are vomiting my poem aren't you? You don't like it!" he says anxiously.

"I do like it! I do..." She says thoughtfully. She does not stress the point. She did like it. It was still in draft form but on the way to becoming one of his best in recent times. Lines from Coca-Cola adverts danced in the poem. That was what he was referring to.

"Subconsciously you don't!" he insists, a little irritated because he cares about what she thinks of his poems.

"On the contrary my conscience is very clear and I think my subconscious! I do like the poem! That's why it's a bit puzzling!"

"But you couldn't have, if you have dreamt about vomiting it!"

232

"Strange!" she says almost to herself. She does not feel the need to over-react or to attempt to convince him.

Are you then vomiting me? which is what you know and won't admit and I won't ask. His eyes remain for a while fixing her with their intense gaze. She looks directly into his. He can't say it. He does not want to accept the inevitability of his own conclusion. *She will never leave me. She loves me passionately, desperately, would do anything for me. I could so easily dominate, control her, if I wanted to. She loves me wants me to love her. I can't. I want her just to be a friend.*

There was jubilation in the Chilean capital yesterday as thousands of people thronged the main streets to celebrate the defeat of President Pinochet in Wednesday's referendum, in which he had been seeking a further eight years in power.
Confetti and tear gas greet victory...

"I am certain of what I will be doing in a year's time from now. Not exactly, but more or less. Because I plan it that way," he says with the smile of wisdom.

"I know… you keep telling me all about these people and your friendships but somehow you avoid talking about me… where do you see me?"

"I want us to be friends. Two-three years from now, I see you as my friend. I want us to stay friends." It was as a-matter-of-fact as buying a painting which was guaranteed to increase in value.

"There are only a few people who are my friends. And I

am loyal to my friends. I am a bit peculiar. Loyalty is one of my virtues. You might not know that," his voice reaches her from a distance.

She is thinking of other things. *It isn't your fault you know. It really isn't. I've put myself into the position of the victim and then blamed you and wanted you to save me from you for me. I blamed you for not loving me. You cannot. Not your fault at all. Just like me you belong mostly to others and minutely to yourself. I was after exchanging your minute details with mine. What you give me is not enough. I want other things I prevent myself from reaching out for as I stay with you. It's not your fault not your fault. I claim responsibility.*

"But her... I will never forgive her. She had no right to do this to me. I showed her so much affection so much care I rang her talked to her invited her to come to meetings to do poetry readings together. But she... nothing. Why? Why was she so mean?" After a moment's silence, he lifts his head up, "Him... Necati, I can forgive him... I may be able to work with him again," he is talking about a fellow poet who cut him out of her life and an academic he was very close to but no longer in touch with.

"Why? Because he is a man and you understand him better?" she catches the mocking rings in her voice as she asks and knows has created conflict.

"No, it's not that. It's something beyond that! I'll never forgive her. She attacked me, when I was being attacked by everyone else. Everyone! Do you know what that means? Not a soul came to my rescue, to defend, even objectively, the role of the artist. They couldn't even grasp that it's me today, them tomorrow. My God I want to be rid of my Cypriotness I want to be rid of it get it off my back! And that other one does not even send me a card... Anyway... I am loyal to my friends," he looks at her with his elbows propped on the table his head resting in his palms, smiling benevolently.

This so-called democratic people's party dictates to the people. They decide who will read poems on an evening organised for peace. I am resigning from the Peace Association. I will not be dictated to by anyone let alone a two-bit poet who comes to Cyprus every five years throws a bomb in the crowd creates havoc then leaves and we have to pick up the pieces. No, I will not do it! I will not allow a party to dictate to me and promote a poet who has condemned the 20th of July and our glorious Turkish Army its sacrifices in blood to save us. He is a traitor who wants us to be friends with the barbarous Greeks our murderers people who buried us our children our women alive! They shoved us into mass graves and bulldozed the earth over us they buried us alive! Never! I want peace but not at any price!

The poet reads his poems of peace on the platform in the square to the people oblivious to the fact that the Committee has banned him in order to protect them from the peace poems of the poet who was a threat to peace.

Traitor! Spy! In the pay of the Greeks! Of the communists! The Greeks pay him to write and recite poetry. Who is the secret hand, carrying messages from the Greeks?

235

Agitation and accusations of dishonest community leaders give way to claims of honesty and the possibility of working together for a common future. There are meetings of leaders in search of unattainable peace in the faraway lands of Geneva, New York, London...

The poet denies all accusations and will not respond to such vile and slanderous allegations. The poet will maintain his silence. He will refuse all literary prizes, interviews, posts and positions until there is peace in Cyprus.

He hands her a newspaper article, "Have a look at this, the most recent attack. Nothing has changed, it is not getting any better; they haven't stopped. I am sick of them!"

"Yes I know my friend. I don't expect them to stop, do you? Why don't you learn to cope with it as you will not get used to it... ever!"

Women walk in no man's land. They come face to face with the machine-gun brandishing soldier from Turkey frightened out of his wits. His generals have told him he can't shoot women and children but his generals have also told him he must not give up even a handful of the soil of the motherland. *But this isn't your motherland soldier from Turkey. Go home! I want to see my friend Pembe. Let me through.* Will he shoot? He paces up and down panic flashing out of his eyes sweeping his machine-gun across the women a spectacle to the world's eyes.

A photograph in their hands held up by the corner, a photograph that is all that is left. Mingling moaning waiting. Black headscarves wet faces the corners of the eyes are wiped with the tips of the scarves. Hope is lost. Black-headed women sway like black poppies in the fields. *Have you seen my son my angel my love my one and only so young... my little lamb. Have you seen him? Have you? Have you? Have you seen hiiiiiiiiim? Answer me! Someone please... answer me...* screams the woman in search of her son lost in war.

He looks at her from top to bottom as she reads the article. Slowly deliberately without turning his face. Black leggings. Black sweatshirt down to the top of her legs. A leather jacket. Wild mane of dark hair swept back. Blown out in layers of candyfloss. Down to her waist. Squares of silver and reds of cornelian drop from her ears. As always passion in her eyes. He feels subdued in a trench coat covering casual blacks. A stubble covers his face. Black wavy hair outgrown his meticulously chosen style and cut when he had some money. His dark delicate brown rimmed glasses hiding honey holes in his brown eyes. With controlled appreciation he says, "It's strange... you look so young!"

Too much is unsaid. They have shared hours, a history, an island, a passion, a loss.

"Have you eaten?" she asks hating her motherliness, liking her sense of care. He nods pointing to the kebab house with his chin.

"I've got AIDS," he says. She studies his eyes as her lips touch the rim of her wineglass. She insists as she has never done to meet his gaze. Her eyes feel cold in the centre, detached pushing away a momentary doubt. "Show me the test and I will believe you!" she says without any emotion.

"I don't have long. The doctor says," his response avoids her comment. A brief silence. He looks away, he feels the need to elaborate to convince her of the truthfulness of his statement. "I had the test done in Greece. Under a false name. You know how it is with a person in my position!" He grimaces. The fingers touch his lips holding a cigarette. Yes of course public poets cannot die private deaths, she thinks. He has not convinced her. She continues to stare at him. His eyes avoid hers. His eyelashes flicker and he searches for signs of pity, sadness, belief, agony, in her eyes. "Have a test here and I'll believe you," the same detached pitiless voice. She is so pitiless not even the faintest of signs of gentleness, empathy, sadness, panic.

"I am a carrier. The doctor told me. I have a maximum of ten years." She controls her outburst, "If you have, your doctor is being very optimistic! Sorry but he can't give you that sort of a guarantee," the irritation in her voice is obvious. She is reacting to his attempts of emotional manipulation. His attempts at extracting pity while rejecting her love infuriate her.

"You always need someone to be sick. You can't love anyone unless they are sick. All your loves carry disease," she says with annoyance and dismissal.

"Love is an illness!" he asserts dismissively.

238

She looks at her hands on the brown table. Her empty wine glass stands next to them. They have lost the brownness of the sun she thinks, comparing them to the brownness of the table. They are sitting in an alcove in a pub. There are books on the top shelves. Old cigarette picture cards of famous stars on one wall lovingly framed for posterity. Who were they? Significant people made insignificant by time or just an illusion of time? A picture of a Turkish frigate in Southampton Harbour on the other.

"Life is normality," he continues. "If life is what is normal then love must be an illness."

"Love is strength, it is power! I want to change your definitions. I want to make love the norm. Love is life." He dismisses her with the casual sweep of his hand and the twist of his mouth. Insists on the sickness of love, the abnormality in a normal world. Speaks over her voice. They lovehate the insistence on arguing their case within the banality of the situation.

Her smile mocks the world but mostly herself. He is irritated by her. Why can she never understand him? She always wants to talk about herself. Everything rotates around her passions. Passing passions. Without permanence. She doesn't even write about herself her history. She is irresponsible to herself to her era of history. Why is she so attached to the state of being transitory?

"I'm going to that congress and I am going to vote for Necati so that he can get elected as Chair. I'll show them. See if they can do what they want then..." he says and she is puzzled by his sudden switch of subject but dives in.

"I thought you had given up all this, little political games. One minute you are giving everything up, the next you are going to congresses and voting. What the Hell is going on? You really are inconsistent!"

"My position is different from yours. At this age, at the age of thirty, I wouldn't join a party but I've been a member since the age of eighteen." He touches his chest with his fingertips trying to convince her of the soundness of his argument.

"So what? So was I. How does it justify you being in one now, unless you are playing some silly game? Do you need to?"

"I am different. My background is that of the political student activist. People from that movement, as distinct from the present political parties, support me. They closely watch what I do and follow my lead."

"That might be the case, but your precious political party would not have supported you if you were not their member. They supported you not because of some ulterior benevolent reason, goodness of their heart or understanding of your independent position as a poet for peace against war. Forget it my friend, if you expect any political party to support an intellectual or an artist, think again. They have difficulties in supporting the independent position of the intellectual and the artist, in more sophisticated countries with a cultural infrastructure. Leave it out! How can you expect a country like ours, which doesn't even have a cinema or a theatre to understand the role of the intellectual or the artist in society? Do me a favour! By your very nature as a poet, as an intellectual, you are in conflict with them.

"The party, no matter how generous, still has to demand obedience and towing the party line on theory, the interpretation of theory, and even what constitutes art. The party is there to do politics and come to power by whatever means possible, not necessarily defend the truth. It is not interested in supporting any outsiders, no matter how correct their line of thought or how moral their way of life. Especially Stalinist parties, like yours. You know them, you have lived amongst them.

"So please don't talk naiveté to me. Why do you think they have never supported me in my struggles or any of the work I have done, no matter how right I was? In fact they have actively sabotaged my work."

"They would support me," he retorts. "They have to! And anyway, I have influence in high places. It's funny... opposing sides support me. And I don't deny or confirm their support," a self-satisfied smile appears on his lips.

"Yes, but you know they will only support you for their own interests and not because of who you are!"

"No, no! No!" he was becoming irritated by her, "What I am saying is finding an echo in the leadership, amongst the executive committee and it's being taken notice of."

"Oh yes... Like who? Your long-standing friend Aşık?"

"Yes, he is on the national executive. They are beginning to take notice of him. We are beginning to have influence."

"Yes and they will cut him down as well. Who do you think he is, in the end? What power does he have? When it suits them, they will dispose of him just as they will dispose of you!

You are expendable! And especially, in a Stalinist party! Don't you know much about the Russian revolution and Stalinism? I thought you would know all this," she counters. She is irritated by his blindness.

"My friend Aşık is also a Stalinist!" he says almost as a provocation because he knows she likes him.

"Of course he is! That is how he was trained. But he is also the opposite because he is an artist and an individualist as all artists are. He paints and the Party can't quite control or have a say in what he paints. They don't even understand his abstract paintings. And so he is a contradiction for himself and the Party."

She is in one of those moods again. She is exasperating! You can't argue with her, bend her, shift her or do anything with her. She now moves in a non-linear way. But her eye is fixed on her target.

"We influenced him. A lot," he persists.

She is losing patience with his assigned self-importance. *Oh how I hate this smugness of yours, this everything was your doing attitude! As though intelligent people don't have the capacity to work out things for themselves. The irritating self-important smile.* She doesn't like it.

"Yes I know. And not just *you*. Others have also influenced him. For example, he says I have influenced him more than *you*, in recent years!"

"When I say, *we*, I mean..."

"I know what you mean," she interrupts him impatiently, "and I am not in that *we* because I am different!"

He is almost on the defensive, "Yes, and that's good. And you should be. Why not!"

"I know I am. And I support *you* which you refer to as *we*, the four of you with my separateness."

She is throwing down a challenge to me. Ah she doesn't understand! She just doesn't know anything. She thinks she knows it. Ignorant fool! Always playing up her own importance.

Somehow there is more laughter too. They are finding each other amusing, engaging. They are competing against each other's intellect.

"Why don't you wear the brooch I gave you?" he asks changing the subject again. "It's beautiful and someone I really like gave it to me."

"Yes I know; you've said."

"Did I? Who was it then?"

"I can't remember her name."

"In that case I won't tell you. Let there be a mystery in it."

"Why did you give it to me?"

"I gave it to you with pleasure and with very deep and genuine emotions. I don't regret giving it to you. I am pleased that I did."

"But why?"

He is puzzled. His eyes dig into his shoulder bag. "Well I wanted to give it to you. Some things you just can't explain. I am happy that I have given it to you."

She gives up and tells him she will wear it because she likes it. There are so many artificial mysteries in your life, she thinks.

"You never allow yourself to be carried away, to float along with someone," she says, smiling, with a touch of irony and teasing in her voice. "You always stop yourself... just in time. At first you let yourself go... and then you suddenly shudder, you have lost control, you are floating, carried away... you put a stop to it. You have a hunger for someone to surrender to, for someone to take you, to carry you off." He blinks.

"Why did you accuse me of doing that last year of carrying you off accusing me for surrendering yourself to me? As though I was to blame. You can never be the one to be carried along... you are the carrier. You pull people along. You are just like me. I carry people off but I let go and float along with them. You will never be able to do it. It's an art!" She is smiling.

A puzzled look on his face. *Where is she trying to get to now? I am not going to be angry with her. And why does she always bring these things up, always back to herself. Why doesn't she accept that I like her as a friend? I want her friendship. Why the innuendos about sex? Why can't she understand it was just pure passion? It is finished. Gone.*

He tries to explain. "There is no Turkish-Cypriot person who could carry me anywhere... ever!" he says with vehemence and then almost apologetically, "Please don't misunderstand me, don't be upset. But really there is no Turkish-Cypriot alive who could carry me off, who could teach me anything! There was only one. I could have fallen in love with her. That will always remain as an unfulfilled desire. But she just cut me out. I knew her inside out. She was my mirror image. She stood in front of me and I saw myself."

"And she couldn't love you because she was in love with someone else," she tries shattering his mirror.

"No! No one but herself!" he smiles.

"Yes that's true! But also in love with someone else!" *How can she insist, she cannot know.*

He is amused by her stubbornness. His eyes overflow with laughter, "Can't you see? She was so beautiful, proud, arrogant... tell me, wasn't she really beautiful? If there are ten beautiful women in Cyprus she is one of them and the most beautiful. She could just cut anyone out, finish everything, that's what she is. Just didn't care. She was my mirror image. And do you know, she was so happy about the poem. She kept showing it to her friend and saying, that's me. I wrote the last verses in a cafe sitting with her and a girlfriend of hers. And, I read the last lines to them; she was so excited. Poor woman she didn't realise that as the poem finished she was also finishing for me. She was just a poem..."

"You should have allowed yourself to love her. You should have let yourself go, allowed her to carry you away."

"Ah you don't understand! You don't understand! Love in your teens is not the same as loving a mature woman. I am going to write about this as well, about all sorts of love. Tears of Loves: that's the name. I've already got the name."

She roars with laughter, "It sounds like a B-movie from the fifties. Shit!"

"Exactly! Precisely!" He is pleasantly surprised by her insight. He likes her sharp mind. She is a phenomenon all by herself! He sometimes loves her...

"Why don't you listen to some of the old tangos of the fifties? I'm sure you'll get great titles for your stories."

He is amused by her suggestion, they laugh as they concoct tear-jerking titles.

"I want to write about all sorts of love. An older man with a young woman, two men, young innocent love..."

"The love of an older woman for a young man. A sixteen year-old boy's love for a thirty-five year old woman... two women..." she completes the list.

"Yes everything! Everything, I've lived through!"

"You haven't lived the love of two women, how can you write it?"

"Well, all the emotions are the same. Replace the young boy with a woman or an older man or an older woman or two men et cetera. The emotions are the same. The people are interchangeable only the emotions stay the same!"

"Yes I've forgotten... it's all destruction, jealousy, pathos, passion, sickness..." she laughs.

"Yes, precisely!" in an almost inaudible voice melting into a soft chuckle. "She doesn't even send me a card!" He is talking about the lover who cut him out, who he finished in a poem. As though to himself he continues with renewed vigour, "I want people to live to admit to what they are, to what they live. I have no patience, I don't accept, I reject people who do not live what they feel. People say I am a snob. Yes I am! I am! On this issue I am." His face had moved closer to hers shoving his points into her face into her eyes. "I find it ridiculous for someone to wear black shiny shoes red socks and pressed trousers when they don't love what they feel. I can never forgive them!" His cigarette smoke is getting into her face interfering with her breathing. She knows he is talking about the academic who is dabbling in politics and wants to be elected Chair.

His limp hand dangles holding a cigarette by the side of the table. He removes it as she grimaces and fans the smoke away. He is chain smoking. When she points it out, he tells her that cigarettes can't kill him, he'll die of AIDS.

He goes into a tirade against the owner of the red socks and pressed pants. The music moves from soul-funk to country and western. To Hot Chocolate! "I like this song!" his eyes light up, his body moves with the music.

"Yes, in the end we haven't even been to a disco together either here or in Cyprus. Despite all this talk!" He is annoyed that she can remember details. She can always come up with something negative. She can never live the positivity of that moment without its history. *Surrendering to her. Remembering that I had attacked her I was furious with her for surrendering myself to her. I rejected her. Now that's what I want, I want a person to surrender to and it must not be her. She wants to be that person. She is convinced that no one can do it, that it is inevitable that I must surrender myself to her. She did everything, controlled everything. She knew everything, everything, about me. And it wasn't enough; she wanted to know more. More than anything, she has an insatiable hunger to know me totally down to every single cell of my body and*

mind! I told her everything, I told her two or three times. Some-
times it was different. She managed everything. She controlled me
by knowing everything. She dominated me. Why did she do that?
Why couldn't I just surrender to her without her dominating me?
Wasn't that possible? She even dictated when we had sex. If I didn't
want to she didn't leave me alone. She seduced me. She made me
make love to her when I didn't want to. I shouldn't have done. I
shouldn't have accepted her. She shouldn't have carried me, accept-
ed me. Why did she? Where does she get this strength? She would
be so nice if she was just a woman. I sometimes find myself talking
to her as though she is a man.

"I'll have another drink. Do you want one?" She was already off her seat walking towards the counter when she had
asked. "You've got me drunk already. Look at me. I am even beginning to like pubs!" he laughs.

"Welcome to living in London!" she says as she walks
away.

She is taken aback by the smile of the barman as he serves
her. The white man standing next to her keeps turning his head
and looking at her. His expression doesn't change. She is appre-
hensive. She expects a racist comment, a racist look. The one
next to him also notices and turns around to look at her. A woman on the other end of the counter with rotten teeth smiles at her,
as she buys a drink.

Slowly she drinks her white wine measuring the strength
of his voice, the mood of his body. "Coca-Cola... that's the meaning of life..." his voice sings. "There was a film once. Should I tell

248

you about it?" she asks. He is not interested.

He watches her hands move around, fingers stretch contract touch the table her wild long hair partially covering her face she flicks back with a swing of her head her earrings flash lips move stretch come together sometimes sensuous. *I could kiss her. She is crazy sometimes.* She is describing something to him. The faint hairline on her upper lip moves. He touches her face with his eyes. She suddenly reaches out to touch his face. He moves back, escapes. He doesn't like being touched by her. No physical contact! No hints of sexuality! *I can't deal with it woman why don't you just become sexless but yet I desire you sometimes I want to fuck you so much I ache. I ache. You are so repulsive. Your insistence on touching on embracing hugging repulsion repulsion repulsion can't you fuck without touching me can't you love without touching me.* How did he kiss this face how did he lie naked next to this body plunge himself into it push himself into this body? She is so old sometimes. He is repulsed by her touch.

She stands still, frozen emotion and motion. Waits for his head to come back in position. He accepts the inevitability of the gesture. She holds his short bearded chin in her palm, strokes the side of his face with the back of her fingers. "Are you afraid that touching is love? Is it affection? Do you know? You do!" She soaks his repulsion and removes her hand with unhurried deliberation.

He slowly leans forward bringing his face close to hers, with smiles in his eyes, he reads with an intimate eroticism in his voice, verses of his new poem,

249

"should we stay?.... why?
should we go? .... where?
should we make love?... with whom?
"Do you like it?" She does. "So do I!" His starry joyful eyes
linger on her.

Iran and Iraq are nearing an agreement. The
Kurds are leaving their reluctant hosts in Turkey,
who are relieved to be losing their potential guer-
rillas and returning to Iraq under certain guarantees. *We might face certain death but it is our country
our land we have to return...* The reluctant host, the
Prime Minister, declares to the world that Turkey
respects human rights as evident from their open-
ing of their borders to the Peshmergas and their
families who have crossed over from Iraq escaping
chemical warfare.

*The PKK is different. Its members are ter-
rorists killing women children and Turkish soldiers.
They will be eliminated. Our troops are winning
against terrorist elements. Last week forty were
killed in remote mountain villages.*

*As an early winter sets in, young children
in the camps are dying of cold. At least ten children
have died every day, about five hundred so far. Turkish officials have been reported to have secretly carried twenty-thousand Kurds over the border into
Iran without prior notification. They are going, we*

cannot stop them, said a Turkish official.

Conciliation is on the horizon.

Seven years ago Nicaraguan contra rebels captured the doctor working in the mission and raped her. What she remembered most was the fact that while the rape was actually going on, her captors were singing hymns and chanting religious incantations.

Conciliation is on the horizon.

She begins to put her jacket on. She puts one arm through. He stirs in his seat. "What, what are you doing?" his face betrays confusion. "You are leaving, are you? I don't believe it! You can't go! Look at this woman! It's incredible!" His voice determined to control her actions. Her movements are deliberate unhesitant not rushed. His eyes scream at her *you can't go, where are you going*? She smiles. A normal smile. There are no hidden messages, innuendos. Calmer than she thought she would be. Where is the heart thump? She smiles with pathos. "Yes, I am now leaving."

"But why? What's happened? After such an evening, is that the conclusion you've reached? Is that what the evening has meant to you... after such an evening that... you have to go?"

She is standing up. He reaches out touches her fingers she takes his hands. He knits his fingers into hers just like on their love-making bed. Knitting both hands into hers stretching her arms above her head kissing kissing kissing her face lips neck lick her salty throat ears eyes breasts as he lies on her. Why do you sweat so much when you are loving me? Uninvited tingles shudders shoot through her body. Sudden tenderness engulfs her. She leans over to kiss his forehead. He instinctively jerks his head back. *Only your forehead. I am only kissing your forehead!*

"It's not just tonight. Thanks for the tenderness, especially yesterday. You were caring. I've been thinking about it for a long time," she says.

He looks at her in panic, "You don't want to see me any more...?" With an imperceptible nod of her head she confirms. *No, I don't.*

"But how could you do this? How could you say that after such... such an evening? How, how could you...?"

"I still love you, I will still think of you, I won't abandon you I will support you I will care for you I do care for you."

He laughs bitterly mockingly. *But why? She must be joking. She is crazy! She's just putting me on! Why can't she see she's the only one I see the only one I meet talk to laugh with invite to my house share my secrets paranoias joys if I have them. I want to make love to her I want to be with her I am afraid I don't want her to love me I want to just love her without touching her.*

"Because you no longer need me," she says. Too simple. Is that all? "I don't want to be a victim any more. I don't want to make myself the victim. I can't live for you with you in you around you together. I must live for me. I count. You need someone who will only live for you to survive only for you. I can't be the patch on your shirt. I AM." A bit like the weepy movies of the fifties why not the liberated woman of the eighties? What's gone wrong? "When we are together only your plans writing poetry projects court case feelings angers dreams frustrations future are important. Where am I in this relationship? I don't want to become a bitter woman. I am worried about that. I don't want to be a victim and blame you. I don't want to regret how I have lived. I want to be the priority in my life. I am setting you free. But that's a disguise for liberating myself!"

"But after tonight... "

"You know it's not just tonight!"

"But I want you to be my friend..."

Ah yes! But it's not enough my friend. I want passion I want love I want to surrender myself I want to be one I want to be lost in the labyrinths of someone I want to be warm angry crazy a child I want to do intellectual battle I want to be strong weak caressed spoilt arrogant I want to fight make love in the sea as the sun sets at midnight under the cypress trees in the stars when they come down to earth I want to sleep with someone on white sheets when my blood warms up in the sun and awaken my womanhood my sun-kissed brown body covered in petals of jasmine wild roses I want to run scream at the top of my voice laugh challenge the world to duels I will win I want to fuck the world I want to be me with someone.

"You are not enough..."

I want someone to surrender their inner-core innocence to me be one with me I want to breathe in tune with someone I want to feel the hunger softness of lips on my mouth neck nipples breasts belly lips the featheriness of pubic hair on my lips strength of a tongue in my mouth I want to feel the suction of my lips of my vagina back to my brain I want arguments I want fights about life I want victories over ugliness deceit hypocrisy oppression over violence rape torture over bureaucracy over falseness over sold-out souls over non-entities over degeneracy I want beauty power gentleness warmth loving over above everything else...

Do you dare enter me do you dare get caught in my whirlwinds in my hurricanes. Poor man. I was once one with you I gave you me I shared with you the woman I have created...

I feel your eyes on my back certain that you are too weak too proud to follow me and I am relieved.

London. October 1988

DESPERATELY
SEEKING...

I can't stay. I am running out of time. I have to fuck! So far nothing that takes my fancy. For the past three days I've been looking really hard. I've turned the place upside down. Under trees, pagodas, inside outside buildings, around the lily pond, even places no one is allowed into… Nothing that shakes my limbs, gets me all flustered. Only a few scraggly miserable specimens. I am certainly not wasting my beautiful body in its prime on them! So I press on…

Look at her… She is always dressed in white and brown speckled white feathers. She never moves during the day. She just sits, blinking her huge eyes occasionally. You think she can't see you, but she does. She just ignores you; you are not worth her attention. She doesn't bat an eyelid or flick a feather or a limb. Just sits in that shaded corner. They say she moves at night. She wanders about silently, slowly; she is in no hurry. Some say they hear her call out with an eerie sound in the night when silence falls. Some consider her bad luck, especially if she crosses their path. Who does she call out to? Where did she live before she found herself in this place? No one knows much about her or what was known has long been forgotten. Only that she has been here for a long time. Was she always alone? She is a funny old bird... Some say she is wise.

The residents are from all over the world. No idea where some came from and why. They are just here. Some by choice, others not. The reasons don't matter after a while. Some survive, some struggle, some go mad, some don't make it no matter what. Some don't want to be here, others can't wait to be approved so as they can stay forever. Others were born here. For some it doesn't seem to matter anymore. Nothing left to return to, yet nothing to keep them.

Some have been here forever. The light in their eyes gone so has the sheen of their skins; grey like the skies. But today is so hot, sunny, exciting, buzzing, heaving, full of colour and hundreds have come to visit them.

There is an old granny here, just here... Come, look through the window. They've just refurbished her house, larger windows, bigger space, all mod cons. But I don't know that she is happy with it or that it has made much difference to her life. I don't even know if they asked her if she wanted the changes. Maybe they assumed she wanted a more modern place rather than her old one. She doesn't look any happier to me or sadder. Has she even noticed? Was it for the visitors? Or maybe to demonstrate that those who run the place are considerate to their residents, especially the elderly? Who knows who made the decisions and for what reason.

There is a melancholy look in her eyes now, slowly being defeated by cataracts. Would they operate on her eyes without asking? Maybe she doesn't want to see any clearer what she knows has changed. Maybe she wants to preserve the images of her life in the surroundings they were lived. Is change always for the better? Maybe being blind to some things is better. She is waiting to die.

She gave birth to all her children here. Some have died, others sent to other countries to other places. She missed her first daughter the most. They called her Shushu or something, as they took her away from her. Her dark-brown hair now covered in silver streaks. She sometimes puts her hand across her mouth and smiles especially when a child comes up to her window. When people demand her attention she just turns her bum on them sitting stubbornly, ignoring them until they leave. She is nobody's fool.

She came from Africa. She didn't choose to come. They adopted her as a baby and brought her over. The story is that her life was in danger, she might not have survived because her mother was killed. Greed for land and hardwood is slowly wiping off her ancestral land and her tribes, they say.

There was this woman who went to find her tribe in the jungle and made films about them, long time ago. Very famous apparently. She once saw her cousin in a flickering box who was also taken away, wearing some strange cloth wrapped around his bum, being ordered to perform tricks, holding this little cloth with straight sticks like the ones they used to stick into holes and pull out honey-ants. Oh what a feast that was! Unaware that with this little trick they were scuttling an established theory and their assigned position in the animal kingdom. This cloth had sticks and stars on it, stuck on another thin long stick. Degrading things they ordered him to do. What were they trying to prove? She could see pain, desperation, anger and humiliation in his eyes and the baring of his teeth, those watching thought a smile.

I sometimes go and sit next to her. Not too close. I see the marvel and enchantment in her eyes as she looks at me and her lips move but no sound comes. She never reaches out to touch me, she knows I don't want to be touched.

Oh just don't look at that one! You'll only feed his ego. What airs… just because he is big and powerful! Look at that mane of ginger-blond hair he flicks around and those whiskers! As though we are all impressed by such show-offs! Such arrogance in those golden eyes as he watches your every move, ready to pounce, so sure you'll fall for his charms. He struts up and down ensuring you have seen all he has to offer from head to toe… his Highness's majestic presence! Irresistible! He even goes by the name of King. King indeed! I don't believe in kings and queens so you can strut all you like. They say he was captured in Africa, then sent to various countries in Europe. No one wanted him, too dangerous, they said. They kept deporting him from country to country. What humiliation for a King to become a refugee, unwanted by all when you ruled a vast open country for thousands of miles with the adoration of your *harem* of faithful wives bearing your adorable offspring ready to follow you anywhere you wished. Of course you had to ensure they didn't challenge your supreme rule by pushing them to the edges of your kingdom… but that's life, they had to make their own lives. Such indignity to feel imprisoned in this cold country, in such a small space, mostly on your own, reduced to rationed sex and only with one female when *they* decide the time is right. And the food is abysmal! No amount of pounding the ground can take away his frustration or his sadness knowing he will die in exile, a refugee.

They say this one was happy as a baby, running in-and-out of the tree-trunk legs of grown-ups, flapping her ears. She was adorable. She was the new baby of the tribe and had taken a long time arriving. She was very special. They say all the grown-ups protected her as their own and accommodated her little antics, pulling her gently out of trouble when it occurred. Everyone watched her with amusement, haplessly inquisitive, bouncing off everywhere, having brushes with members of other tribes.

She loved bath-times the best, squirting water she hadn't mastered yet, while grown-ups teased her by showering her, as she slipped and fell in the pond, rolled over, scrambling to get up, feet slipping, doing the splits with her chin in the mud, trying to balance her feet only to be nudged ever-so-gently by a grown-up and fall flat in the mud again wondering what had happened.

They were the happy times... There were also others so harrowing and frightening she tries to bury deep in her memory while she watches her visitors trying to understand them. But the other day, they say she just went berserk. She wrecked the place. No one could placate her. She just gave out these long,

long heart-rending screams, calling out, almost waiting for a response. She cried like a baby and she is an old girl now. Everyone watched helplessly, upset by her agony. They say it was triggered by a machine gun a boy aimed at her. It was a toy but for her, it was so real…

Apparently, she had watched boy-children no higher than her knee walking around with these, slung across their bodies, as big as themselves, barely able to carry them. So heavy. She could see the pain in their malnourished faces and wounds or sores on their bodies. And they walked for miles. Sometimes a small group would emerge from one direction wearing dark-green leaf coloured clothes with strange patterns, then another group from another side wearing the same clothes but with dry sandy earth colours with the same strange pattern and the same heavy black guns. She never understood why boy-children the same age were killing each other, just because they were wearing slightly different coloured clothes…

Her elders would sense them and steer the tribe away before the loud thunder noises came. But once they just appeared and suddenly her tribe was caught in the middle of such fire, from both sides. Even the long-memoried grannies and the strong leader of the tribe didn't know which direction to run. They were trapped in hell fire. There was panic, dust, confusion, running in circles until one of the wise grannies led them out to safety.

When the blinding sand and dust clouds settled and the unbearable screaming and fire thunder stopped, they stopped shivering huddled together. They waited for the bird sounds, a signal for returning to normality. When she looked around from between the tree-trunk legs she saw blood oozing down some of them, creating small puddles by their feet. She panicked they say and started crying but she really lost it when they searched for her aunts, uncles and cousins who were missing.

They found them lying on the ground, in pools of blood, their faces mutilated, their beautiful teeth pulled off breaking the jaws, their faces torn apart. She just stared, frozen. They say she never recovered... her mother was there, she couldn't recognise her. For days she called out for her, inconsolable when the mother didn't answer. They travelled for miles but she would still call out for her...

And now she is here... I've only been here a short while. It's a fascinating place! The residents so interesting. Worth a visit but I am not staying.

This one is a snapper. I don't go near her... She likes water. She keeps going in and out. Sometimes you just see her eyes above the water and a little of her head. Dead still. She just waits... just waits... waits. Such patience! But what a temper! Everyone tolerates her eccentricities. I suppose that's her way of dealing with things...

Did you see those tall fellows? Ginger haired, big eared? You can see them from anywhere around this residence. They are my landmarks if ever I lose my way wandering about. I glance up and there they are... with those slightly puzzled enormous eyes and to-kill-for eyelashes sending me an amused wink.

Around the corner there is this one who is always on the floor. He prefers to crawl. You never see him upright. He curls up at the bottom of that tree trunk and just watches with sleepy eyes. Every now and again he decides to make fun of passers by and flicks his tongue out at them. That's all. People think he is dangerous or revolting. Some shiver as they look at him, revulsion in their eyes, making squeamish sounds and funny hand movements. I've never worked out what these mean. He seems so harmless. He moves about under the tree picking up leftovers or what people leave for him minding his business. His teeth must have rotted. You sometimes see him trying to swallow things whole or in big chunks. Now, that's revolting. And he keeps peeling off all his garments and discarding them all over the ground or leaves them dangling on the tree, wandering around stark naked.

He looks such an unlikely character for murdering someone. Many years ago, apparently. He just hugged this man and crushed his bones. They say he didn't intend to do it. It's just that he was provoked and brutally abused.

He has been blamed for all sorts of things including seducing some woman, long, long time ago, causing havoc and damnation on earth. Only the males of the species can believe that we can be seduced just with an apple... they really lack imagination! But he does have a beautiful copper-brown body with these intricate tattoos. They say his home was India.

Time is getting on. I need to find a fuck! Still nothing in sight... Have you seen anything? No! Maybe I'll have better luck around the lily-pond. It's balmy hot, sunny, the water attracts all sorts. I've already scoured the pond but no harm in trying again. They come to see the water lilies with pink, purple, yellow, white heads resting on the water amongst the beautiful green plate-like leaves. Can you hear the frogs? There... there are two sitting on those leaves. One here, next to the giant white lily with its mysterious orange protruding central cone, the other over there by the cornflower-coloured one with delicate petals reaching up so elegantly. Breathtaking sight this time of year, when the lilies are out. Everyone rushes to gaze in admiration and wonderment. Captivated by the images long buried in memories of childhood journeys embarked upon while reading storybooks. There were the beautiful flowers and flat plate-like leaves. And frogs used to sit on them, butterflies fluttered and my ancestors danced on the water. And honeybees, wasps and bumblebees came. And tiny fish jumped into the air from below the plate-like leaves trying to catch flies with rainbow wings. And dainty little fairies in flimsy pink skirts twinkle-toed from leaf to leaf, flower to flower some carrying sparkling magic wands... Anything could happen here...

Did you hear that? Hush! Listen... A muffled noise behind the purple-flowering creeper dangling in curtains from the ceiling. A deep sigh, soon followed by another. Some undecipherable words. What language is that? So many in here, those of the residents and the visitors who speak so differently. A ruffling noise. Something knocked over. Silence. Then giggles. More whispers. A squeak. Then another. A rhythmic squeak betrays movement accompanied with deep sighs and audible occasional grunts. The squeaks gain momentum and so do the accompanying sighs and grunts. Few whispers in between, urge, in desperation...

I have to see... And there they are, a blonde young woman in a short skirt rolled up to her buttocks, straddling the young man in a pin-striped suit, too hot for the day and even more so for the lily house. His hair up-right, wind-swept, fashionably short cropped, moussed, with his hands pressing her tightly against his groin. He is sitting on the white garden bench the brass plaque says was donated by the family of Lilly Waterhouse who spent hours painting the lilies, slightly hidden by the purple and orange flowering creeper weaving a curtain. Fucking to their hearts' content, oblivious to the plight of the residents with their regimented eating, sleeping, visiting and precisely timed mating programmes.

This pool seems promising... I better keep a close eye on those who are very keen on my body. I am not going to give them the pleasure before I have mine... a once-in-a-lifetime experience. I have no intention of dying a virgin!

Across the pond... Look! What a beautiful body, what a colour! How he moves! Such an elegant dance! Definitely fit for my babies... I feel the heat even more as I begin to tremble. I sense my own body smells rise. The groaning couple are not even trying to muffle their voices now. Very disturbing, while

I am trying to focus on attracting this gorgeous creature from across the pond. He has sensed me. I can see he is approaching with small dancing movements. Then I see he makes a sudden move, too close to the water. My eyes zoom on the frogs on the plate leaves. They have sensed him; they don't move an eyelid. They have been transformed into fairy statues. Uncontrollable desire has made him drunk. He is taking risks. The frog by the cornflower-coloured lily snaps as he goes past. He misses... My eyes suffer a shock of lightning. The one enamoured not even aware of his own near extinction, drunkenly dancing towards me... This is not a choice! The couple on the white bench have a choice, not I. This is survival. This drunkenness cannot deprive me of my future generations.

I fly in and force him to come with me to a place high above the pond away from the tongues and bulging eyes of the frogs staring into space without batting an eyelid. I make sure he straddles me tightly from behind, wrapping my body with his. Finally relieved, basking in the pleasure of imagining the beauty of my future babies...

The young woman emerges from behind the flower curtain, brushes her blonde hair back from her flushed pink face and looks around surreptitiously. No one around. She is relieved. Her eye then catches the beautiful blue-turquoise dragonflies clasped tightly, copulating on the twig above the lily pond. She laughs thinking everyone is at it in this zoo.

Famagusta. December 2007

TONGUES
OF THE CITY

Dec 25, 2010 - Christmas day. Beirut! What amazing images it conjured up in me as a child in Cyprus. Such diversity, cultures, cultured people, boundless wealth, buildings, boulevards, glitter beyond my imagination… fed by the 'suitcase-trade' of the women in my impoverished neighbourhood in the 1950s on the outskirts of Nicosia, which didn't even have tarmacked roads or running water. Where we carried clumps of rust coloured mud under our shoes as we dodged the puddles. It remained stubbornly glued under our newly polished shoes, gathering twigs or straw, creating precarious platforms on which we wobbled, constantly in danger of slipping into the mud… unaware of our innocence before we descended into the sewage of decades of war, colluding in corruption, immorality and selective amnesia.

So this morning's Beirut… Hamra, where we have a four-star hotel. I have never stayed in these places wherever I've travelled. I go along with the wishes of my companions. An Australian bassoonist and a Georgian diplomat. I know they want to stay somewhere 'safe', expensive hotels are… but from whom?

Confusion of streets, languages, melange of communities,

269

music, faces, smells. But I love the sense of this place… and I've only been here two days. The orderliness, which emerges from the seeming disorder, leaves me in awe, despite my disappointment in my first espresso in this metropolis of civilization and ancient home of Turkish coffee.

New tower blocks, old tower blocks surround me. The city grows upwards; straight and narrow and stretching, just stretching upwards, reflecting a soullessness I am unprepared for. Why did they knock down the old so mercilessly? Why didn't they preserve it? Is this an interpretation of being 'Western', modern, copying the West? Why? Then slowly I notice gaps between the buildings. Wastelands. *But Beirut was BOMBED!* escapes my lips as my eyes blink, imagining the carnage, explosions, dust, deaths in the streets… and so often, for such a long time… So indiscriminately. Almost with vengeance. Nothing was spared. Nothing! Then large craters, holes, no electricity, no water, no phones, buildings burning for days. My memory catches up with my eyes, ears, sense of smell. Israel bombed the shit out of it! Then the Syrians. They pulled the guts out of the body of this city.

> *TEN THOUSAND BOMBS HAD LANDED, AND I WAS WAITING for George.* Rawi Hage later tells me in his novel *De Niro's Game*. … *Heat descended, bombs landed, and thugs jumped the long lines of bread, stole the food of the weak, bullied the baker and caressed his daughter. Thugs never waited in lines … War is for thugs. Motorcycles are*

also for thugs, and for longhaired teenagers like us,
with guns under our bellies, and stolen gas in our
tanks, and no particular place to go ... I climbed
onto George's motorbike and sat behind him, and
we drove down the main streets where bombs fell,
where Saudi diplomats had once picked up French
prostitutes, where ancient Greeks had danced, Ro-
mans had invaded, Persians had sharpened their
swords, Mamluks had stolen the villagers' food,
crusaders had eaten human flesh, and Turks had
enslaved my grandmother.

Ahh! I knew we had some common ancestors in these streets...

They tell me, *No part of Beirut was spared.* Then someone would say, *Around the American University of Beirut was not bombed too heavily.* Later still, I am told that the great hall housing the library was totally destroyed. And, rebuilt with the same stones exactly as it was, so in some sense, what you see is not the real thing but rather a replica, out of the rubble of the old.

I become aware that what I might consider West Beirut as on a map I took from the hotel reception may not be the actual West Beirut or North or East Beirut as referred to by those who are witnesses to the history/herstory of this city. What I had initiated in Cyprus to avoid nationalist discourse in the 1980s - that of, 'north' and 'south' Cyprus, north and south Nicosia, as opposed to 'Greek-side' or 'Turkish-side' - leaves me without a sense of certainty in another geography. Is what I call "North" really the north?

My espresso coffee cup is full of imagery I am fascinated by. My fascination the only compromise with coffee readings supposedly telling my future, some had insisted. All my own creation, I would retort, summoning the power of my Goddesses! Months later, I would smile reading about Robert Fisk sitting in a café, in Place de L'Etoile, musing about his city.

> *My café au lait is always served piping hot, just like Beirut's history. And everything I look at in these streets was restored post-civil war by the company whose largest shareholder was Rafiq Hariri.*

New, quick, substandard buildings, harbingers of temporality more than transience; just so it will serve its purpose until a better one is built, if ever... If those who are building them live through the next war or don't emigrate to Africa or South America, Australia or... never to return. "There are thirteen million across the world, only four million of us in Lebanon," the taxidriver had said on the way from the airport.

Later in the day, I go searching for the spirit of Christmas in the Greek Catholic church, not far from the hotel. L'Eglise Pierre et Paul leaves me cold in a bare concrete building of the nineteen-sixties, early nineteen-seventies; the typical functionalist concrete box... complementing the vastness of the space, bland icons, probably bought from the corner shop. While in search of the Greek Catholics of Lebanon, I enter the church to be faced with a congregation of women; Philippinas, a few drops from Sri Lanka, a few more from Africa in search of spirituality in this soulless space on Christmas day. Just like in Cyprus. The only male, the priest, from China or perhaps the Philippines. They are waiting for something, or rather, the words of God in languages they can understand. For the moment they are making do with the American drawl filling the space with *The Word*, projected onto a temporary screen in front of the altar. To ease the sense of total incomprehension, a little dot bounces from word to word enabling the followers to pretend they can understand them. Religious or maybe Bible Karaoke…

A few words from the priest, then the service begins with a hymn, in which language, I have no idea. They sing, all of them, a naïve song from another part of the world, not the Arab one they inhabit. I catch the words *amen* and, every now and again, *selam*. And then 'participation' is ensured by one of their own women wearing a uniform of sorts - a special dress between that of a choirgirl and a nurse - reading out something while the congregation, those who can understand, respond. The grand chandelier of crystal glass twinkles a little above the heads of the faithful, cold fluorescent bulbs have displaced the candles up front but are submissive to the chandelier's imposing, almost aristocratic grandeur.

They stand up… time to rescue my atheist spirit from this soullessness. I can't handle the bleeding heart of the blue-eyed Christ in this olive-skinned, dark-eyed world, his roots, of literally bleeding hearts of wars! I prefer the chaos and melange of the streets!

***

"The Wall came down," says Jean, our driver for the day. It's past midnight, we are re-entering Beirut. "Now they are building..." He points at the heavy concrete boulders on the side of the road as we drive past some roadworks playing havoc with the heavy Beirut traffic. He points left, "This... was Christian," points right, "This was Muslim." A pause, "There was a wall..." Quickly my mind's eye flashes to Nicosia, to Berlin, two cities I have experienced closely, working out how to penetrate the walls, violate the borders, prevent the walls from keeping me either in or out. "Now... no wall!" I hear Jean say. I can't work out if that pleases him or there is confusion or regret, almost as if to say, *What the fuck was that about?* Was it necessarily followed up by, *Why did the Muslims and Christians kill each other?* or maybe, *Why did you make me kill so many or shoot or hate and now you tell me everything is OK? As though all that didn't happen?* Would he think that?

Earlier he had taken us to his house in a valley for mint tea, coffee and fruit and on the way back he wanted to show us a place. He stopped at a vantage point on the hillside, a balcony overlooking Beirut. It was already dark. Such a stunning view of the city at our feet, down there in the distance, with its star-like lights. I joked, "Now I can see Cyprus..." He was all serious, "Yes, on a clear day you can!" I imagined him looking towards my island as I looked into the unyielding dark Mediterranean from the other side, from Famagusta, making myself believe I could see the lights of Beirut.

As we were walking away from the railings he said, "In

the war people used to come here to watch the bombing of Beirut…" I looked at his face thinking this is macabre, how can people come to watch destruction and death as though it is a film! "I also shoot," he says, making a machine gun, an AK47 probably, with his hands, arms extended, making a sweeping movement around himself, from one side to the other. He responds to the unmasked question in my eyes, "I was a Christian militia…" A momentary fear, regret of those days, the justification from someone probably shit scared for his life but finding himself in a situation of having to shoot, to kill in the devastation and chaos of an area, reduced to concrete rubble and steel rods, or in neighbourhoods which once overflowed with the sounds of music from different communities, weddings and circumcision parties, love stories, family squabbles, women running off with lovers, corner stores selling cheese, balloons, bread, *baklava* and other pastry sweets, vegetables, fruit, coffee and nuts. *What was it all about?* passes as a shadow across his dark eyes, nodding his head imperceptibly as the beholder of knowledge no one can access; he is condemned to carry.

***

I am searching for bookshops aware that I will find traces of these lives and more, in the literatures of Lebanon. And I do, as I rummage through novels, memoirs and poetry in the Beirut and Byblos bookshops, Saqi, Librairie Antoine and Orientale, and even more in London. "Closed for Xmas," signs attached

275

on the doors of the two I found on al Hamra Street, the Oxford Street and Champs-Elysees of Beirut apparently; the prices
match. Does that mean they are Christian owned? The rest of
the shops in the street are open, business as usual. I am familiar
with the generosity, appreciation and energies of multi-cultural
cities with layers of languages and faiths; they never sleep! A
few weeks later, I discover my sense of this city echoed by Hala
Kawtharani; he had escaped it and war, and went to the States
to study,

> *I became fascinated with my mother's account of*
> *Beirut in the fifties and sixties: a time when the*
> *faces of many colours from many lands walked al-*
> *Hambra Street and all the languages of the world*
> *could be heard. In Beirut, everything was toler-*
> *ated: 'every idea, every identity' as I read in the*
> *conclusion of that wonderful book by the thinker*
> *Edward Said ... that shares his title with Mahmoud*
> *Darwish's poem 'After the Last Sky'.*

***

Images of Beirut still flash by on my way to Famagusta...
Sitting in a café with Jean, waiting for Miriam who has gone to
the see the first bassoonist of the Beirut Symphony Orchestra;
Ekaterina has returned to Cyprus. A café with a large semi-basement for jazz and alternative music. The customers could have
walked in from the US, UK or any other European or Austral-

ian city. A corner of Beirut! So distant for Jean, who seems alienated by these places, looking around with disoriented eyes, whereas I walk in and out of them without discomfort. He is waiting for Miriam, with whom he has a special affinity. With me, he is uneasy. I am older, but increasingly, I get the feeling it is because I am 'Muslim'. He is having difficulty placing me in that category. I upset his categories based on religion, ethnicity and Allah knows what! I am different, but still sense his unease, like rumbling, deep in the earth, vibrations of heavy vehicles, tanks rolling. *I am an atheist* I had said when he broached the subject not so tangentially. But to him, it's what you are born into. After all, that's the politics of Lebanon; all its wars were fought on those issues. People were and are killed, solely because of their religion and not just on the broad base of Christianity or Islam. The minutia also a factor and cause for killings within Christian congregations and within the Muslim faithful. The arbitrariness and deliberate cruelty of the killings is what stuns and numbs me! The mass slaughter of innocent people in refugee camps alongside the individual senseless (is any killing sensible / senseful?) killing by a sniper lodged on a rooftop, of a pregnant scared woman venturing onto her balcony to hang the washing of her family or the killing of a hungry dog rummaging through rubbish bins for food... My intellect tries to make sense of the senseless, the absurd... and being an atheist is just as irrelevant in that configuration. Months later, wandering around the Tate, in London, I am reminded of the absurdity, as my eye catches the Mediterranean faces in an arts video installation, by Lamia

Joreige. In the video, he holds a 1983 photo, tenderly,

> *...in the Party they started killing each other, killing*
> *my friends. I was ordered to shoot into a dark corner*
> *and nearly shot my brother; I heard his voice and*
> *stopped. I had killed so many... war had eaten all*
> *our ideas, flesh, politics...*

Jean makes polite conversation but uneasy when on his own with me. His eyes follow every move in the café. Then he seems to come to terms with it because I am not Lebanese. In his consideration, I can be exempt from the political alliances he lives with and survives through. Suddenly, he offers to take me to a bookshop he has heard I'm looking for. This is also a means of escaping the alien surroundings of the café, a million miles from the world he had to survive through, a world of mental and physical scars the geography of the city carries, of bullet hole-riddled buildings, glass window panes, mangled steel rods sticking out of buildings, roads; *his* reality of the same city. He knows how to navigate that geography that destruction that pain not this cosy little world of foreigners with no pock mark in sight, the untouched and untouchable foreigners... except for kidnappings.

He knows Beirut like the back of his hand. Like the *palm of his hand,* as we would say in these parts of the world. He has a mental map. He says, *just tell me what you want and I will take you,* with a certainty challenging the uncertainty of this place. And he does. He finds things for you with the ease of someone who had to find, take, commandeer, in situations where the normal rules break down and survival instinct takes over. My request not a piss in the wind. His whole body, hands on the wheel asserts, "This is my city!" reminding me of my own claim, *London is my city*. He has created Beirut just as I've created London; in turn, they've created us.

He tells me about his French lover; later I learn she is Belgian. Much younger than him. For some reason I remember he might have said he is forty-seven. His lover? *Twenty-five twenty-six*, he responds with a sigh. A lover for three or four months, it transpires. A journalist and photographer. Went to live with him and left a huge gap in his soul when *she left to live with the Palestinians*, he gestures with a swing of his arm into the air indicating faraway distances. My grandfather's gesture whenever he implied too long a distance, in reality, of un-attainability. *Come,* she said but he didn't. Beirut is his city. He is a Christian militiaman, how could he end up amongst the Palestinians. She doesn't even consider he might be in danger. She comes from a country, a continent without borders for its citizens. Schengen protects her. He didn't go. But his soul bleeds with her absence, the hollow she has left. "She made me speak French," he says with a vague smile. Taught him to be silent, when she painted or wrote her articles for various European magazines. She came back and took her things; his pain concentrated in his mouth as he replays the scene. "The house is empty now," he says, passing the inside of his thumb across his lips. He goes late, to the house of emptiness.

He smokes. Annoyed at first that I had voiced my opposition to him smoking in the car, he apologises, politely, whenever he forgets and lights up. He tells me things my two companions don't hear. Or if they do, it doesn't form a missing piece in their jigsaw. He earns a lot of money. He crumples his face, lowers his voice and tells me, *I go gambling because she is not there*, and after a moment, *the house is empty*. He tells us about his divorce and how he gambled away all his money to spite his wife who wanted everything. He tells me about the wars, the others I realize don't know much about. They have no reason to see the city in a different way. Whereas I have a herstory, I dig in her past. I know so much about herstory, we have crossed paths many times and yet I have never been here.

***

I am puzzled, intrigued by Jean's relationship with the two bankers we met on our second night here, who took us to visit their childhoods, swimming off the rocks, gazing at the stars on a moonless night and dark waters of the eastern Mediterranean. Still unspoilt. Escapees from developers, they fund. What is it that binds them together beyond the fact that he is a driver they ask to drive special people around Lebanon and Beirut? And in our case, they paid him for our journeys, an act of generosity. None of us have met them before. But do they owe him? What are the expected but unstated rules which govern their connection, between the driver and the bankers? What's their history? The fact that he is an astonishing driver is unquestionable! Driving fast with precision and the astute risks he took were phenomenal. I had a sense that he would get you out of any situation. He was in total control – not a thing escaped his attention! Not just the driving, he was there to protect you. You had been entrusted to him, so he was absolutely in charge of your safety. A bodyguard, I suppose - in other words...

He took us to places he liked; through the mountains covered in pine trees saying repeatedly how much he loved the mountains. Not the city, swiped away with the flick of the hand and crumple of the face. He kept asking or rather asserting, "Beautiful, no?" Was that the recently acquired French intonation, I wondered? Or is it Arabic? I smile realising the same expression in Cypriotturkish, *"Güzel; değil?"* And it was beautiful, especially in the last rays of the sun reflecting against the pink bodies and the dark green of the pine needles. Breathtaking and unexpected. It went on for miles, covering every hill and mountaintop, almost rolling along as a torrent of fast-flowing stream. Trees of the same height, the same style of pruning with three-four thick trunks rising from the main trunk, and covered with a flat canopy of leaves, only at the top.

"I take you to my house, yes?" is greeted with silence. Each one of us developing a separate scenario. We are on a mountaintop. Isolated. It is getting dark. Once the sun sets, darkness descends with speed. Then pitch darkness and we are nearing that time of evening. He drives without a word. I can feel the tense silence. "Where is your house?" asks Ekaterina and I smile thinking, *but you wouldn't know even if he tells you* and he does. None of us have a clue. "Where is that exactly?" is the next question which comes from Miriam. The spaces between us in the car fill with tension. How do we handle this? After a while I ask, "Who is in the house?" Silence. He is aware of the tension in the car. Ekaterina glances back at us at the same time trying to extract more information. I sense her fear at one stage but realise that I have none. Miriam shifts next to me uneasily. Jean is unwilling to give anymore information. He just drives with amazing skill through mountain roads, where there is hardly any traffic. I begin to have a different sense of him. He is sharing what he likes with us, these mountains; he has offered us the hospitality of his house. He is saying nothing more. But he is aware of the tension his offer has caused. Ekaterina is probably writing the scenario of, *Georgian diplomat kidnapped in Beirut,* headlines, and about her father who probably told her not to go, not to take risks, not to leave the city, to ring every day… that she has disregarded her embassy's advice of *danger in Lebanon.* I suppose that is the fear she will have to live with wherever she goes as a diplomat. I note she holds her mobile in her hand. Miriam has sensed her unease and has become agitated, or maybe she also has her fears. We don't know this man, we have spent one day being driven from Beirut to Baalbeq and now somewhere over the mountains, into darkness, somewhere we don't know. What happens if we need to escape? "Is there much traffic on this road?" she asks. "No," comes the easy noncommittal answer. He voices his invitation again. There are invisible electric sparks flashing all over the place, held breaths, furtive looks. "Yes, why not," I hear myself say, "is it far?" *No* comes the answer with a sense of relief and joy. The others are a little shocked and I read the looks. I have made a decision, which implicates all of us. And what if I am wrong? It doesn't make sense to me that he will try anything on. I get a feeling that he has begun to like us, having spent the day with us, haggling with us and for us, eating with us, cracking jokes we mostly miss and teasing us. I get him to talk about the house. It belongs to the family, his brothers live just above, it is his mother's house. "I stay there. I like it." The road is getting narrower and narrower and darker. "Is it still far?' asks Ekaterina; I'm not sure she realises her voice is trembling. Is he taking us to a remote place? It looks like it. The road becomes a dirt track. No other cars. No street lights. Some houses but no light in their windows, no sign of life. The tension is becoming unbearable. He stops in what looks like a driveway of a house in pitch darkness. I find I am totally at ease, totally relaxed. I don't get a sense of imminent danger, but I watch carefully.

Jean jumps out with a spring in his step. He is happy. There is a moment of absolutely no movement in the car. A state of being frozen stunned. I take a deep breath, open the door and say, *here we go*! I try to adjust my eyes to the dark. The others don't budge; they are glued to their seats. Jean has disappeared into the darkness. We seem to be at the edge of a terrace, some lights in the distance, a dark house on the next terrace up above us, no life anywhere. A cool air, fresh, crisp, even cold, which surprises me; down below, in Beirut, it is much warmer. I can hear some fiddling in the dark by the house. No idea what might emerge. A light comes on in the hallway, barely seeping out through the front door. I walk towards it; Miriam and Ekaterina come out of the car and follow.

It is a cold house. An unlived-in, house. A house where there is no human warmth. Is it deserted? "It is my mother's house," he says. *And where is she*? A chorus from us three. "She is in Beirut," he shrugs his shoulder. Eka and Miriam look at each other, has he lied to get us here? I watch them. "It is too cold here," he offers. "Everyone goes to Beirut for the winter and everyone comes back in the summer, when Beirut is too hot. Here is beautiful. But I like it in the winter here also. I can sleep. In Beirut, I can't sleep. I can't sleep."

Later we had tea he made from mint from the garden and ate tangerines he picked for us, with a photo family album on each lap, comparing images and his history, his whole existence captured. He had lived in Cyprus for seven years. We didn't offer him such a glimpse into our lives. At one stage he motioned for me to follow him, the others watched worried, albums on laps. How did I risk going outside into the dark with him? He led me to the tangerine trees to pick the fruit myself as I'd told him earlier in the day I preferred to pick them, gently guiding me away from the edge of the terrace, just in case, and lowering the branches for me so I could reach the fruit…

I ask him if his French lover lived here, with him, as I reach for the tangerines. He nods with that special sadness that descends on him out of the blue. Later he shows us his house.

284

Takes a torch to show us a room at the back. A bucket full of snails, sliding over each other. He kneels, holds the torchlight on them and watches. I make mocking lip-smacking sounds while Miriam holds onto her camera as she screws up her face. "Come, come!" he urges and shows us a plant cut up on a round metal tray. I crush a few leaves between my fingers and smell. A whole Cannabis plant, drying out on the floor. I smile. It was so obvious; it had been drying for a long time, hardly any scent left. Later, on the way back to Beirut, Miriam says, "Look at this," she holds up her hand. A sizable bag dangles, a couple of months' worth of happy smokes… "What do I do with it?" she says. I laugh remembering my student days when I first heard of the best Lebanese, alongside the Afghan and Moroccan, "You certainly can't take it back to Cyprus!" For the rest of the trip Miriam was trying to find a home to donate the 'gift' without hurting Jean's sensitivities by such rejection. Some of the clubs she frequented were into designer drugs accompanied by de-signer clothes and accessories; I don't think anyone would have even looked at the simple weed!

That morning we had driven over the mountains, covered in snow which had created zebra ridges above the Bekaa valley; lush and green, full of fruit trees on one slope and bare moun-tains on the other. "Two minutes, you are over the border! In Syria…" he clicks his thumb and forefinger to demonstrate the speed of getting there. Then veers left without reducing speed, towards Baalbeq on the single lane road. Roadblocks, militia-men and tanks interspersed along all the roads since we've left

Beirut. They look inside the car, over our faces, sometimes they ask for IDs but not ours. He probably tells them we are tourists; we are exempt. It is such an uneasy situation to be going through so many roadblocks and militiamen, all in different colour uniforms, all armed, cold black machine-guns strapped across their chests, in control of your life. There is a sense that life is worth so little. There is a sense that at any moment anything could happen and you could be dead. On the mountain sides, you notice dug-outs, walls with sentry points, holes to shoot from, you are at the end of the barrel of a gun pointing at you, watching you through a viewfinder... "Why so many tanks, guns, soldiers?" I ask. "Political problem," he says, resigned. Naked, rugged, stony, rocky hills, brown, not a shade of green, just different hues of browns and rusts, hills you drive through on this thin strip of road you cannot escape from. Later I learn that the UN report on the murder of Rafiq Hariri, killed by a bomb on Valentines Day in 2005, with twenty others, was due to be released in December 2010. It was delayed to allow Christmas and New Year celebrations and was due in the new year. Communal fighting was expected between the Sunnis and Hezbollah Shi'a, the government was certain to collapse, they said, and chaos would ensue. More killings were inevitable. Some thought it was not the Hezbollah but Syria that had organised the assassination. Was that so as to avoid inter-communal fighting, the new balance achieved in Lebanon by pointing the finger to an outside power?

For lunch he took us to an Armenian village on the way

back from Baalbeq, so neat and so pretty, almost a picture post-card. It was interesting to experience an Armenian village and not just an Armenian neighbourhood which is what I am famil-iar with in Cyprus. The Armenians run this village. They don't have to align themselves with some bigger community as part of the constitution. They exist in their own right! Or do they? Jean insisted we ate there, "The best chicken *sandwich*," which turned out to be a wrap or *dürüm,* in Turkish. Different names for the same thing. We tucked into it hungrily standing around. "I tell you, no?" comes from Jean between stuffed mouthfuls, happy that I took his advice on chicken and telling off Miriam and Eka for choosing fish which they couldn't eat. They didn't need his admonishment.

***

The mountain road seemed endless. The tension rose with every curve with every hope crushed of finding a street-light, a house, a sign that this was not a dark, deserted mountain road with no end. The held breaths, intense staring into darkness, the constantly shifting borders of the headlight beams revealing nothing but the same. A disappointing release of held breaths… for the cycle to be repeated. The sight of buildings, sparse street-lights create a sudden lightness in the car. No one on the streets. A little village with no lights. Shutters, doors shut. None of the normality of a village. No café, no bar. Suddenly some flag car-rying young people become visible. Jean scans around the car

rapidly. He is a little agitated. Is he looking for an escape route?
I've noticed him doing this constantly. His eyes scan all around
the car, especially the sides and rear, in any situation where
the car is forced to slow down. Suddenly there is a rush to our
car. He is forced to slow down because of the cars in front. He
becomes even more agitated, quick darts of the head, left then
right. Then he smiles. Large trays of chocolates push through
the car windows, precariously balanced. Wrapped in lurid reds,
greens, gold, silver, Yves Klein blue creating pyramids. Urged
to take more than one by the young people who had surrounded
our car, now smiling, laughing at us with curiosity. Miriam the
centre of attention with her blonde hair, broad smile, camera-
clicking finger. We notice all cars driving through the village
subjected to the same custom, ritual.

We get out of the car still a little cautious, on the insistence of the young people. We wander in the square, an impres-
sive church and connected buildings. Pose for photos. Become
the focus of jokes around language. Full of life, fourteen-, fif-
teen-, sixteen-year-olds. Young men and women with laughing eyes, light hearts, dreams of a future. An eighteen-year-old,
cropped hair, stockier than the others, enthusiastically directing
the scene, acting as 'leader', court jester. "Whose idea was this?
The chocolates?" we ask, thinking of an ancient custom perhaps.
"The Commander asked us to distribute chocolates," the leader
says. I realise some cars would not be passing through this village.

My repulsion of flags keeps drawing my eyes to the one
they are waving about, pose with, including the photos they in-

sist we become part of. A cedar tree. A version of the Lebanese flag, I think. A symbol of unity, an extension of the demands of thousands who marched not long ago, forcing the leaders to stop carnage between communities, faiths, ethnicities. A red circle around the cedar tree. Not quite the Lebanese flag. Although it uses the same colours and symbols. I look at Jean for clues. "They are OK," he says. "I know them." Later I learn it is the Christian militias' flag, the Phalangists, responsible for massacring thousands of women and children in the Shatilla and Sabra Palestinian refugee camps, surrounded by the Israeli army to prevent anyone from escaping, the same army that had also trained the Phalangists. And my stomach turns imagining the transformation of fifteen-sixteen-year-old chocolate offering hands into killers and rapists.

***

The White Virgin from the mountain called. We take the cable car to the top where she stands. Whitewashed concrete, I assume, but perhaps marble, with an external spiral staircase to just below her gazing eyes and lips, provocative arousal and innocence wrapped in one, only Michelangelo could attain in his David. Is this a *trans-ing* of him into the Virgin? The external staircase, a take on the Leaning Tower of Pisa. The enormous church, modern, filled with near enough a thousand worshippers more reminiscent of the rootless, grandiose American Christian Road Shows than a subtle Middle Eastern church, steeped in history and quaintness. The beautiful voices of the Christmas carol singers and songs, none I can recognise. Melodies and rhythms so far away from those I am familiar with in the West. And suddenly, I recognise Sufi melodies and Ghazals escaping from the polyphonous renditions, possibly Amharic or Maronite, I am uncertain. My thought that it was a Maronite church, later confirmed. I realise my experience of Christianity is primarily of the West and not of the Middle East where it was born. People milling around, some having arrived by cable car, others in posh four-wheel drives or Mercs, Land Rovers, Audis. Opulence and glitz, signs of big money arriving from the Saudis and other Arab billionaires who are behind the big building complexes as well as sustaining the economy. They rent large suites in hotels or luxury apartment blocks, for years. All stand empty except for the short periods when the billionaires arrive at their Beirut playground of women, drinks and casinos. Good Muslims that they are, they come for prostitution, alcohol and gambling while back home, they can stone women to death for falling in love, having a relationship with a married man or being raped.

All under the benevolent eye of the blue-robe-clad Madonna, the all-forgiving. I want one of those kitsch statuettes, arms extended on either side, welcoming, with a tiny red light bulb in different sizes to match any purse. In the gift shop. The symbolic embodiment of the perfect woman; pure, virginal and a whore. She would feel at home on my mantelpiece, above the fireplace, in Nicosia.

***

290

Months later in Famagusta… I am still furious with the UN man. He had attached himself to us, on our first day, as we were looking for the entrance to the American University of Beirut, from the shore side. Miriam had had a *narghile* at the café on the rocks full of head-scarfed women doing the same. Light conversation ensued as we found ourselves walking around back streets to the visitors' entrance we were directed to. We walked in the University grounds, watched students, smiled at the 'installations' of forgotten or lost/found items since the early 1930s-40s in glass cases at the entrance; watches, reading and sun glasses, pens, lighters. All with a silent and maybe lost story. He joined us at a small restaurant, *tabakh*. While Eka was telling the story of a determined and capable Georgian queen who was called a king, he held his palms up as though holding something big and round. Astonished, we realised he was making a gesture for big breasts. Silent, we looked at each other.

Then, I just couldn't hold it back; I was livid! I let rip. I couldn't even remember precisely what I had said to him! Miriam, Suzie (half-Syrian half-American) and Eka months later in Cyprus, reconstruct the story for me: after challenging him, I had made a crass masturbating motion with my hand around my groin, holding an imaginary penis, *so if it was a king you would have done this?* My anger seems to have erased my response to the provocation! I remember thinking, what shit UN man! And maybe typical! He couldn't let it pass without bringing sex into the conversation in such crass manner with three intelligent women travelling together. His mind was trapped between his legs. Did he think he was going to pull us into his innuendo or that we would choose embarrassed silence, both providing him with some sexual titillation? UN internal sex scandals, involvement in prostitution in war zones flashed before my eyes. Our saviours? He was on his way to Iraq as part of a team to sort it out; *infra-structure*, he had mumbled. *Economics* he had said. *Micro- or macro-?* I had asked, which led him to express surprise at knowledge I should not posses as an 'attractive woman' and even worse that I had a political stance on the illegal invasion, plundering and destruction of Iraq and the continued attempts to go fuck it up even further with 'experts' like him! From Canada...

***

London, Jan 28, 2011 - Beirut thoughts still rumble... Demanding to be written but even more so to be finished. Maybe to morph into a new object, action, phase. From experience into an article with photos secured for posterity. Beyond the transience of experiences, thoughts, emotions, analyses, to be frozen forever.

I've just spent a brief time at the Tate Modern with Miriam - who is on the conveyor belt of getting her sister into marriagehood - looking at the transient works of Orezco. Mexican artist/ photographer who seemed to have produced his most radical, pushing-the-boundaries work in his early thirties (born 1962, exciting work 1992-1997). His latest circles of various colours and ellipses, in gold leaf. What happens to artists who at one stage of their lives turned the ordinary and the gutter into gold and as they become 'establishment' or in their ardour to become so, end up painting in gold-leaf, turning art into the sewage of the gutter?

Back to Beirut... "I feed the ants," he says, as I look more and more amused by his line of thought. Jean-Paul Guiragossian pauses, deep in thought and imagery. He was introduced as, "And this is Jean-Paul..." an assumption which did not find resonance with me. I had no idea who Jean-Paul was, especially as I catch his cursory glance in our direction, two women, strangers who had just walked thorough the gallery doors. He is preoccupied with his laptop. We are whisked off on a tour of the Guiragossian Gallery. About fifty minutes later, we are on the way out, saying our goodbyes near the exit, to our host, his younger sister, Manuella, as she has another appointment. "Would you like tea?" comes from the body with the laptop to my surprise, shattering his seeming indifference and setting us off on a journey of stories and questions which lead to even more stories we were not prepared for, over the next four hours.

I watch him for about twenty minutes without saying a word. Miriam is asking questions. He is answering to please the guests. She puts him at ease with her polite, non-intrusive questions. He is aware of my silence and watchful eye and that I am taking everything in. In a sense, I feel he is trapped in my silence and aware of my watching every move, eye flicker, finger tap, glance. He has pulled me into his story but he has trapped himself in my unflinching attention.

I asked a question, I can't even remember what or even his answer... then another. His gaze turns from Miriam to me. He is hooked on my questions and I don't aim them deliberately or plan them. They stumble on my lips then just fall out. I watch Jean-Paul's reaction. He wants to continue the superficiality of the conversation but he begins to fall deeper into places he doesn't want to go.

"Me? I feed the ants. I can't even kill *them*. When they come into my house and they invade everything and crawl all over, I don't crush them. I don't exterminate them. I don't zap them with poison. I just take some food, walk around the room, until I find where they enter, how they enter my kitchen, then I put the food there... So they don't have to walk so far. And that way, they stay there. I contain them where they come in, instead of walking all over my kitchen looking for crumbs." I smile. It reminds me of my brother in London who last summer having been invaded by ants, put hard watermelon skins close to the holes of the ants outside the building. When they lodged themselves into the thin layer of red flesh in their thousands, feasting on the sweet juice, he took the boat-shaped skins to the bottom of the garden, two-hundred meters away from the house, liberating himself and his kitchen on the first floor of the house from their invasion.

He pauses after he talks about the ants having explained his philosophy of life. In Turkish there is a saying, "He can't even hurt an ant!" I shift in my chair amused by his response in a country where probably almost everyone has been involved in or witnessed killings… I think I had asked that and how he ended up abroad. He looks at me straight and says, "I watched my best friend die in my arms…" he winces in memory of the moment. I silently gasp. Hold my breath. He describes a typical love between childhood friends, living through the innocence of youth. The beauty and kindness of his friend. How inseparable they were. How he was from a poor background but had made it. How he was the cleverest of the bunch and many boys looked up to him. How the poor neighbourhood adored him; he was their inspiration, role model, the elders praised him and looked upon him as their hope… that others could also make it out of the neighbourhood. He was studying medicine, second year.

"Then one night we were walking to some place, arm in arm, joking laughing. The war had started but there was no danger where we were, not that night anyway. He was telling me about this girl who liked him… was there anyone who didn't?" he asks with pleasure in his voice, arms outstretched. "He was so kind and so special." A pause. "As we were going around a corner, suddenly a shot rings out. We dived onto the ground. I looked quickly to see if I could see anyone. In those days everyone could get hold of a gun, too many guns about. Snipers! Everywhere! We crouched. I am scared. Our hearts are thumping. I carefully stretch my head around the corner to see if anything was there, all the time so scared and nervous, talking to my friend aloud. I turn around and there is no sound from him. Nothing! He is silent. He is on the ground, slumped. I grab him. Nothing. I don't understand. Then I notice the blood. And I am nearly out of my mind! The impossibility of it! How could he be shot? We had seen no one, we had heard no one! I was beside myself. I couldn't believe what had happened. I held him in my arms, talking to him, shaking him, hoping he would open his eyes. I started to scream. More to wake him up than anything else. But he died. I was devastated. He died in my arms."

After a short pause he continues with the story. His friends and the neighbourhood were determined to find the killer and take revenge. After a few days they heard that the boyfriend of the girl was the killer; he had confessed in tears. After some drinking, he found a gun and had apparently followed them. "Nothing had happened between them!" Jean-Paul insists after all these years. "And this mechanic boy was such a gentle guy, he wouldn't hurt a fly. He was so quiet and gentle." He describes how when the news went out that the medical student was shot, the whole neighbourhood was mobilised to find the killer. He talks of their shock when they discovered what had happened. "The boy was so hurt that she was abandoning him in favour of the star; he just wanted to show my friend he was upset. He found a gun, not because he wanted to kill my friend, because he loved him too, they were also friends, but just to express his pain. Apparently he followed us after we all had spent some time together in the sports club. He broke down and told some people the story. He had shot in the air to draw attention to himself. But what he didn't realise was that he was standing under a balcony,' Jean-Paul is holding up his hand into the air simulating a gun with his fingers, "when he pulled the trigger it bounced off the balcony; there were two metal supports under the balcony. The bullet ricocheted against the metal and went through the body of my friend just as we were walking along arms around each other." He slumps in his seat. Silent, he stares at the floor.

"I was devastated. I wanted revenge. I vowed I would kill whoever it was. Me, kill?" he asks in disbelief, gently. "So many others felt like me. We went into the neighbourhood looking for him. We were still shocked having discovered who it was, this lovable gentle person. But I had vowed I'd kill him. We discovered he had left the neighbourhood. He was in hiding. We then discovered he had gone to the mountains. We tracked him down. We got into cars and went to find him. It was in a deserted village. Because of the fighting people had fled to Beirut and other places. We found the house and broke in. It was all dark. He could've shot us as we were breaking in... but nothing. Someone found him and called me... I'd told them he was mine! When I saw him in the corner of the room I was still fuming. I wanted revenge, so badly! I was shaking. My friends looked at me and stayed behind. I walked up to him. He was cowering in a corner on his knees, curled up. I looked at him. I looked and I couldn't do anything. When I saw him, I didn't recognise him; it wasn't the same boy. He was big, chubby like a cuddly bear and gentle. This person in front of me was not the same boy. He was totally wasted. Skin and bone, his skin sallow, almost like a skeleton, eyes sunken, dirty, dishevelled hair. He was so pitiful. Suddenly I felt so sorry for him. My heart broke. He broke down and started to cry. He told me he didn't intend to kill our friend… just to show him how hurt he was. He didn't want to kill him because he also loved him. I just looked at him and I couldn't do anything. I couldn't pull the trigger. I couldn't beat him up. I just turned my back and walked out. Other friends, surprised, asked if I wasn't going to… I told them to leave him alone and not to touch him. I shouted and told them no one was to touch him." They left him in that deserted house and went back to Beirut.

"What became of him?" I ask after a while. He tells me years later he traced him, when he himself had left Beirut because of the wars coming back about seven-eight years ago. He discovered that his family managed to get him out of Beirut. "He now lives in the US," he says, "West Coast, somewhere…" Ironically, Jean-Paul tells us he spent years in San Francisco, in poverty, as an artist. "He married, I hear; has three children. Maybe I'll see him someday…" is his closure of the killing of his friend. And I sat, my whole body tense, my mind quickly running through the nightmare of friends killing each other at the age of seventeen-eighteen or even younger, becoming victims both in being killed and becoming killers and losing what it means to live their youth and the 'normality' of non-war regions or cities of the world. Later, Elias Khoury's mesmerising *Yalo*, reminds me of how some young people try to escape their Kafkaesque situations,

> *I ran away from the war because I could no longer understand. No, I wasn't a coward … and I left the war because I'd got fed up with it. At the beginning I*

was like all boys. I wanted to defend Lebanon. Then I discovered I was fighting other poor people like me that I would remain a stranger whatever I did ... When I discovered I was a man, I fled to Paris and I suffered, and Khawaja Michel Salloum rescued me (while begging on the streets) and gave me a job as a guard at the Villa Gardenia in Ballona.

It took me back to the wastage of youth in Cyprus in the 1960s and 1970s wars, and even to the ghettos of civilised big cities like London, where I've spent much of my life trying to throw life-lines to young people sucked into gangs to shoot or stab each other on the flimsiest of reasons - just like the Lebanese boy, because his girlfriend happened to express her admiration or fancy for the medical student – in the inner cities of the West, the wrong look, the wrong colour, wrong language, wrong religion is good enough for a murder... and another gang fight!

✳✳✳

December 31, 2010. Nicosia. The last day of 2010. And I seem to want to be with myself... Since my return, Beirut sounds are knocking on my ears, images are plastered over my eyes. My vision struggles to get through Beirut images, to reach the 'ordinary' images of Nicosia. The Beirut sounds so dominant! Arabic and the languages I can't make sense of, except for a few words, remnants of the influence of Arabic in Ottoman Turkish, survivors of the pogroms of the *Türk Dil Kurumu* (Turkish

299

Language Authority). I smile when I catch the individual word in a turbulent sea or fast-moving river of Arabic or Armenian as though I've caught a big fish... gleeful that I have managed it in such fast-moving language waters. Then I wonder about other languages I've missed because my ears are not attuned to the nuances... of Egyptian, Syrian or Palestinian Arabic. There must also be Maronite somewhere, plenty of it. Amharic? But is it Arabic-based as that of Cyprus? And then, French, as once it was a French dominion. How easily layers of society switch into perfect French or English. And they have all left those lands, gone back and left again, packing a bag and leaving for Canada, Greece, Cyprus, Britain, France, Australia. I even came across them in The Gambia and Jamaica where the locals thought I was Lebanese.

My confusion deepens trying to work out the religions. Can I discern the differences without reference to a book/internet? I scan the names of churches, mosques, places of worship for clues. For me a guessing game but for others a matter of life and death not just an academic pastime or simple curiosity. The Lebanese killed and were killed based on religion, no longer merely a private choice of worship but a yardstick for identifying targets to kill. My brain resists; my soul even more so. I am looking for logic, reason, where none exists. It is a matter of belief... Some of those people walking the streets of Beirut, around me, were murderers! And not so different to those in Cyprus.

Our recent most devastating wars are about the same age; the invasion of Cyprus in 1974, the Lebanese war, 1975. Many

300

came as refugees to Cyprus. They have managed to hold onto one country; ours is divided and may stay so in my lifetime. But the extent, the enormity, the duration in Lebanon, overwhelms me. And the reason or reasons? As many justifications as perpetuated deaths and constructed myths… Unjustifiable acts of brutality, of becoming brutalised! I am aware that my search for reasons is partly to come to terms with what happened in Cyprus and the perpetuation of myths by the very mythmakers.

In Cyprus, I am dealing with two communities, polarities within a framework of the denial of all other existing communities. In Beirut, the 'polarities' perhaps are the tips of a six- or eight-pointed star. I try to identify the groups on religious grounds then superimpose ethnic groupings as the same religious group can have several ethnicities and vice-versa… the Palestinians can be Christians and Muslims. In a conflict which side are they forced to take? Or does their ethnicity obliterate religious distinctions? I draw boxes on a sheet of paper, Christians on one side, Muslims on the other. My arrows come out of each, naming the groups I have managed to identify. So far the Christians are Maronites, Armenians, Greek Orthodox (who may or may not be Greek), Greek Catholics, Catholics, Assyrians/Syriacs (Suryani in Turkish, who I had come across in Holland in 1984 while doing research; refugees from southern Turkey), Copts, Latins, Anglicans and other familiar Western Christians in small numbers. The Muslims seem to have Shi'a, Sunni, Alevi. Then the Druze, a prominent force in politics, many people could not tell me much about their religion, some said Christian, others

Muslim. "They become whatever situation they find themselves in..." was a short-cut explanation. I've heard the same said of the Roma in other parts of the world. Much later I learn they are Muslim of Ismaili origin, esoteric with eclectic beliefs and different lifestyles not necessarily devout or practising, but loyal. Later still, I am surprised to discover that the Druze and Cypriotturkish communities, especially males, share a common rare genetic heritage. And much later, I learnt of the seventeen religious groups. And I enjoyed the adventures and non-conformity of Sarah named after Sarah Bernhardt by her Druze grandfather, and learnt much more through Alamaddine's novel, *I, the Divine*,

> *I met Fadi on my first day in class... his first question to me was "Are you a lesbian?" My response was swift: "Your mother's cunt, you brother of a whore." The Lebanese dialect is filled with delectable curses, a luscious language all its own, of which I was a true poet, trained by none other than my father. He thought children's use of adult curse words tremendously amusing and trained all his children in the art of insult. I grew up an avid practitioner.*

I attempt superimposing layers of ethnicities on religions. Lebanese, Palestinians, Syrians, Assyrians/Syriacs, Arabs, Armenians, Maronites, empire remnants of Russians and French, recent arrivals from Sri Lanka, Philippines, Turkey, Kurdistan, Iraq. In addition to the thousands who arrive for work, to escape wars, to be educated at universities with gateways to the West, including the American University of Beirut, work in banking and finance (the Switzerland of the Middle East) or live away from oppressive home countries (in the Paris of the Middle East). A city of hope, a metropolis of the Levant and from time immemorial unmatched... And later reading Hala Kawtharani, an Arab New Yorker, born in Lebanon, made me feel a little better,

> *I still don't understand Lebanon. I don't understand the relationships between its parties and its politicians. I don't understand the articles in the newspapers. I don't understand who loves who and who hates who. I don't understand why one war started and another came to an end, why young men in the streets carry knives in their pockets, or why they call Lebanon the Switzerland of the East and Beirut the Paris of the Middle East... All the talk of the Switzerland of the East was a mirage.*

And if diversity is the norm and has been unbridled for centuries, am I now entrapping myself in problematising it through the value systems of predominantly monolingual, mono-cultural, single-faith discourses of northern Europe? Even though I know they have not been as mono-cultural as they wish to be portrayed. I have lived amongst them for over forty-five years. Empire societies versus nation statehood philosophies. I do not need to make sense of diversity, potentially explosive and yet essentially normal. And who is Lebanese? Echoes as to who is Cypriot, British, French, German... Constructed definitions imposed by outsiders or insiders. All within nationhoods and geographic borders. I am reminded of my boredom at the assumed superior knowledge or insights espoused by some British or German person challenging my stubborn definition of myself as Cypriot, since the 1960s. "You can't be Cypriot, you can only be Turkish or Greek. There is no such thing as Cypriot!" Is there such a thing as Lebanese? When does a young man with Syrian heritage in the Christian militia become Lebanese? When does a Palestinian born in Shatilla, become Lebanese?

I am amused by the Lebanese immigration officer looking at my British passport, on my way out at Beirut Airport.

" You are Turkish…" he says.

"No, I am Cypriot." I reply taken aback by his need to put me into some category.

"But where were you born?"

"Nicosia," my response is assertive.

"But your parents, where?" comes his certainty that he knows.

"Cyprus!" now a sense of agitation and impatience enters my voice that he stops his line of questioning, searching for something, positive or negative in my categorisation, "…and my grandparents!" I add not giving him an opportunity to continue. An imperceptible smile develops and lingers at the corner of his mouth. I respond in my thoughts, *You and I may share confusions of identity around us, but I've worked it out. Why do you insist on trying to fit me into a box? I've learned to smash them long ago.*

***

Months later... The deliberately exploited and provoked Beirut conflicts linger in my mind; there is much detail I cannot reach. Its end game is absolute devastation and aftershocks; the repeated cycle, its driving force. Always restarting with a vengeance between other groups or from the outside, if there happens to be an internal lull. Constantly shifting alliances and allegiances, erasing held values, customs, respect, honesty, kindness, compassion, love, cherishing life... everything human and humane becomes a commodity, trampled or derided. Unholy alliances of religion, ethnicity and class become possible.

The indiscriminate brazen bombing by Israel of South Lebanon and parts of crowded Beirut or invasion, always without sanctions. Their bombs are selective; they don't kill children and women! And in any case, it is the fault of men who leave the women and children in those high-rise blocks of flats where they live and go fight elsewhere or go into hiding or were long ago deported...

In *Mornings in Jenin*, Amal looking for her husband and deported brother holds me in a vice, forcing me to experience the sheer brutality, repeated traumas, the enormity of war crimes gone unpunished with the collusion of the world leaders, against innocent people, mere 'collateral damage' in wars. After intense bombing for two months and invasion on 6 June 1982,

> *By August the results were 17,500 civilians killed, 40,000 wounded, 400,000 homeless and 100,000 without shelter. Prostrate, Lebanon lay devastated and raped, with no infra structure for food or water.*

Israel claimed it had been forced to invade for peace.
"We are here for peace. This is a peacekeeping mis-
sion."

The ludicrous argument of war for peace brings echoes of
the invasion of Cyprus by Turkey, July 1974; the continued occupation is referred to as a, "Peace Operation".

"Decades later, still searching for the fate that forgot me,"
Amal continues, *"I sifted through the accounts of peace. In his*
epic memoir, Pity the Nation: The Abduction of Lebanon, *Brit-*
ish correspondent, Robert Fisk describes phosphorous Israeli shells:
Dr. Shammaa's story was a dreadful one and her voice broke as
she told it, 'I had to take the babies and put them in buckets of
water to put out the flames,' she said. 'When I took them out half
an hour later, they were still burning. Even in the mortuary they
smouldered for hours.' Next morning Amal Shammaa took the
tiny corpses out of the mortuary for burial. To her horror, they
again burst into flames."

Invasion in 2006 leads to 1,700 dead, one million displaced. Figures, which strangle my mind…

When Israel stops… Syria starts bombing from the East
or north then invades and decides the outcome of 'free' elections! Both of these countries only recently withdrew, Syria in
2005 and Israel in 2006. Cyprus is still under occupation.

The perception that more or less every MP is or has been
involved in murders, including Ministers… More than once, I've
heard the story of the leading Christian militiaman who went
into a church and shot dead six people, at point-blank range and

yet became a government Minister. A fact confirmed later in London while browsing through old articles of Robert Fisk and later still, discovering it in the pages of Ghada Samman's *Beirut Nightmares,*

> *... it happened whenever she received a visit from a certain influential bey, who always arrived surrounded by bodyguards who would stand waiting for him outside the door. The moment he entered the room she would feel a heavy 'presence' weighing on her chest ... She wasn't certain if it was because of a rumour she'd heard to the effect that he'd murdered several people in a local place of worship without batting an eyelid, or whether it was...*

Fact fictionalised; the safest way to record it for posterity. What I do. A painful reminder that murderers in Cyprus are also walking around free; hailed as heroes of the 'Cause' and rewarded, some as MPs, others as Ministers. "And people still vote for them!" says Jean, frustrated, the Lebanese communications manager who has opted to live in Cyprus for the past nineteen years. Will he ever return, I wonder? Do people deserve the political representatives (not leaders!) they get? Probably! Unless individuals decide no longer to collude and demand they are tried as war criminals and murderers that they are, they will continue to leer at the cowardice of the majority! There is a need to redefine heroes and heroines, based on humanitarian acts, taking care of the human not that of war and murders. I don't need to be told it is about controlling and appropriating resources and wealth… I hear the woman narrator of *Beirut Nightmares* echoing my thoughts,

> *No one is innocent in a guilty society … there can be*
> *no neutrality in a society devoid of justice. There can*
> *be no neutrality in the city of nudity and the veil, the*
> *city of hunger and surfeit. Those who remain neutral*
> *are the principal offenders. The silent majority is the*
> *criminal majority.*

I keep hearing myself arguing the same points in relation to Cyprus, human trafficking, prostitution, gambling, the Mafia. How do people move beyond the present and envisage and create a different future outside the 'traditional' traps, which lead to death or cul-de-sacs?

***

Second day in Lebanon… We are on our way to Baalbeq, north east of Beirut, about a hundred and fifty kilometres over the mountains. As we climb the terrain changes and so does the width and look of the road. No longer the well-manicured plants, gardens, pavements, buildings, witnesses and products of wealth. Poverty begins to peep, muscle through the wealthy cousins and after a while dominates. Drabness rules. The colour has gone. The flashy, glitzy billboards no longer loom over the road. The houses have a sense of being temporary, no carefully designed gardens, well-ordered roads; a mishmash of everthing dominates.

Then the Ayatollah appears. In the middle of the road.

You can't escape his gaze; he follows you everywhere. Dressed in his long black *jelabiah*. Is it called that in Lebanon? It looks as though it is flying caught in the winds from the sea, so far inland. His hands emerge from the black cloth, maybe there is a finger extended, making a point. The eyes demand, the eyes cajole, the eyes expect... young men to act in particular ways. They demand, women will behave, in particular ways, they will obey. He has the authority to say so on Earth interpreting the Book. And in bleak places with very little to do but watch in awe the wealth of others symbolised by Mercedes, BMWs and four-wheelers zooming past this highway, while they sit by the roadside, selling sheepskins to tourists prepared to pay fifty dollars because they have no idea of local prices unless their driver says ten dollars or even better ten Lebanese pounds and whips the skin off the barbed wire on the side of the road, they will believe him, the Ayatollah with the manly, urging, demanding eyes and dignified wise beard. Especially, if it is his clan bringing in medicines, schools, food, support to those who cannot even bury their dead. And, who are the only ones to defeat Israel in South Lebanon. When the call comes, some will go.

I watch the Ayatollah zoom past in the middle of the road. No other image competes with his. But aren't images idolatry in Islam? So why this huge image, cardboard cut-outs of the Ayatollah every hundred meters or so on the way to Baalbeq? Has he no shame being seen with the only other image allowed, that of the wedding-dressed bride leaning from the side of the road on a huge billboard? But she is on the side, above an ugly concrete building, lit up; he is in the middle of the road where trees and flowers would be seen in the West, providing protection from the glare of oncoming traffic. The Ayatollah wants the limelight… no bashfulness, no shame… pure politics!

He accompanies us all the way to Baalbeq. He doesn't leave lest we lose our way, take the wrong turning, go off the rails… Our driver is the other one keeping us safe after the initial hesitation that we might have ended up with a reckless driver. He came recommended and arranged by the two bankers who took us to dinner last night. As the oncoming traffic approaches at high speed, he puts his foot down trying to overtake a slower minibus in front. We are new in the country. Our sense of traffic is that of the West or, nearest to it in the Middle East, Cyprus, although each has experiences across the world. We all lean back, put our foot on the imagined brake pedal, tighten our bodies, wait for the imminent impact… He swings by, glides more likely, in front of the minibus. *Woow!* is accompanied with the intake of deep breaths, and *that was close!* He just drives his attention on the road, giving no sign of acknowledging our fear. I momentarily question if this is a show for the three women tourists and conclude that it is not. He knows this road; he has been down it with hundreds of tourists but also for other reasons. He knows it only too well… and as the day progresses it becomes more obvious that he is someone special.

We wander around the Roman ruins in Baalbeq. I take my time feeling the stones, which challenge my imagination, lying on their sides after earthquakes in ancient times, with radii one-and-a-half times my height. My fingers can't reach the top. A little further away columns stand erect created by these carved boulders of marble. My knees shake uncontrollably standing at the edge of a high rock looking up at the three columns reaching into the sky. My ears are blasted by the mosque opposite, six loud speakers attached to the minaret, transforming it into a bizarre structure of science siction tower representations, circa 1950s. Someone demands I take notice of his presence. Me and the whole town of Baalbeq. Not withstanding my transitory presence, the sound must be inscribed in my mind. I must not leave this town without registering the words of Allah, whatever religion I am immersed in, or dare to defend my atheism with dignity. This is the town to which Robert Fisk travelled in March 1985 looking for his kidnapped journalist friend, Terry Anderson,

> ... where we guessed he would be taken by his kid-
> nappers. We handed out his photograph to militia-
> men, shopkeepers, gunmen, Syrian soldiers and Is-
> lamic extremists... years later I learnt I had given his
> picture to one of his kidnappers, earnestly entreating
> the stunned man to find my friend.

It is the town of an annual jazz festival and where Um Kalthoum left not a dry eye in Lebanon during her concerts.

> These days I avoid Umm Kalthoum, but not because I
> hate her. I avoid her because every time I hear that Egyp-
> tian bitch, I cry hysterically. Sarah says in, I, the Divine.

First, a prayer blasts my ears, then a call to prayer I am

familiar with, from Cyprus and my travels across Muslim countries. Then a harrowing, hammering, harassing, berating voice reaching a hysterical pitch assaults me, demanding I take notice of it, rather than of the remains of thousands of years of 'civilizations' and their Gods, and temples built in their honour reaching up to the skies. It calls me to war, to kill, embellished in the will of Allah, revenge, promise of Heaven and the rest... He does not let off. This hysterical frustrated man sent off young men to their deaths. My hair stands on end, not only because of its fatalistic connotations but also the inevitability of its attraction, especially for the poor, dispossessed young people, the refugees, the unwanted. Someone wants them, makes them feel important, significant, not an ant to be crushed on the pavements and roadsides, while trying to eke out a living surrounded by such opulence; someone is promising justice... so close, in Beirut.

***

Flashbacks come of walking in Downtown with Miriam, amidst the rapid building of skyscrapers, constant noise of caterpillar diggers, cranes swinging across vast building-sites, their scoops carrying building workers with a cement mixer on their lap, precariously balanced on long steel cables, thirty floors high above. A swing no one wants to be on... Still there, working in the light of generators, on another day, when we go past after midnight. Miriam takes a photo of the 'swing' and the workers who wave and smile, happy being deemed artistic enough to be photographed in grey concrete splashed clothes, hands, faces. She takes me along to choose a dress for the impending wedding of her sister in London, from the exclusive Elias Saab *haut couture* house amongst the new emerging quarter of the rich rising from the rubble of war.

After a quick look at the clothes, I am outside; not my scene. While waiting, I am drawn to the stones of the surrounding buildings. I touch the light pink sandstone. I can't tell if it is new or newly polished, no matter how carefully I look. There is something unsettling about this old building, I can't work out. The brain stumbles on, is confused by the information my fingertips and eyes provide. I move onto a building I can handle; no confusion about its origins, steel construction and glass. I am captivated. I like it, but like the art piece in the foyer even more, in perfect contrast yet perfect harmony with the steel. Reds, blues, blacks, yellows, abstract thick lines reminding me of sacred objects. A totem pole or even a modern mummy. I want to know what the building is. No sign I can see, no plaque. I am convinced it is an art gallery; I'd been looking for one since my arrival. I walk over to the security guards, the area their haven, private or public, and ask pointing at the building. They are puzzled, look at each other, at the building then back at me. I am about to make fun of the incompetence of security guards unaware of the nature of buildings they guard. "A bank," comes the puzzled response. Of course, what else! Later at dinner with the two bank directors, I smile as they describe the location of their bank with the modern hieroglyphic mummy in the foyer. An art piece by Jean Dubuffet. They tell us the bank workers are still waiting for the boss to unwrap the bandages and reveal the real sculpture, the real piece of art within.

The bankers tell their stories of how each time there is a war, they pack and leave. Later I discover the literature is littered with the Lebanese trying to leave, to anywhere! They come back after some years, trying to pick up the pieces knowing they will pack up and leave again. *Where to,* I ask? *Anywhere!* Each time, a different place, whichever country will take them. "It is not *if* there will be another war; it is *when*?" Abel says. And I look at him speechless. There are no words or solace for such a statement and knowledge. They know! And they keep building, high, higher, offices, apartment blocks, shopping centres, galleries, restaurants, hotels, casinos, hospitals, schools, knowing they will be bombed and destroyed! Almost a frenzy of building, racing with time… The bombs the guns will come, there will be no electricity, water, petrol, telephones. Roads will be blocked by collapsed high-rise offices, apartment blocks, all reduced to ruin in a few minutes, just rubble. There will be no food. Just paralysis! They will be stopped, searched, humiliated, beaten up, blackmailed, killed by little nobodies with mega egos who become somebodies through the barrel of an AK47, seizing their moment of 'power' knowing full well it is temporary and transient. They will lose it just as fast reverting to being nobodies. How do people live with, stay sane through such destruction?

And what of the artists I search for desperately aware that *they are both instigators of and fodder to revolutions…* as the

314

woman narrator of *Beirut Nightmares* also knows.

Miriam and I find them... *I feed the ants*, Jean-Paul's paintings are bouquets and clusters of flowers in brilliant colours, mocking the superficiality of Beiruti society, those who do not want to see the carnage, bomb craters, destruction, gaps in between, corruption, immorality, absurdity. For acting as though life is a "bunch of roses", no stink anywhere in Beirut. "I'll give you flowers!" is his challenge. There is a madness, desperation in the gaiety of his work, a sense of Isherwood's pre-World War II Berlin.

Dazzling colourful skeletons of mangled buildings is Manuella's, his sister's response. "I refuse to paint the remnants of war, the grey, bombed-out buildings," she says as a stance of resistance against being depicted as a painter of war, as though painters of Beirut should only be painting the carnage of wars. And yet, amongst her brilliant multi-coloured structures of fairy-tale castles, puzzles, I wonder if she can see that she paints carnage and skeletons of buildings in dazzling pinks, purples, orange, blues and yellows.

Plays with sexuality, gayness, gender cross-over... The Palestinian contemporary painter, exhibiting at a prestigious art gallery in the middle of a modern complex of skyscrapers, glass, concrete, with a sprinkling of modern water fountains, lit by extra-modern underwater Yves Klein blue lights. Large canvasses depict large beings in agony, frightened expressions of pain, torture, confusion, possibly pleasure, duality, double existence, identity, represented in two heads coming out of a single body or

315

trunk at times in contorted postures. I am gut-wrenched!

In the gallery opposite hangs the work of contemporary Lebanese artists including photo-based nudity. Is this a world away, from Hezbollah-controlled areas in the same city or from Baalbeq? A city living on the edge. The edge is not always a descent into war.

We set off to find the new Beirut Art Centre, after haggling with the impish, perpetually smiling, off the street, taxi driver who agreed to take us but is clueless as to its location. Housed in the old industrial area, under busy flyovers, it is rapidly turning into a hub of an Arts and Media industry. Chris Marker, French artist and filmmaker, had an inspirational show on. Such a political commentator! I carry away two eloquent quotes from the December 2010, *Par quatre chemins* exhibition, we saw,

The mindlessness of power sometimes creates a memory from what was meant to be amnesia.

Gods and heroes will seek asylum in art collections like political refugees in foreign embassies.

***

As we approach a crossroads a shrill whistle goes off. An armed traffic policeman is waving his arms. Behind him stands a military or militiaman, an AK hangs from his shoulder; I can't tell the difference between a militia and a military man. Someone in uniform is the closest I can get. Both are watching something intently. I look in the direction of their gaze. Just then a car makes a sharp left turn, away from them. Just as I was expecting him to drive away, he does a full circle in their full gaze, in front of them in the middle of the road across both lanes, blocking the traffic in both directions. The traffic stops. Jean, our driver, watches the scene with pure attention; nothing escapes him. He is silent, his body is taut, every muscle is ready for whatever action will be required. The outcome of this showdown is not certain… gunshots may come from any direction, from the young man in the car, from the armed traffic policeman or the militiaman behind him, standing in front of an armoured vehicle, from a tank blocking a side-street, or from anyone in one of the cars at a standstill in either direction. The young man in the car is on a high, no one will stop him. He will not be caught. The wheels screech, the tyres burn, smoke billows from the tarmac, he holds onto the steering wheel, almost locks it permanently in a tight left. The car keeps skidding, turning around and around. He is going nowhere! He keeps circling in a cloud of screeches, daring the policeman and militiaman to take action, to do anything! They don't, but watch intently. There are nervous breathing and muffled comments in our car. I say nothing. I am watching with held breath. I am watching Jean who is also silent. I keep my eyes on the swirling screeching car and the militiamen. It will take only one second, one move for the whole thing to blow up into a disaster. And all those in the know are aware of it. Someone's nerves have to give… Is he a suicide bomber? Then, after about three-four full circles, the young man behind the wheel speeds off still screeching, burning tyres in the opposite direction. I notice Jean exhales, his hands on the wheel relax, flex. I know my life is in his hands. Whatever action he chooses to take will impact on my life. *Nerves of steel,* that stupid phrase is my reality, as I watch him.

"Why didn't the police do something? Why did they just stand there? Crazy!" a subdued comment in our car. Jean doesn't reply, he carefully picks up speed and moves away from the spot. Did he hear? I think he did but his choice of not answering betrays a knowledge and experience he doesn't think he needs to share. "What could they do?" I ask after a while. "They could not stop him. Whatever mind-frame he was in, no one was going to stop him. He was making precisely that point; he knew no one could do anything." They are not convinced. "And they can't shoot at him. Any accident would block this road, both ways... it would be chaos! The city would be paralysed." I try to imagine what it could have been about and thought of that one second it would have taken to turn the situation into a blood bath.

Overlooking the Downtown area I notice a church, glittering, no sign of age on its stones. A Greek Orthodox church, I am told. Beautiful. Then another. "Armenian," says Jean. He watches my eyes through the mirror move towards a lapis blue domed mosque at the other end of the square dwarfing the two churches, "and Hariri had that one built," comes the quick answer. As we go past a square piece of wasteland - a sight I was familiar with in the 1970s Hackney, East London with signs of inner city decay and neglect - "And that's where they blew him up; they left it as a memoriam," continues Jean's matter-of-fact commentary still following my eyes through the mirror. No love lost between them. The Prime Minister of the time, Rafiq Hariri, a Sunni. Later I learn that the PM is a Sunni, the President a Maronite and the Speaker of the House is Shi'a; political power-sharing amongst religions. I wonder how the economic power sharing spans out.

An elliptical building on stilts comes into view a little down the road. Not a building anymore, a grey concrete structure with steel rods poking through. "A cinema... that used to be a cinema," continues Jean, "They have left it as a symbol of the war." I think of the bombed Gedächtniskirche, Berlin, the church I had walked around in the nineteen-seventies, imagining the falling of bombs, thunderous noise of bomber planes, the choking dust, fear, greyness of WWII. Suddenly things begin to make sense. Earlier, as I was walking around, I was aware of vast green spaces between buildings. There were beautiful lawns, bright green, well manicured. My mind kept asking questions about these vast spaces in 'Downtown' as they called it. Were the streets planned with these huge spaces in-between? Parisian boulevards and palace parks? But something refused to make sense. Suddenly, seeing the elliptical capsule-like cinema, I realize that this whole area was bombed, devastated, razed to the ground. Then in time cleared and sanitised with the laying of lawns, rebuilding of churches and a few other select buildings. These churches were not really those churches; they were full-scale replicas…

And yet there was the taste of Arabian nights in rose-petal sprinkled nougat, avocado fruit salads, *manao'iche*, the crispy pitta stuffed with thyme and sesame seeds hanging from the bicycles of street sellers, snapper sushi at Sultan Ibrahim restaurant, the name turns out to mean red-mullet. The breathtaking wonder of the world, the magic of Jeita Caves, the karaoke of unrequited love at the Christian kebab house on the hill… This is also Lebanon.

And why can I not go to the Sabra and Shatilla refugee camps? I asked Jean to take me; he stiffens and says *dangerous. What you want to see? Nothing there.* He replies to a question I have not asked. Accompanied by the dismissive swipe of the hand. I am not one to take no for an answer. Why don't I insist? Every time my eyes catch their presence on the maps, only fifteen minutes away, I wince. I work out what stops me. I need to go on my own. I will need to deal with the barbaric images, which will ambush me. I cannot be a voyeur…

***

Before I leave I go looking for earrings. My usual present to myself encrypting stories of my journeys. *Silver,* I say, *big,* imagining silver songs of the Middle East dangling from my ears. Definitely Arab. Similar to those I have carried from Morocco, made by Berbers. "You like a Berber woman," the poet, reluctant keeper of a tiny cupboard-sized shop, had asserted. A speaker of four languages, well educated, in the dusty desert town of Tafroute, rising from the pink quartz of Western Sahara. When I asked why? "You bargain like one!" We had laughed. Maybe I am looking for the experience of bargaining not just for the earrings but for life. A point of learning, watching each other's shifts as snippets of lives, world philosophies, experiences cross paths. A short convergence from across the world then dispersal, leaving only the earrings and fragments of conversations.

We park under a fly-over, a bridge. Jean points to it with his car keys, indicating its significance. Only after my return and submergence into the literatures of Lebanon do I get a glimpse of its secrets. It was the dividing line, border; so much happened under that bridge. Where the innocent teenagers in *De Niro's Game* sat at the all-night juice bar *at the other side of town, in the Armenian district, far from the Turks who had enslaved my grandmother* drinking mango topped with white cheese, honey and nuts, licked their fingers and talked about the silence of the gun to be used against a neighbour for a mere parking offence. Later, where George tells his friend, *I killed today. I killed many,* sitting with... *fresh blood on his military pants; a large black patch of it almost glowed,* describing the butchering of innocent Palestinians in the refugee camp, Quarantina. Still much later, towards the end of the novel, the gun between them,

> We sat in the car, under the bridge ... George and I
> had quarrelled ... (He) was sent to take me back to
> my torturer, and then they would have killed me. But
> he said that he would give me a chance. He played

with his gun. He filled it with three bullets and spun
it. He smiled, and then he said to me, I am giving
you a chance.
I took the gun from his hand, and without blinking,
without giving myself the time to think about the sea,
the ship, the new place that I wanted so much to go
to, I held the gun against my head and pulled the
trigger. It clicked, and it did not go off.
I laid the gun on the car seat … I buried him under
the bridge…

As we saunter through the side streets and narrow lanes
the shop door metal grills suddenly begin to roll down, there is
a commotion, people become agitated, murmurs. I watch the
faces for clues as to what might be happening. I can't decipher
them. A silence descends on the street but people still move
about. I try to dash out of the shop as the metal grill is coming
down. I am only aware of an intense feeling of not wanting to be
in an enclosed space, being trapped. I say sorry to the shopkeeper as I duck under the metal grill still rolling down. He smiles
apologetically saying, *we have to do this.* My mind on overtime
trying to work out why? Was there an order from 'above" for
some reason? I look around. Other shopkeepers are also bringing the metal grills down. Suddenly, I realise they are only half
down. Then people cross themselves. A few stand on the curb. I
scan the street, houses, above the shops, rooftops of buildings,
both ends of the road. Am I missing something? Only then do
I notice a line of people walking steadily, unhurried, dressed in

black. Mostly elderly. Behind a coffin. So simple. Silence, reverence, acceptance of the inevitable. A walk. The last walk through his neighbourhood, before he is taken to the Armenian church tucked away in the side street for the funeral service then forever driven away from the street where he had spent his life. Where was he born, I wondered? Was he a survivor of the genocide in Turkey or was his mother?

The metal grills rolled up as soon as he passed. The shopkeeper said he was in his late eighties. *He had a good life* he added with a smile. Life was back to normal, the music, the laughter, loud banter across shop doorways, reclaimed the street. I wondered if they did this for each funeral in the days of bombings, snipers and indiscriminate killings. And I noticed this neighbourhood was intact but at the end of the street there was a wide avenue lined with modern shopping plazas on both sides. I have learnt to decipher the tongues of the city...

On the way back, I notice a sticker on a whitewashed wall, a little high up. The "Keep Britain Clean" stickers plastered everywhere promoting environmental awareness. I smile at the familiar symbol also travelling the world. Then notice the red letters falling into the bin on the sticker. T-Ü-R-K-İ-Y-E. The A.R.F. Zavarian Student Association would like to clean up - not original but a clever little sticker! I wondered where the Turkish-speaking neighbourhood of Beirut was? I was certain there was one... And whether some of the Turkish-speaking Armenians, exiled from Turkey, ever lived there? Would I find similar stickers there with sentiments of cleaning up the Armenians? A war conducted with stickers on the walls of neighbourhoods.

I stretch up and remove it carefully from the wall. I want to have it as a memento of this neighbourhood of Beirut. The shops only had silver earrings mass-produced in Bali, none from the Middle East. I was obviously in the wrong place to find the large, bold, rough-cut, expressive – maybe even considered vulgar - earrings I was looking for. These were too tame for me. I needed to be in the Palestinian neighbourhoods, perhaps. And Jean could not take me there. Perhaps he had already seen the ghosts I knew would ambush me, as had Robert Fisk...

> *What we found inside the Palestinian Shatila camp at ten o'clock on the morning of 18 September 1982 did not quite beggar description..."* he begins, then continues, *"...we were unable to register our own shock ... there were women lying in houses with their skirts torn up to their waists and their legs wide apart, children with their throats cut, rows of young men shot in the back after being lined up at an execution wall. There were babies – blackened babies because they had been slaughtered more than 24 hours earlier and their small bodies were already in a state of decomposition – tossed into rubbish heaps alongside discarded U.S. Army ration tins, Israeli army medical equipment, and empty bottles of whisky ... one lay on her back, her dress torn open and the head of a little girl emerging from behind her. The girl had short, dark*

curly hair, her eyes were staring at us and there
was a frown on her face. She was dead. Someone
had slit the woman's stomach, cutting sideways
and then upwards, perhaps trying to kill her un-
born child. Her eyes were wide open, her dark face
frozen in horror.

***

At the airport, I kiss his cheeks three times resting my hands on each shoulder wondering if the Egyptian custom also applies in Lebanon. He lowers his body so I can reach him, resting his hands gently on my back. Slight confusion in his eyes sits alongside controlled emotions. "If you come to Beirut, I am here," he manages, allowing me to read it as I can depend on him. A brave offer to a 'Muslim' woman he allowed into his affections, going against his prejudices. Perhaps within that brutalising history, at some level, it was still about not forgetting and about forgiveness, and the individual responsibility of taking care of the human. Of the three of us, he knew that I knew who he was.

Beirut-Nicosia-Famagusta-London. December 2010 - October 2011

WOMEN
OF NICOSIA

They are dressed in their Sunday best. It is Sunday. Shimmering black hair. Straight. Short or long touching their invisible buttocks. Dark skins created by faraway oceans hold onto their lustre touched by the Mediterranean sun. Only the hands have swollen, cracked, cut, scarred, dotted with raw pink patches, nails worn down, barely growing beyond the tender flesh line.

The geranium still hangs from the balcony. In bright clusters of crimson blooms. A saddened thirsty cactus droops. Bright purple freesias on slender string-like necks, upright, lined up next to each other, funnels open to the skies, sway in the slight breeze brushing by the balconies on its way to the Pentadachtylos mountains in the distance. Lines of dark washing, discarded, forgotten chairs, a child's bike nestle in the corners of high up balconies.

Laughter. A high pitched voice from the darkness of a half-closed window up above crushes onto the voice of a Turkish speaking man in the street below passing the dark-skinned woman with laughing eyes, hanging onto her friend's arm. Brown, bare feet imprisoned in high heels and Nike copies and tight jeans with American flag patchwork, symbols of success and acceptance into this 'civilised' world. An illusion of equality. A passport. The insistence for its necessity only to be left outside the park gates when dissolving into a sea of dark skins and dazzling smiles under the shade of trees force-migrated by the Empire botanists, dropping their seeds eager to leave their mark on their return journeys to the 'motherland'.

The new women of Nicosia. Carrying plastic bags of lurid pink and blue. And maybe one from Fendi. A cast-off of her employer. Walking in Nicosia, up and down. Up and down. Claiming it as theirs. In groups. Always in groups. Claiming and reclaiming the streets of Nicosia. It is now theirs. The Cypriots have deserted her, moved onto other places, other interests. Discarded her. She is no longer chic.

She is hospitable. Takes care of them with her broken windows, rotten doors, missing distorted shutters, collapsed roofs, shut-down shops, lattice metal shop shutters, balconies, gaping wounds of fallen plaster, narrow alleyways, courtyards with palm trees and thick layers of dust. *Attention Dangerous Building* signs in three languages, none that of the new women of Nicosia. They walk by oblivious, only aware of the smile and touch of the women in their group savouring the single day of freedom and the new friendships of forced migrations.

A white peace flag sways gently in the breeze from the balcony above the street where two women in crimson sarees return my smile as they go by. To the woman of old Nicosia, migrant in another faraway cold land.

The laughter of a woman from a side street bathes us.

Nicosia. March 2004

LONDON IS
MY CITY

This is where I became a grown-up. Where I became the woman I am. Where I created the woman I have become. Where I fell in love. Where I first made love. London is where I came to seek refuge from a war. My arrival a historical accident, a history created by others, one I was forced to live. My stay, a choice. London, I love. She created me as I created her. She would be something else if it were not for me, and others like me who came to stay.

This is where I ate my first curry, volcano in my mouth wondering at the limitations of pain for pleasure. Where I discovered old China Town in Limehouse and later at Gerrard Street. Where I watched, awestruck, Margot Fonteyn and Rudolf Nureyev dance against Apartheid in a concrete maze I thought unfinished which later became one of my cultural oases. Where I walked through the escaping steam and pungent whiff of hops of the old Truman Brewery, mesmerised by the mural of buxom women on Clifton's wall in competition with Nazrul's, squeezed between Jewish materials shops. Now I can hardly cycle my way through the Bengali restaurant touts who have squeezed out the

Jewish communities and converted the synagogue into a mosque in Brick Lane. The old Truman still holds onto its fig tree leaning on the red-brick wall unnoticed by the drum 'n' bass thirty-twenty-something crowds of the Vibe Club. Salt beef and salmon bagels still the pit-stop late at night for the black butterflies and tailed suits donned by men and bejewelled older women in Rolls Royces or Jaguars on their way back from the Opera heading to the ends of this City. I notice more people begging on the pavement at the corner by the traffic lights where I demonstrated against the fascist National Front who wanted to send the likes of me back.

The city where I became the guest of languages, some I could not decipher, sitting on the Number 38 bus from Piccadilly to Hackney sometimes to the music of the harmonica-playing conductor. I would smile when I could guess the language. The city where I learnt to distinguish the Caribbeans from the Africans and then those from their different parts. Where I learnt about slavery and met the great-great-grandchildren of the slaves. Where I saw wealth and experienced poverty. Where I stared at the muddy waters of the Thames in search of the sea, trying to impose the image of the crystal waters of the Mediterranean. I discovered towns in London: China in Soho, Bangla in Brick Lane, India and Pakistan in Green Street, Beirut and Arab in Edgware Road, Caribbean in Brixton, Cyprus along Green Lanes and Hackney, my town, a mini London with all its communities.

I go around the world in 80 minutes or less walking down

Ridley Road Market. Alfie the cucumber-man is gone, so is Foreman the smoked fish hut reminding me of the Jewish communities, escapees of fascism and WWII. Navarino Mansions, their safe heaven, with its Art Nouveau iron window railings now houses refugees from other wars in Africa, Kurdistan, Afghanistan, Pakistan, Iraq. The Hasidim Jews in Stamford Hill remain and still walk around on Saturdays, men with wide-brimmed fur hats, long twisted locks dangling on either side of their faces, women pushing prams in their Saturday-best, wearing wigs of unchanged styles. At night, after the cacophony of the market has died down, I watch lone men in the dim light of the streetlamps, sit on stalls pushed against the darkness of the walls waiting for dawn. Only their orange cigarette lights sparkle. The old sweatshops have become barren lonely hostels for lonely men escapees of persecution. Bare bulbs hanging from ceilings, washing left to dry on windowsills and sometimes music in different languages the only life in the deserted dark market street.

Hackney, where I am educated and informed of the world political and economic events, conflicts and wars through the changes in the people, faces and languages in the market. The Cypriots, leftovers from the 1960s and 1970s conflicts, the Caribbeans, the Indians, Pakistanis, Kashmiris, the Vietnamese, East Africans and now West Africans, the Nigerians, Bangladeshis, the Kurdish and Turkish communities, more recently the lone young men from Kosovo, Albania, Serbia, Bosnia, Somalis, especially the tall women in their long dark robes and more women in *hidjab* and headscarves. And even more recently blonde white

333

women, fashion conscious, from Poland and other East Europe-an countries and well-built stocky young men carrying pots and pans, brooms, microwave ovens and electric kettles ready to set up home. And now languages I can't even begin to decipher...

I watched the only market pub close down and become a beauty shop full of nail, hair, skin products, wigs and false nails. Even the local Hackney Action for Racial Equality has become a nail parlour. The Vietnamese experts in nail fashion. Outside the pub, the Caribbean elders no longer bring their chairs out to bang the domino pieces on a board precariously balanced on an orange box from Morocco, commandeered from the discarded pile behind one of the stalls. Ganja doesn't whiff across adult conversations and flirting amongst baby-mothers and baby-fa-thers while children run in-and-out of the telephone boxes on the corner, giggling and climbing on empty stalls. No longer the Rasta locks flying through the air with the flick of the head and bright green, red and yellow dress code and Supermalt in hand reminding you of tropical places. And the old working class white East End market families, sprinkled in-between, at first re-sentful that we dared touch their fruit and veg now sell pok-choi, beansprouts, flat-leaf parsley, passion fruit, mango, water mel-ons and varieties of other melons, mint, coriander, aubergines, spinach, French beans, rockette, eddoes, plantains, yams, sweet potatoes, star fruit as though they have always sold them. They will even give you recipes and instructions of how to cook or eat them. They will even shout the weight and price in Turkish, after all, the largest language group in Hackney after English.

I watch the garment factory with its Stars of David at the end of the Market become the Turkish Food Centre from a small shop with a hill of watermelons on the pavement on the side, to a Mecca of food where you can buy anything on sale in Turkey. Freshly baked baklava and its twenty or so variations, breads and pide, fresh and dried vegetables, dried aubergines and peppers hanging from strings, fruits, nuts, drinks including wines and *rakı*, music cassettes and CDs, variations of olives and white cheese (feta), *mangals* (BBQs), skewers, Turkish coffee sets, shapely tea glasses, even short reed brooms to double you over in old age. And of course from the minute to the large vulgarly ostentatious blue glass 'evil-eyes' dangling in their hundreds like a surreal installation from walls used to protect your car, house, newborn at a price from the 'evil eye'. All attempts to reduce the longing for 'home', places, tastes, ornaments, people, smells, music, images left behind. Above the food centre the Alevi Cem Evi, replacing the mosque as a centre of spirituality, where young people walk through the market with their long necked *saz* stringed instruments gently carried under their arms. And of course similar food-shops run by the Turkish Speaking Communities (TSCs) are spread all over London, open all hours of the day and night, generating and creating a different way of life, energy, buzz and excitement with an entrepreneurial spirit not there before their arrival. They have changed the face and rules of shopping. Follow these food Meccas, small or large, and you follow the nomadic adventures of the TSCs across London and beyond. When did the *kebab* replace fish and chips as the local dish of London? Now you can find a kebab take-away in the remotest market towns in Wales, north of England and Scotland.

Back on Kingsland Road, the old Roman road, your soul is safe from Shoreditch to Stoke Newington, with Süleymaniye Mosque in the south to Aziziye, a converted bingo hall, in the north. Both covered in beautiful blue-azure Kütahya tiles especially imported from Turkey. Lit up green during the two religious celebrations, *Kurban* and *Seker Bayramı* (Eid), they are a hive of activity distributing food to the poor and needy and Quranic wisdom to those at the precipice of temptation. The left-wing radical revolutionaries escapees of political coups and persecution in Turkey offer salvation to others in the numerous centres set up in the 1980s, walls crowded with the portraits of the martyrs to the cause, some still perpetuating sectarian animosities amongst dwindling Marxist congregations. Half-way up the long road, Rio Cinema sustained my love of world cinema. This is where the Cypriotgreek and Cypriotturkish communities descended from all over London and beyond in the 1960s and 1970s to watch Greek and Turkish language films. This was before the time of videos. Alternate weekends ensured that the animosities generated in Cyprus didn't spill into the cinema at the same time it offered opportunities for some to go to both films. Of the five cinemas on Kingsland Road, when I moved into the area, only the Rio remains. For the past eleven years each November the London Turkish Film Festival attracts thousands from the TSCs and others to celebrate achievements of films some with world cinema award garlands from Cannes, Venice, Berlin, Istanbul,

336

while film shorts create opportunities for the new emerging TS actors and directors of the future London-based cinemaphiles.

A little up the road, Mangal II where Gilbert and George, the famous art duo enjoy their kebabs served by polite waiters usually studying for a 'solid' degree, mostly unaware of who they are. "I think they are filmmakers," said one when I asked once. I smiled. I could see why he thought that as I've witnessed more than once the American accented palm-sized expensive equipment-wielding bods filming them at their table. While the interviewer sweats and fluffs, they demurely get on with their food. I've witnessed a young woman waiting to be seated refuse a table and insist on waiting for Gilbert and George's. Gilbert usually smiles shyly and says Hi when he becomes aware that you are Turkish Speaking and know who they are.

Mangal in Arcola Street, gave birth to Mangal II by feeding workers from the local sweatshops and garment factories producing clothes paraded by long-legged catwalk models in the West End and beyond. At the numerous weddings, engagement and circumcision parties each weekend, undistinguishable from each other in the type of music, food and dance, the same dress parades and wiggles to belly-dance on the dance floor, to some love song from the depths of Anatolia on a short-legged plump body. The short bursts of "ziiiiirt, ziiiiirt" of industrial sewing machines no longer overflow through the open windows, accompanied by the music of heart-wrenching longing and unrequited love in Turkish. The factories have gone, first to Bulgaria and Romania with the blessing and funding of the EU and now probably on their way to China leaving thirty-thousand Turkish Speaking (TS) and others unemployed. The increased TS Mafia activity soon after, is no coincidence. Arcola Theatre set up in one such ex-factory, by Mehmet Ergen, a young dynamic TS director, brings world-class theatre and plays to Hackney. This includes Stafford-Clark's *Macbeth*, which played to full houses, creating a beehive attracting creativity from all over London.

Saturdays and Sundays I call pantomime days for the TSCs. Young women in satin fancy dress, in all colours, line up at the hairdressers adding flowers and tiaras to their hair, impervious to the plight of the cars covered in flowers and ribbons and their drivers waiting patiently by the curb in front of the flower shops next door. Yet another group of young people bowing to the pressures of getting married, some too young. Some young girls seeing marriage as an escape from parental pressure only to hand themselves over to the pressures of a husband and marriage. An agreement between families and clans more than between two young people. Living together not an option as it brings heavily punishable dishonour and curse on seven generations! But the flowers spilt onto the pavement especially on Valentine's Day with red hearts not only make good photographs but also prepare you for a softer landing just before the police station with a history of deaths in custody, it is barely getting over.

Green Lanes is where Cypriots created 'Little Cyprus' along the 'Ladder' from Newington Green to Wood Green. While divisions and nationalist discourse raged in Cyprus, Cypriot men quietly drank coffee and played backgammon and cards in the sanctity of the mixed coffee houses, named after villages in the 'homelands' but most importantly away from women. The same men both perpetrators and victims of acts of violence and generosity, some as servants of the colonial empire. I watch as that generation is dying out and the second and third generation move into larger enterprises or professions in other industries. The Turkish and Kurdish communities have recently taken over the inconspicuous Cypriot corner shop, café and fish and chip shop and transformed it into the loud coloured, flashing light decorated signs offering tastes of Anatolia rather than the Mediterranean. Yasar Halim who in the face of Turkish nationalist fervour insisted on putting signs up for freshly baked bread, pide/pitta, hellim/halloumi and olives in Turkish, Greek and English is still there. People from all over London came to buy a little bit of Cyprus until the next visit to the village where, to the amusement of customs officers, luggage would be dragged along the floor packed with these goodies not available in London, now staple foods in all supermarkets. Now it is illegal to bring in halloumi cheese. Yasar Halim was beaten up and hospitalised in the 1990s for refusing to make 'donations' of about £10,000 per week, some say to the TS Mafia, others to left-wing revolutionaries and yet others say to the Kurdish PKK. A practice, which still continues. Kurdish, Turkish and eastern Europeans work in his bakery and expanded shop and the products reflect it. Across the road Patisserie Halepi still holds onto the old recipes from Cyprus for *pilavuna, gurabiye, lokma* and *shamishi* amongst gory multi-layered wedding cakes, giving away the Middle Eastern fusion of cuisines; Halepi, Aleppo of Syria. I make a special trip sometimes to close my eyes and taste the crumbling shortbread with almonds, *gurabiye*, or the syrup filled little pastry balls, *lokma*, to take me back to being a child in Cyprus.

Green Lanes at the corner of Newington Green reminds me of the hundreds, arriving and leaving from the offices of the company running overland trips between Cyprus and London, well before the days of cheap flights. The screams, laughter, tears of joy of separations, excitement, the long waves goodbye, the kisses, the silence of sorrow, wiping of the eyes with the corner of the headscarf still linger on. A little further north, the Fleet Street of the Turkish language press where four out of five newspapers printed in London exist side by side with the Turkish Bookshop struggling to survive. Local newspapers are available free in all the supermarkets, off-licences and shops run by TSCs alongside papers from Turkey and Cyprus. Just as important as the news are the smiling faces dressed to kill posing in the hundreds of clubs and restaurants plastered all over at least three-four full pages in each paper. The owner of Kıbrıs Studios a little down the road is now over seventy and has photographed Cypriots throughout the decades. He must have a phenomenal archive. African babies and newlyweds smile from his shop window now. A couple of shops down was the soup shop where all the nightclub musicians and singers would congregate for hot soup, a chat and catch up with the news before daybreak. At the Wood Green end of Green Lanes, Turkish London Radio broadcasts events, news, music amongst jingles for property investment, catering wholesalers and even more. With satellite dishes popping up like mushrooms all over London buildings, the TSCs can access over fifty channels from Turkey and Cyprus. The links with the 'homelands' of some and the Turkish language is as strong as ever.

Football has always been big in the TSCs with its own Football Federation and League. Over four hundred teams take over Hackney Marshes on Sundays where big business rules, players are bought and sold and where winning the League is mega. Nationalism and prejudice seem not to have a place in the League as African-Caribbean and even Cypriotgreek players play in TSCs teams. The European successes of the big football clubs and the national team of Turkey in the World Cup have boosted the confidence and profile of football in London.

Green Lanes and Kingsland Road are but a small reflection of the life of the TSCs across London and beyond, their hopes, aspirations, loves, preoccupations and thirst for life. From the respectable to the most hidden, from the honest, hard working trying to make it in this city despite all odds to the money launderer, people smuggler, credit card fraudster, those exploiting women for prostitution. I feel the pain and anger as I walk past basement cafes where young blonde women serve tea and coffee and I suspect sex and feel their desperation and helplessness. I don't pretend not to see the adverts for sex in all the local Turkish language papers bar the Toplum Postası while '*namus*' (honour) and morality are shoved down the throats of TS young girls and women. I note the community centres providing much-needed services to desperate people and note those who receive large sums on behalf of the communities but fleece them. One thing is certain: the TSCs have set up networks and systems that do not require going 'outside' the communities. The chain of jewellers, accountants, finance companies, lawyers, travel agents, import-export, catering, household goods, building, ICT companies and its millionaires are a testimony of economic self-sufficiency. Some of these companies are suppliers to British supermarkets and the catering industry while others like Hüseyin Özer of Özer and Sofra restaurants chain is mentioned as one of the three chefs with the most influence on the new developing British cuisine. Weekly cultural events of theatre, music, festivals including singers from Turkey and the high visibility events such as the Turkish Fest at the Southbank, a Turkish harbour at the Boat Show, Eurovision and Miss World successes, Mercan Dede and Whirling Dervishes at the Queen Elizabeth Hall coupled with the new political developments in Turkey have made a positive impact on the TSCs in London and the rest of Europe. The lack of going 'outside' can be interpreted as strength necessitated by isolation, racial prejudice and sheer determination to survive, no different to other communities. At times a weakness, as it may exclude others and the self and may not contribute to the creation of new multi-cultural societies. However, it seems the wars in Iraq, Afghanistan and Palestine, and the inevitable bombings in London have become the pretext to rob us of rights and freedoms as citizens of this City and take us back to the dark ages leaving race equality in shreds. But I would like to think that we are more resilient than that and we are all still learning...

London. July 2005

ACKNOWLEDGMENTS

My special thanks to Selma Canver, Münevver Özgür Özersay, Kathy Kattashis, Kathy Cosimano, Gregorio von Hildebrand, Achim Wieland and Navid Gholipour for their dedicated technical support and ideas to bring the stories out into the world and the care they took during the process.

Lincoln Williams for sharing childhood memories and an island. Hasan Kunter, Mahmut Kunter, Ozzie Redjeb, Altan Halil, Hafize Ece, Gülgün Mustafa, Türkan Tuncel, Jean and many others, including children, my storytellers, who fired my imagination and determination to retell the stories.

My thanks to Türkan Tuncel for the back cover photograph at a reading at the London Poetry Café, Miriam Butler for the Beirut photographs and a wondrous journey, together with Ekaterina Lortkipanidze, Kathy Kattashis for the Nicosia photographs and the unknown artist for the photograph detail used on the cover.

I am indebted to the following writers and their stories of Beirut, Lebanon and beyond, which enriched *Tongues of the city* and my experience,

Susan Abulhawa (2011) *Mornings in Jenin.*
Bloomsbury, London. p.219

Rabih Alameddine (2002) *I, the Divine.* W.W. Norton
& Company, New York. p.7, 229

Robert Fisk, *Life, death & café au lait,* The Independent
on Sunday. 13 February 2011.

Robert Fisk (2008) *The World of Robert Fisk Volume 1,*
1989-1998, From Beirut to Bosnia. The Independent
News   and Media. p.16

Robert Fisk (2002) *Pity the Nation: The Abduction*
of Lebanon. Nation Books, New York.

Rawi Hage (2008) *De Niro's Game.* Harper Collins,
New York. pp. 11, 12, 13, 15, 173, 270, 271

Lamia Joreige (2006) *Objects of War, No 3.* Arts Video
Installation at the Tate Modern, London.

Hala Kawtharani (2010) *Lebanon/Switzerland? Beirut/Paris?*
In Beirut 39 – *new writing from the Arab world*, ed. Samuel
Shimon. Bloomsbury, London. pp.94-95

Elias Khoury (2009) *Yalo.* (trans. by Humphrey Davies)
London, MacLehose Press. p.237

Ghada Samman (1997; reprinted 2010) *Beirut Nightmares*
- *a novel.* Quartet Books, London. pp. 49, 170

BIOGRAPHICAL NOTE

AYDIN MEHMET ALI was born in Cyprus. She lives in London where she came to seek refuge from a war and in Cyprus. She was educated in Cyprus, USA and Britain. An intellectual activist she contributed to the creation of multicultural, anti-racist, bilingual societies and cities. She set up and managed numerous international empowerment projects focusing on women and young people. She has worked as a chief education officer, international education consultant, arts projects manager, researcher and as an adviser to the London Mayor, universities, schools and Local Education Authorities. She is a passionate campaigner for justice and equity in Cyprus, UK, Turkey and Greece and against the militarisation of communities and societies globally.

She has performed her work at international events, at a variety of venues, to diverse audiences. She translates and edits poetry and short stories. Her articles, creative writings and translations have appeared in numerous international anthologies, collections, journals, and magazines and performed on radio, TV and at festivals. She is an advisory editor of Cadences literary journal and founder of Literary Agency Cyprus (LAC) – winner of Stelios Foundation Awards, 2013.

347

COMMENTS

I am an island a Cypriot poet had said with a sense of self-importance, once so long ago, when he was a friend, to which I had responded, *That may be so... but as a woman I am the sea.*

This is an appreciation, acknowledgement, an 'outing' of those who contribute to my creativity and to literatures beyond barriers. I want to move away from the mythology and fantasy of the sole solo writer, poet, artist, intellectual by making visible the strands and dialogues between us, essential for our survival as creators...

Unlike most stories they are unique explorations of the identity and memory of women and form a project of feminine self-discovery the aim of which is not to settle the past or prepare the way for an imaginary future but to always question and illuminate, going beyond certainties and conventions and often articulating truths that conventional morality would rather pass over in silence. In Aydın Mehmet Ali's stories, femininity is synonymous with an irrepressible desire to name and discover, especially when the truth involved is painful to oneself, shameful to oneself and others or simply not in line with dominant notions of identity.

Angie Veola, Senior Lecturer, University of East London

Mehmet Ali's short stories are her life stories, a fictional life writing that focuses on gendered and diasporic experiences and mobility between spaces and time-zones: from those in 1950s colonial Cyprus; her departures and dwellings between Cyprus, UK and beyond; and her return and crossings to postcolonial partitioned Cyprus. In Mehmet Ali's process of literary production disruptive modes emerge individually and nightmarishly, yet they intimately connect successfully to generate a hybrid inter-generic network and solidarity.

Bahriye Kemal, PhD candidate, Writing Cyprus: Postcolonial and Partitioned Literatures of Place, University of Kent

Aydın's short stories are a powerful antidote to the rift and tear that have affected her island. While relentlessly showing the killing and the rapes, all the forms of violence that were let loose, she also shows moments of love, or less dramatically, eyes that meet, hands that join, everyday instances of living together, often focused on women or homosexuals.

Christine Pagnoulle, Senior lecturer, Post-Colonial Literature at the University of Liège, Belgium

350

I remember how connected and moved I felt when she first read part of her short story "Pink Butterflies". I was awed by her voice, and her words, that so effortlessly filled the space and transposed it to another world. Since then, I've had my copy of her book with me in London, with her inscription scribbled inside, 'Here's to childhoods which create us as we recreate ourselves.' Her words, wise and true are as meaningful to me today as they were then. I am lucky to know this remarkable woman and writer. Her creative restlessness, honesty, and fearlessness are a ceaseless source of inspiration for me. Not only has she consistently supported me in my creative endeavors, but she's also been a great friend... Her writing is a treasure, just as she is.

Eleni Skarpari, MA, singer/songwriter, actress, award winning writer.

... both the woman and the work are radically, unapologetically, dare I say, intransigently unaffiliated. To choose to work in a country with a history such as ours, in a society that has arisen as a direct result of that chequered past, within its own incestuous literary microcosm, and to remain so vehemently independent, not just politically and philosophically, but most importantly artistically, is a minor miracle. Her fluidity is what I value most because it means she has a seat prepared for her at almost every table in every scene. And she is one of the only writers I've ever met who listens considerably more than she speaks, feels far more that she opines, who is open and generous and enthralled to all the young artists of this island. This has always been pre-

sent in her work, which is touched by the present and haunted by the past. But the radical cultural changes currently sweeping across this country see her in a unique place and I have a sneaky suspicion that she's only just getting started.
Evros Stylianou, writer, MA in Literature

Aydın's poetry and short stories are fascinating allowing insight into her life and experiences. I am always moved by her writing. She is an inspiration to all writers; she never ceases to amaze me.
Gülgün Mustafa, *MA, Education and Behaviour Specialist, Artist*

The most courageous woman writer in Cyprus...
Gür Genç, poet, short story writer on "Caught Out"

One of Aydın's stories which I have translated into German, the story of Tony who is Greek and Ozzie who is Turkish and one mother, all from Cyprus, has touched me deeply. Aydın has caught the essence of the Cypriot character; on the one hand unforgiving because of tradition and perhaps religion, and on the other, ready to open the arms when one is in need. In the thoughts of the mother, there are many of the stories I have heard, while conducting interviews in Cyprus.
Heidi Trautmann, on "Bedtime Story", Artist, essayist and author of, "Art and Creativity in North Cyprus"

Aydın's work is powerful and shocking because it is explicit in exposing the abuse and suffering of Turkish speaking women in London… Her short story 'Daughter-in-Law', provides an insight into the situation and dilemma of one such victimised woman who is totally isolated and turns to a Turkish speaking community worker who is herself threatened by men. Although the narrative insists on the power of women in a feminist discourse, it also raises the question of the potential power of feminism in a community long accustomed to patriarchy.

Jennifer Langer, founding director of Exiled Writers Ink; MA in Cultural Memory, and doctoral student in literature of exile.

Aydın's work challenges and breaks taboos in her communities. She is a courageous writer.

Judith Vidal-Hall, Editor of Index on Censorship. Know Your Place: Diaspora cultures & the subversion of borders Conference, 2005. Goodenough College, London

Aydın's work is powerful. Her descriptions vivid. Her "butterflying" words ask for no wings, they are the wings.

Maria A. Ioannou, award winning poet and writer.

Aydın's prose attunes to the pulse of the city, a city whose heart is revived with all the endearing details of everyday life. A narrative about women embracing Nicosia despite her old and fragile state as surrogate "motherland" poignantly juxtaposed with insightful commentary. Immediate as a smile which lasts enough to make us reflect.

Marianna Foka MA, on "Women of Nicosia"

Mehmet Ali's "London is my City" exemplifies an anxiety to rescue her own version of London from being erased. In this process, 'home' and 'abroad' are blurred since the narrative seems to be shifting between the two, interrogating them both in the process, and advocating at the same time identity politics of becoming or rootlessness. The story traverses London both spatially and temporally, a journey that critically revisits orthodox notions of 'home', 'nation', 'community'.
Marios Vasiliou, PhD candidate, Cypriot Anglophone Literature, University of Cyprus

Some words and memories cannot be translated or rather if they are, they become dull, lose their power and life. There is only one language in which these stories can be told. This is the language of those who live away from the lands on which they were born; they have been either invaded or forced to migrate. This is the language of the dispossessed, of rootlessness.
Metin Şenergüç, www.acikgazete.com, *on Pink Butterflies/Bize Dair*

A creative short story, travel notes, daily ethico-political thoughts, post-event considerations, observations or any other writing... The format might change but for Aydın one basic truth is essential and underlines all her work: we are all connected and equal. An ant on the kitchen worktop is as important as the president of the USA. Sex, love, body, the individual, society, politics, art, human rights, languages, music... Her work is a timeless, delicate and colourful patchwork of nature, humanity and equality.

Münevver Özgür Özersay, PhD Architect and Lecturer

So often her short stories read like collated poems. Her sentences, punctuated by colours, sounds and images that disrupt and divide them, remind me so much of the disruption and division in our lives, in the lives of all of us who live and feel Cyprus. *Dr Nicoletta Demetriou, Research Fellow in Ethnomusicology and Life Writing, Wolfson College, University of Oxford*

In this incisive collection of stories, award-winning writer Aydın Mehmet Ali reflects the experiences of women caught up in conflict, both personal and political. It is beautifully written yet thought-provoking, giving voice to issues often silenced by taboos. Aydın skillfully uses fiction to raise important and universal political issues.
Shereen Pandit, South African award winning writer, Lawyer

Aydın describes symbols of division, such as barbed wire, which created a focus for the reunification movement, and how it has now gone. The next step for Cypriots is to face the crimes of the past, she says, and advocates a process of truth and reconciliation. Then we have to start looking at Cyprus in a multi-cultural context, she believes. "The more you talk about bi-communal, the more polarized you become," she says. The stories are colourful, and at times painfully intimate. She does not shy away from painful memories and lays her heart, body and soul on the line... *Pink Butterflies/Bize Dair* is an important insight into the

Turkish Cypriot psyche, both from the point of view of one who has been away for a long time, and from that of one who never left. It also reveals a great deal on the nature of Turkish Cypriot womanhood.
Simon Bahçeli – Cyprus Mail (2005)

In terms of Cypriot literature, the most astute representation of migrant women is Aydın Mehmet Ali's short prose piece "Women of Nicosia". The writer depicts their otherness in terms that turn their othered presence on the Nicosia scape into a source of potential empowerment. Their very presence, their walks in the old town give them entitlement to the culture and history of this place. In other words, they are integral to Nicosia just as Nicosia is integral to their life. Aligning them in a certain, limited sense with Aphrodite, emerging through the ruins to beautify and transform the landscape blessing it with her sensuous abundance.
Stavros Karayanni, Associate Professor, Department of Humanities, European University Cyprus; Editor of Cadences literary journal

London is my City is a fine literary essay that celebrates the sharing of cultural experiences in the multicultural society that emerged in post-colonial London. Mehmet Ali's voice is all the more vibrant and moving as she brings together her coming-of-age in the metropolis with her personal and social engagement.
Stephanos Stephanides, FEA OSSI, Professor of English and Comparative Literature, University of Cyprus

OTHER PUBLICATIONS BY FATAL

Pink Butterflies / Bize Dair – (2005)
by Aydın Mehmet Ali and Gülfidan Erhürman.
pp.166. Price £8.00
Two Cypriot women scattered by the winds of war. Two sisters. They have been apart since 1963. One lives in London and writes short stories, the other writes poetry in Nicosia. For a long time neither knew the other wrote. They write about lost childhoods, friends, places left on the 'other' side, divided by barbed wire and mine fields. Theirs is a rebellion against personal and political injustice. Voices of longing and love for the past and the future. They tell it with passion…

Turkish Speaking Communities & Education - no delight
(2001)
by Aydın Mehmet Ali. pp.232. Price £10.00
The Turkish Speaking Communities (TSCs) have been part of British society for over fifty years yet have been made invisible in the education system. Their selected visibility in parts of London reinforces stereotypes of "kebab culture" and criminality against

a backdrop of hostility towards refugees and asylum seekers. This is a unique book combining a rigorous academic approach and using "their voices", to explore the educational needs and aspirations of the Cypriotturkish, Turkish and Kurdish communities. It brings together analysis, experiences, expertise and recommendations of different stakeholders in the TSCs. The nine chapters cover the history of the TSCs in the UK, an analysis of the educational underachievement levels at each Key Stage in nine London LEAs, the changing patterns of Turkish language use, parents' views of bilingual nursery education, the diverse educational needs and aspirations of women as adult learners and mentoring. The book contains an unparalleled reference section.

"A book long overdue. I found it to be an invaluable source of information. The first book, which coherently analyses the educational needs of the Turkish speaking communities as seen by a true insider. It is on the highly recommended book list for our PGCE course."
Dr. Tözün Issa, Director, Centre for Multilingualism in Education, London Metropolitan University.

"It says things that needed to be said which have been kept quiet for a long time."
Enver Gürsev, Artist and Associate Lecturer at Chelsea College of Art and Design.

"This book is a 'bible' that anyone interested in the educational and

social situation of migrants and asylum seekers in England and Europe should refer to over and over again. Highly recommended."
Veronica Alvarez-Cordova, Widening Participation Project Manager for six London universities.

"The underachievement of Turkish Speaking pupils has been a long-standing issue in this country. This book contains the evidence to prove it and will be an invaluable tool for those in the field who have been struggling to bring it to light. Thank you for writing this book. It has helped so many of us."
Ayşe Ahmet, Science teacher, London secondary school.

"An informative and insightful account of the education of these children, who have been represented in British schools for half a century now ... and the need for 'an emergency rescue operation' to the 'educational genocide' of these young people. A welcome resource for teachers."
Dr. Gillian Klein, Editor, *Multicultural Teaching;* Vol. 20, November 3 Summer 2002.

"Teachers found the book groundbreaking. Aydın first sets the contexts in which Turkish, Cypriot and Kurdish children and their families live in London and Europe and then proceeds to outline the way whereby families and children are excluded and disempowered by the process of schooling. But where the book makes its outstanding contribution is in the articulation of the voices of the young people, which she weaves into concrete sug-

gestions which schools and teachers can act on."
Mike Vance, Acting Head of Ethnic Minority Achievement
Service Team, Hackney.

*"It is one of its kind and a 'must read' book, a valuable resource
for professionals working with TS children, young people, women
and refugees. It is full of ordinary people's voices. Aydın not only
describes the situation as 'educational genocide' and deals with the
issues in depth, but also offers solutions in a chapter entitled, 'An
emergency rescue operation – what needs to be done'. When I read
the book it shook me; I found it necessary to redefine my work."*
Mahmut Kunter, London Metropolitan University Widening
Participation Coordinator for TSCs.

**Turkish Cypriot Identity in Literature - Edebiyatta Kıbrıslı
Türk Kimliği** (1990)
edited and translated by Aydın Mehmet Ali.
pp.230. Price £5.00

This is a collection of papers presented at the First International Panel of Turkish Cypriot Young Intellectuals held in London.
The book is published in Turkish and English. It is a sincere,
questioning and inspiring collection of studies courageously
searching for answers and challenging the status quo at a time
of heightened nationalism and chauvinism in Cyprus. The con-
tributors were branded as traitors to the "national cause". It en-
abled the voices of oppositionist intellectuals to be heard outside

Cyprus and for their work to appear in English for the first time. Niyazi Kızılyürek, Filiz Naldöven, Mehmet Yaşın, Neşe Yaşın, Hakkı Yücel and Aydın Mehmet Ali have since become internationally known in their own fields.

"Historically the most significant book dealing with issues of identity in Cyprus using an analytical approach and focusing on research, which was unheard of at the time. It is still unique and unsurpassed."
Tufan Erhürman, Vice-Dean, Faculty of Law, Eastern Mediterranean University, Cyprus.